My Heart's for You

HUMOR, LOVE AND ADVENTURE

MERCY SERIES
BOOK ONE

JAN REA JOHNSON

FARMHOUSE

For
Sidney Johnson

My Heart's for You

Published 2022

Farmhouse Publication

94436 Mustonen Rd

Astoria, Oregon 97103

Printed in the United States of America

ISBN:979-8-9863725-3-2

E-ISBN: 979-8-9863725-2-5 This is a work of fiction. All of the characters, organizations, and events portrayed in this book are either products of the author's imagination or are used fictitiously.

Also by Jan Rea Johnson

I Will Enter His Gates, A Walk with God

Mistletoe @ Christmas Tree Lodge

Mercy Series

My Heart's for You

Windows of the Heart

Acknowledgments

This story would not have been possible without the ever-present advice from nurse Sidney Johnson, who made herself available to me to spur ideas and medical corrections. Not to mention the additions of humor along the way.

I'd also like to thank her coworkers (partners in crime) Morgan Burdick, David Iverson, Brandon Tovey and Debra Vitorelo who were willing to chime in on plot ideas and fictitious patient stories.

Jodi Henley, developmental editor, who helped and encouraged me so much as a new writer. Kate Johnston, developmental editor, who helped me see that great characters need flaws.

And for the willing listeners from my writing group led by Julie Bonn Blank.

Chapter One

The internet icon circled, the tap of Kaitlyn Monroe's fingernails drumming on the wood of the kitchen table, pinky to pointer. Pinky to pointer. She swallowed; her eyes glued to the screen, waiting to deliver the results of her search for reviews of online dating sites. Which one should she choose?

Fresh memories flooded in—her near miss at the altar. The playlist she and her roommate had put together rang out over the small Bluetooth speaker. Kaitlyn's white satin dress flowed as she walked slowly down the aisle, admiring the white satin bows attached to the front pews. Tina's bride's maid bouquet of sunflowers, white poppies, and bachelor buttons almost made her forget how nervous she was. The thundering beat of her heart matched her shaking hands, making the flowers in her bouquet shutter.

She'd made the right decision, right? Sure, it had only been a few months since she had met Robbie, but let's face it. Time was running out. She was already twenty-three and still not married. And everyone who was anyone had their ring by spring.

Kaitlyn looked out at the few friends she had invited. Friends from her nursing cohort. Megan. Tricia. Kelly. Kelly looked exceptionally good- long blonde hair done up with a pearl clip, false eyelashes. Made Kaitlyn a little self-conscious— she wasn't exactly a trophy bride.

And where were Robbie's eyes? Not on his bride-to-be, that was for sure. They were glued to Kelly, her hand with perfectly manicured nails covering a hint of a smile.

Earlier, when she had confronted Robbie about flirting with others, Robbie had told her she didn't have to worry. He only had eyes for her. Obviously not true. She should have listened to Tina, who had seen the red flags. His white lies, the lack of a job, and how he treated his mom.

Kaitlyn pulled herself together to listen to the pastor.

"Thank you for gathering here today to witness the marriage of Kaitlyn and Robbie." At the sound of his name, his eyes snapped to Kaitlyn. He shifted from one leg to the other. The pastor beckoned him to stand next to Kaitlyn, their backs facing the guests. Robbie turned his head and snuck another glance at Kelly.

Kaitlyn felt a tear slide down her cheek. And not the happy kind. She thrust her bouquet at Tina, turned, and ran down the aisle and out the door. She slid the cubic zirconia ring off her finger and threw it, where it landed in a clump of thistles. Right where it belonged. The jerk!

♥ ♥ ♥

That had been over a year ago. She'd looked in all the places where she might find a good match. It'd be nice to go on at least one date. But it just didn't seem to be in the cards.

Who's to say God couldn't work through a dating site? She ran her fingers through her curly brown hair and twisted it into a bun.

The Google list populated. She clicked on reviews and made a comparison.

"Oh. My. Gosh! Who knew there were so many sites?" It was easy to eliminate those for fifty and over and those who were just looking for a meetup. She settled on Perfect Match and took a deep breath, her pulse thumping wildly. The full moon shone through the slatted window shades, casting striped shadows on the wooden kitchen table.

She downloaded the Perfect Match app on her phone.

"Okay, here goes." She straightened her shoulders and typed in her name, her profession, where she had gone to college, filled in the checklist of activities she enjoyed. Would she prefer to be contacted through emails or text?

What would be your ideal date? She checked coffee, movies, cycling.

She wrote and rewrote several descriptions of herself. Looking for eyes you could lose yourself in? Someone who likes adventure? Sweet tooth? I make the best ooey-gooey cinnamon rolls smothered in cream cheese icing. Look no further!

Kaitlyn scrolled through at least a million pictures, trying to decide which photos of herself she should submit. Her with her bestie Tina Halverson? Maybe not — they'd skip her and go for Tina with her amazing auburn hair.

Kaitlyn hiking with her dad? That would do. How about the one next to her new bike? The background was a lake with fall leaves. And of course, she could post the one with her little scruffy Maltese mix, Bentley.

She paused with her finger hovering over submit. With a nervous glance over her shoulder, she pushed clicked the button and fell back in her chair. A long breath escaped her.

What had she just done? This was stupid. It was just this type of impulsivity that had landed her alone at the altar.

Chapter Two

Kaitlyn held Bentley's leash as he did his thing in the grass. She fingered her phone in her pocket. Was it too soon for someone to show interest in her? What if someone did? Would she even know what to do? What exactly was the protocol here?

"Hi, my name is Kaitlyn. I'm the girl you've been waiting for and dreaming about all your life."

Or "Hi, you have the dreamiest eyes ever! Oh, could you wait just a minute while I wipe the drool from my mouth?"

Or "Hi, I'm Kaitlyn. I'm the Ruth to your Boaz."

OMG! Lord, you are going to have to put the words in my mouth like you did for Moses if anything good is going to come out of this.

She walked down the sidewalk, oblivious to the passing cars and the school bus stopped to pick up the neighbor kids. She pulled her phone out of her bag and checked the app. Nothing. She wasn't sure whether to be relieved or rejected.

She returned home where she found Tina pouring herself a cup of coffee.

"You're out early." Tina pulled out a chair at the round oak table.

"If Bentley didn't need a walk, I'd still be sleeping." Kaitlyn yawned.

"You didn't sleep well?" How was she going to answer this?

Kaitlyn sat down and rested her arms on the table. She locked eyes with Tina. "Okay. So." Kaitlyn scrunched up her nose. "I," she stalled.

"Yes?"

Kaitlyn drew a deep breath and let it out, the words rushing from her lips. "Signed up for a dating site."

"Really? Let me see."

She handed Tina the phone where she flipped through a few pages.

"What is supposed to happen? How do I know if there's anyone interested in me?"

"You're asking me? I've never done a dating site. Did you fill everything out?"

"Yeah, I think so." Kaitlyn scrunched her shoulders and put her fist to her lips.

"Did you swipe through the profiles?"

Kaitlyn gave her a deer in the headlights look. She took the phone back and started swiping through, holding the phone so they could both read.

Kevin, 28.

You're smart. You're not about to fall for the lies made by so many of the profiles on this site. This ain't your first rodeo, now, is it? Here's the deal. I'm an honest man. I have a great career and I pay my mortgage on time. I even wear matching clothes. And clean underwear. As a side benefit, I may even introduce you to my pet gerbil. What else could you possibly need to know?

Could it get any better than that? Not to mention his intriguing eyes and dimpled smile which moved her to swipe right. A heart icon pulsed red to indicate he was bookmarked.

"I hope you like alpha males because I'm your guy. That's right, I'm the whole package. I'll defend your honor in public, won't take any crap from waiters. I'll warn you, though, that I'm hopelessly addicted to video games. Seriously though, I'll quit now so you can get back to looking at my photos.

"Ugh! Too geeky. Too full of himself. Nope. He lost me at the video games." She swiped left.

Ladies, your time has come. Seriously – stop what you're doing and message me right now, because I am the best thing that could ever happen to you. Better than Tik-Tok videos. Better than ten Insta likes. And even better than cute puppy GIFs. Okay, maybe not better than those. But let's be real- HMU!

Tina shook her head in a violent no. "Not this one. He looks like he's only got one thing on his mind." Her right eyebrow rose a fraction.

"How about Bama Boy, 26?"

I'm a born and raised Alabama boy- charming, love a good BBQ, and I clean up pretty good if we're going someplace nice. My lab is always at my side, ready for a good duck hunt.

Last night, I was reading in the book of numbers and realized I didn't have yours. Wink emoji.

"Bama Boy? Seriously?" Tina wrinkled her forehead.

"He might be fun. I mean, I grew up on a farm, right? I should be used to that kinda living. And besides, he'd probably get a laugh out of me."

Kaitlyn sucked her bottom lip in and swiped right. She'd choose several. Better to have too many. Kenny, 25.

When I'm not in the ER saving lives, you can find me with my passport in hand, exploring destinations far and wide. I'm the kinda guy you can take home to your family. But beware. They may end up liking me more than you, which might end up kinda awkward.

She laughed and swiped right. "Okay, that's enough. I gotta get something to eat."

Tina laughed. "I can't wait to see how this turns out. This should be interesting. Be careful, though. You don't want a *Robbie* repeat."

♥ ♥ ♥

Kaitlyn brushed and re-brushed her hair. She and Bama Boy were meeting today at Coffee Corner. Should she wear makeup? She rarely wore any. Maybe she should just be herself. She chose a navy cabled pullover and skinny jeans. Which earrings? She decided on some small dangly silver ones. She checked herself one last time in the mirror. Why couldn't Tina be home to help her with these important decisions? She was the kind of friend that could take your anxieties and turn them into strengths.

Kaitlyn parked her Prius and clicked the fob—not before looking in the mirror one last time. She walked slowly, taking in deep breaths, trying to will her anxiety to stop. Okay God, I'm trusting you here.

The bell on the door tinkled as she stepped into Coffee

Corner. Fortunately, the place was nearly empty. This was already feeling awkward, and she didn't want to run into anyone she knew. Coming to her normal stomping grounds might not have been the best choice.

She scanned the room but didn't see anyone who matched the profile photo. She tugged her sweater down and redid her sloppy bun. Kaitlyn chose a table in the far corner. Just in case of... what? She wasn't quite sure. But it seemed like a logical option. Then again, it was a long way to the door where she could make a quick escape if needed.

She didn't need to look over the drinks menu — she had them memorized from hundreds of trips here. The hiss of the espresso machine, the sun reflecting off the stainless steel, paused her swirling thoughts. A man's hands suddenly covered her eyes.

"Guess who?" His voice was a little louder than it needed to be, considering they were inside.

Kaitlyn's mouth fell open. "Uh, I'm hoping you're the guy I've got a date with." She peeled his hands off her eyes. Unlike what she expected, he was actually cuter in person. He had his Alabama football cap on backwards, light blond curls peeking out, sunglasses and a freshly shaved face.

He smiled. "Yep, that's me, little gal. I'm your guy! Hey, can I get y'all a coffee? Do you want anything else?" His southern drawl was kind of cute. He glanced around the room as he took off his Carhart jacket.

"Mocha mint — iced — whip cream. And a brownie."

He walked to the counter to order. His muscles rippled under his tight white t-shirt. Plus. The round chew can in his back pocket. Minus.

He walked back to the table, hands full of coffees and

treats. He turned his chair backwards and straddled it. Typical guy. Reminded her of her brother.

"So," Bobby reached out his hand. Kaitlyn took it, surprised by his firm grip. "I'm Bobby. Bobby the Bama Boy."

She couldn't help the smirk forming on her lips. "I'm Kaitlyn the, uh... Oregon Girl. Pleased to meet you, Bobby." Awkward. Her sip of mocha gave her a minute to ponder her next brilliant conversation piece. "Tell me about yourself." That should be a good way to start—keep him talking so she wouldn't have to.

"I guess y'all could tell I'm from the south. I grew up there in Alabama. I came here for a job. Been working at Intel as a welder. It's amazing pay. What about you?" He took a bite of muffin. He sneezed, and bits of it spewed onto the table.

Kaitlyn backed up. Woah now. No need to share. She gingerly offered him a napkin, held between her thumb and forefinger.

"I just finished my nursing degree. I'm looking for a job. I've got an interview next week at Mercy Hospital."

"You're one of those caring people, aren't you? My grandma would probably like you."

Bobby pulled out his phone. "Here, let me show you a picture of her." He scrolled through until he found what appeared to be a family barbecue. He stretched the screen to show a closer look at a woman relaxing in a metal framed lawn chair, a beer can in her hand. Were they shot gunning?

Her perfectly curled, greying hair looked like it had just come out of those round, plastic curlers. Wasn't there some kind of product? Dippity Doo or something like that, which held your hair in place?

"That's Grandma. She's always taking care of everybody.

She once took a barbed fishhook out of my hand. It barely even hurt. Only got infected a little." He took a swig of his Red Bull.

A text buzzed.

<Coming over tonight?>

Kaitlyn tried not to read it, but hey, it was right in front of her. Another text.

<Beers and Cards Against Humanity. Abilene will be there.> Wink emoji.

"Party tonight?" Kaitlyn asked. Bobby quickly swiped back to the photos.

"Um. Yeah, just getting together with some of the guys."

And gals.

He glanced over his shoulder. Who did he think he'd see?

"So," Kaitlyn said. "What do you like to do on your weekends?"

He balanced his chair on the back legs and crossed his arms. "Go hunting for crawdads, mud trucking, catch up on video games." He downed the rest of his drink.

Alrighty then. She checked the time.

"Bobby, I hate to cut this short, but I've got to get home and walk my goldfish." She stood. "It's been nice. Thanks for the treats." And now to hightail it out of here. That was a close call.

What was she getting herself into? Cute wasn't the only ingredient for an excellent date. Maybe a guy with some manners. Or someone able to carry on an intelligent conversation. I know I said I wanted someone with a sense of humor, but really? But how about someone with more of an attention span than a gnat?

Chapter Three

In the plaza outside the seventeen-story skyscraper, Luke McCarthy locked his bike and looked up at the endless glass windows wrapped in trendy shades of blue, teal, and brown.

He pushed through the rotating glass doors, waved at the receptionist, and stepped inside the elevator.

A tall blonde flashed him a smile. "Which floor?"

"Ten please."

"That's where I'm headed. Do you work at Healthy Kids?" She shifted her shoulder bag.

Luke shifted his bike helmet to his left hand and offered her his right.

"Luke McCarthy."

"Gracie St. George, glad to meet you. I was just hired yesterday."

"Welcome! It's a great place to work. I've only worked here a short while, but I love the people and believe in the mission." The doors slid open, and he ushered her through the door.

Finding a job that fit Luke hadn't been easy. Unlike his

12

younger brother, Ryan, who seemed to walk into any job effortlessly, Luke had changed majors several times and finally settled on a degree in non-profit management.

Which had led him to work for an NGO in Mexico, doing meaningful work with families. That was until.... He shook his head at the memory. No sense going there and ruining his day.

The elevator doors opened, and they sauntered down the hall past a large logo of Healthy Kids International. A photo of a couple of bright-eyed, dark-haired children peeking out of the window of a mud and stick house filled an entire wall.

Luke hung his bike helmet on the coat rack and retrieved his laptop from his locker. Natural sunlight filtered through the floor-to-ceiling windows onto the golden bamboo floors.

He sat in one of four orange lounge chairs surrounding a teak coffee table. He gazed out the large picture window at Mt. Hood as he waited for his computer to boot.

His mail populated. Subscriptions to Fundraising Authority, Funds for Good, and Nonprofit Success filled his page. He scrolled down, searching for anything important. He was expecting a reply from a speaker for the next banquet.

Overseeing fundraising and the face of this non-profit was extremely gratifying. Meeting people and making connections was as easy as breathing. And planning the events was so energizing—finding the locale, booking the speakers, signing up sponsors who believed in a faith-based non-profit. He hoped he could live up to his boss' expectations. Which he was sure he could do. As long as she didn't find out about what happened in Mexico. But since that organization no longer existed, he should be safe.

Luke heard the click of Brianna Bradley's boots before he saw her.

He glanced up. She could have been the model on a Vogue magazine cover. Her brown and white striped high-waisted pants and gold patterned scarf covering her bright pink hair made him smile. Stylish short boots finished the ensemble.

The pink hair. Yeah, well, he'd gotten used to his boss changing the color every few days. Heavy eyeliner framed her intense eyes behind her cat eyeglasses.

"Hey Luke," Brianna said. "Did you check out the latest report on our website? We've got an increase in donors by twenty percent."

"No—hey! That's great!" Luke said. He leaned back against the blue suede of his lounge chair and smiled.

"That increase is because of the outstanding job you've done getting out there and schmoozing people. That charming smile of yours must be your recipe for success." Brianna smiled.

Luke stroked his chin. He didn't really think of himself as having a charming smile. He just did what came naturally. Still, Luke buffed his shoulders and sat up straighter, enjoying the praise.

The type of praise he had hungered for in his last job. He was supposed to build a school, help people in need, change lives. Yet here he was, living with a memory that still rattled him.

"I've finished the draft of this month's newsletter. What's next?"

"I'll look it over and shoot it on to graphics. Take a look at our website and see how you can spice it up. I'd like to see it before closing tomorrow." She walked off.

He spent some time looking over other websites of Non-Governmental Organizations. The one thing NGOs had in common was some cute kid smiling and something making the donor into the hero. In the case of Healthy Kids, their banner photo was of sickly kids, making the donor give out of guilt.

That needed to change. The verbiage was just a little too wordy and technical. Brianna was right. It needed a makeover, for sure. Maybe he could suggest a video clip that would draw people in. Something with kids before and after. Sadness into joy?

He opened Adobe and sketched out a storyboard. First scene: kids in, where? India? South America? They wander aimlessly down a street. Their tattered clothing highlights their poverty. Two: a marketplace with lots of fresh produce, poultry hanging, pig's heads, vendors placing food in baskets for customers. Three: Back to the kids. They jostle each other. A motorcycle whizzes by with a man and wife riding, a baby strapped to the wife's back. One boy stops and looks longingly at them. Four: A man and woman from Healthy Kids walk through the village handing out fresh fruit. Five: The kids encounter the HK people. They take the fruit and run, laughing.

Luke rubbed his hand through his brown hair and stretched. He grabbed his coffee cup and headed to the Keurig. And glanced at Brianna. Who was she under her boss' bravado? She was a hard one to figure out.

Gracie came up beside him.

"What are you working on?" Luke selected a dark roast pod and placed his cup under it.

"Just trying to make sense of the health records. The last person didn't keep outstanding records—just sayin'. I've spent hours poring over them and trying to fix the disparities."

"That sounds like a lot of work!"

"It is. But it's what I enjoy."

"No thanks. I'll stick to my job." Luke shook his head. He filled his cup and headed back to his desk. Teamwork. Everyone using their own gifts.

This job held the promise of what he longed for—purpose, passion, and belonging. He was becoming convinced he was right where God wanted him.

Chapter Four

Kaitlyn had accepted a date to the exclusive Portland City Grill restaurant. But not before she had started messaging Kevin. She wasn't going to make the same mistake—a cold first date. Based on the few conversations and texts, he seemed okay. She'd shown them to Tina, who had thought they showed promise.

Kaitlyn's freshly plucked eyebrows framed her sparkling brown eyes. This had to be better than the last time. If nothing else, she should get an excellent dinner out of it.

Kevin was waiting for her at the front door of the restaurant. His grey sport coat and slacks made a good impression. He obviously prided himself on his good looks. She breathed a sigh of relief when she saw he wasn't wearing a tie. She would have felt underdressed in her simple teal dress.

"Hi, you must be Kaitlyn." His face broke out in a wide smile. "You look just like your photo." He reached out his rough hand. Up close, she wondered if his profile photo had had a little digital enhancement. There was only a slight resemblance. For starters, she didn't remember his face being that round. Or a unibrow. He did, as his profile said, wear matching clothes.

"Kevin?" He nodded. His eyes swept over her face approvingly, wandering past her dangling necklace to the hem of her dress.

The host led them past a man with distinguished grey hair dressed in a tux who ran his fingers over the keys of a piano, filling the room with soft jazz. The host seated them near a fireplace in a cozy corner.

Kaitlyn studied her menu, sneaking a glance at Kevin out of the corner of her eye.

"What's your favorite food?" Kevin peeked over the top of his menu.

"Anything that isn't green." Kaitlyn wrinkled her nose.

"No salad?" She shook her head decisively.

"No asparagus?"

"Absolutely not! What do you like?" Kaitlyn's eyes peeked over her menu.

"Carrots. Those little bitty ones. Especially cooked with brown sugar and butter." Kevin placed his hand on his heart and looked up. Kevin, the carrot guy. Yeah.

The waitperson returned, and she ordered steak and baked potato. He ordered scallops and halibut with quinoa. Carrots and quinoa. Not looking good.

"So, Kevin, where do you work? Your profile didn't say."

"I'm actually between jobs right now. I was working construction on a high-rise hotel, but the job was finished, and I got laid off. You?" His hazel eyes gazed into hers.

"I'm starting work at Mercy Hospital this week."

"A job like that should be food for all kinds of stories." He placed the cloth napkin in his lap and reached for a piece of artisan bread.

"Yeah, if it's anything like my clinicals." Maybe this guy might be alright. He's got great manners, anyway.

"Where'd you grow up?"

"A lot of places. We moved around a lot. Military kid. You?" He took a sip of his beer.

"On the coast. My dad's a farmer- sheep and blueberries. It's a beautiful area. Fishing, hunting, kayaking. You do any of that?"

"Nah. I'm more into sports. Watching football, playing basketball. I play pickup games on the weekends."

The server came by to take their plates. "Dessert?"

Kaitlyn glanced at Kevin. "No, not tonight. I'm stuffed."

He placed the bill on the table.

Kevin laid his phone on the table and fished in his pants pocket for his wallet. He patted his shirt pocket.

"I must have left my wallet at home. I am so sorry. Any chance you could cover dinner?" He glanced over his shoulder.

"Yeah, I guess." Kaitlyn frowned and pulled out her credit card. *No offer to pay me back, I see.*

Kevin started texting someone. Kaitlyn signed the slip and looked at him quizzically.

"Oh, sorry, I gotta go meet some friends. Hey, could you give me twenty dollars to take the max and get some beer?"

Not a chance, loser. She resisted making a L with her fingers and putting it on her forehead. See? Tina would be proud of her. She was acting more adult.

Kaitlyn turned abruptly and headed to her car. She couldn't believe she had made two bad choices. Maybe taking things into her own hands wasn't such a great idea.

Really, was she that desperate that she needed to play the dating game? All she wanted was a companion. Neither of these idiots were in the league for a friend, let alone life partners and soul mates. She lifted her open hands in the air.

Okay, God. You gotta help me with this. Either help me be satisfied to be single or get me a good guy. Emphasis on good! A guy in flannel would be nice, too.

Chapter Five

K aitlyn groped for her phone as the alarm sounded. She stumbled out of bed and looked at the circles under her eyes as she brushed her teeth. She was sure she hadn't slept for thirty minutes last night. Her mind kept spinning thinking about her first day at Mercy Hospital. She'd gotten up twice, sure she was going to throw up. She never should have ventured into the dating world. Having a new job had enough anxieties of its own.

At least she had a friend who would be with her. If she could just look past day one, she'd be okay. But right now? Not happening. What if they found out what she'd done? At least her mistake was safe with Tina. She took a deep breath and stepped into the hot shower.

As she toweled off, Kaitlyn remembered how hard she had worked to have grades that had been stellar. Her dad had been so proud of her. And her internship had gone well. Until...

She shook her head. What if she didn't fit in at Mercy Hospital? What if her supervisor was death on her like the one she had been assigned during her senior practicum? What if she had to put in an IV and couldn't find the vein, or worse, put in a catheter and missed the right hole? They would all think she was an imbecile, and they'd probably be right.

"Kaitlyn, you up?" Tina hollered up the stairs. She tucked her thoughts into a box and hid them somewhere in the folds of her brain.

"Yeah, I'll be down in a minute. What should I wear?"

"I'm just gonna go with business casual. Wait, were we supposed to show up in scrubs?" Tina asked.

"Yikes, not sure." Kaitlyn quickly confirmed with her email.

"Scrubs," she called.

She quickly threw on the blue Dickies she had from when she was a student. She'd play it safe and not wear her puppy dog scrubs this time.

"Tina, check me over — any blood or bodily fluid stains I've missed?" Tina scrutinized her scrubs and gave the thumbs up.

They grabbed their coffees and headed out the door. Kaitlyn set her cup on the roof of her Prius and slid in. She pressed the start key and backed up.

"Wait!" She panicked and pushed the brake. She jumped out and watched as coffee dripped down the windshield and her travel mug slid under the car. She squatted and tried to reach it, but it rolled to the center, where she hoped, she could avoid hitting it when she backed up.

"I can tell what kind of day this is gonna be. I'm already starting to sweat."

Tina laughed. "Just calm down. You'll be fine. I'm nervous too. We'll be great! Maybe we should pray before we go!" She folded her hands together in prayer and looked up. "Jesus, we need you!"

"We really need you!" Kaitlyn echoed. Short prayers to the point were as good as long ones, right?

Kaitlyn circled the parking lot through all levels before she finally found a slot. By the time they made their way to the lobby, took the elevator to the third floor, and walked to the nursing station, she was a nervous wreck.

Kaitlyn linked arms with Tina. "What if they find out?"

"They won't. You don't have to tell them. I'm sure they did a comprehensive background check and if they hired you, I'm sure no one told them."

Kaitlyn squeezed her eyes shut.

"You'll be fine! This is no time to let your anxieties grab hold of you."

Tina was right. Of course she was right. She was the level-headed one. And if anyone knew her, it was Tina. You couldn't be friends since kindergarten and not know each other through and through.

❦ ❦ ❦

Kaitlyn and Tina walked through the entry gazing at artwork covering the walls. A painting of an elderly couple holding hands by a pond, a sculpture of a girl dancing and lifting her hands in praise, a quilted wall hanging of women laughing with subtly interwoven pink breast cancer logos. A huge picture window overlooked Portland with a snow-capped Mt. Hood in the distance.

"There're the two guys who were at orientation yesterday.

They must be working our shift." Kaitlyn nodded her head towards them.

Dozens of employees with white coats and scrubs filled the halls, clipboards in hands.

"Who are all these people?" Peter swung his lanyard around his finger like a propeller.

"Attendings, residents, students, pharmacists...Did you grow up in a barn? Short memory?"

Kaitlyn sidestepped just in time to avoid Peter giving Dan a friendly shove.

"Yeah actually, I did. Just a little out of my comfort zone here."

They followed Dan and Peter into the elevator. Kaitlyn backed up to the wall while Tina pushed the fifth-floor button.

"So, are you guys ready for the day?" Dan raised his eyebrows.

"It might be a bit of a challenge." Tina pulled an elastic from her scrubs pocket and pulled her hair back. "I mean, Delores? What the heck?" Kaitlyn gave an involuntary shudder. The charge nurse hadn't been exactly friendly. When they had approached her station, she didn't bother to turn her six-foot frame from the file cabinet to welcome them. Her lip curled when she finally faced them, making her feel like she was gum on the bottom of her shoe.

"I think she just wants to intimidate people. She's probably a softie at heart." Peter shrugged. Kaitlyn could only hope he was right. The doors slid open.

Kaitlyn looked up at the light fixture made of several organic paper shapes. The gentle sound of water streaming over a large slate wall was peaceful. Huge picture windows overlooked the Willamette River.

They walked down the hall, passing enormous patient rooms. Kaitlyn marveled at the individual vitals machines on the walls and state-of-the-art equipment. They hadn't had anything like this in the small rural hospital that she and Tina had trained in.

"You could do cartwheels in these rooms!" Kaitlyn said. "They're huge!" They had been used to double occupancy rooms where you had to scrunch against the wall when trying to bring in carts of equipment.

"I wonder what these nurses had to do to be assigned to such a nice floor." Dan's deep voice was close to a whisper.

"I don't know, but I hope we get paid more than them. Our floor is going to be a challenge." Tina led them past a Hawaiian vacation motif sitting on the nursing station counter where a hula dancer wobbled. Was this floor pretending to be a vacay? Maybe it had a spa. And the patients were here for tummy tucks.

They followed Dan and walked what seemed a city block, through a long corridor, past an information booth, down another long hall, and finally arrived.

Kaitlyn made her way over the old, thread bare purple carpet. A carpet string caught on her shoe and unraveled as she took several steps. She stopped and gingerly unwound it. This place looked like it hadn't been cleaned since Noah built the ark.

Peter laughed. "A little sketch. Ghetto."

There wasn't one piece of artwork. The peeling walls were painted hospital green. Ceiling tiles overhead had water stains.

"Good morning, Delores." Peter gave the large woman a salute. Delores narrowed her eyes.

A call light was flashing, a small beep sounded with each flash.

"Log into the computer and read the reports so you know where to start."

Kaitlyn's pulse was rising. Was she really going to be able to work with this woman? PTSDs were setting in. This was too much like clinicals, reminding her of her tragic mistake.

"Don't just stand there. Y'all should know what to do," Delores snapped.

Kaitlyn wrapped her arms across her chest, willing herself to remain calm.

They moved to the computer, where Dan took the lead and pulled up the charts.

A large man shuffled out of room 4, hanging onto his IV pole. His bare bottom showed through his open gown. Kaitlyn glanced at Tina.

Peter whispered, "Shut the curtain!" Kaitlyn's lips turned up.

"Nurse," the man said, his voice raspy, evidence of a lifetime of smoking. "Nurse! I pushed the call button, and you didn't come!"

Delores turned around, straightened her shoulders, and stood to her intimidating height. Her hands went to her broad hips. "Who elected you king of the floor? You think you're all I have to think about?"

"I think my IV is coming out." He rubbed his whiskered chin. The tape on his hand hung by a thread, the tube dangling to the floor where he nearly stepped on it.

"Get back to your room," she commanded. "I'll be there when I get time. Can't you see I've got more important things to do?" She looked at Kaitlyn. "You—go take care of him."

"Man, looks like we've got Nurse Ratched here," Peter whispered.

A nurse appeared from around the corner, his black hair pulled into a man bun. "Oh, hey! Glad you guys are here. I wasn't sure if you'd come back after the way she treated you yesterday."

Kaitlyn's shoulders relaxed when she saw Sahid's broad smile.

"We've had to learn our way around Miss Grumpy Pants." Sahid looked over his shoulder and laughed. "Her bark's bigger than her bite."

"My meds, somebody. Give me my meds."

"Hey Gus, we've got you covered, man. Let's get you back to your room." Sahid took his elbow and guided him to his room.

As they walked down the hallway, the strangled cry of "Hel-lllppp!" came from Room 8.

Kaitlyn felt like a deer in the headlights. Be the hands and feet of Jesus, they said. Bring compassion, they said. Spread the love, they said. It'll be fun.

She couldn't shake the feeling that sooner or later, Delores would uncover the secret she held buried in her heart.

Chapter Six

"Who's that?" Dan peered over Kaitlyn's shoulder as she scrolled through several pics.

"A guy I went on a date with the other night." A gorgeous guy. "He's from Honduras. He'll be over in a bit."

Kaitlyn and Tina had invited Dan and Peter over for dinner and game night. Turns out they made up a pretty good team on their Mercy floor. A balance of crazy and got-your-back.

"A guy, eh?" Daniel raised one eyebrow.

Her face flushed, scooting her lasagna around her plate with her fork.

"Ooooooh," Peter made a heart shape with his hands and held them over his heart, making them beat.

"Stop! He's a really nice guy who doesn't know very many people and wants me to tutor him. Don't give him a bad impression of America."

"Yeah, okay. But here's the thing. If you get all lovey-dovey with this guy, who will marry me?" Peter said. His face fell with mocked pain.

Kaitlyn rolled her eyes and shook her head. "Not a chance, friend. Not a chance." Peter was cute, in a dorky sort of way. He was always pushing his straight brown hair out of his eyes. And freckles scattered over his nose and cheeks. But let's face it, he was fun.

The doorbell rang. Dan rushed to open it.

Francisco looked confused. "This is right house?"

"The right house for what?" He crossed his arms as if he were the sentinel.

"I look for Kaitlyn."

"Oh yeah, come on in." Dan grinned and stepped aside.

"Hey Francisco. Don't mind him." Kaitlyn rolled her eyes and made quick introductions. "Sit here, I saved you a plate." She passed Francisco the lasagna. And the salad. He shook his head at the greens. Kaitlyn smiled at him. Just earned himself a point.

So," Peter began. "Kaitlyn says you're from Honduras. You're going to school?"

"Si, am in year one and am study science. Is very difficult," Francisco said.

"Where are you living?" Dan said.

"I live with una familia who sponsors me, very nice family, very nice home." He took a bite. "This very good." He placed his fingers on her hand. Kaitlyn smiled, a warmth traveling up her arm. One point for the cook.

Tina placed salad on her fork. "Are you working too?"

"Can only work at college, I no have green card." *That wasn't a problem, right?*

After dinner was done, Kaitlyn helped Tina clear the dishes.

"Francisco, how about I beat you in a game of poker?" Peter

said. He pulled out a deck of cards from his backpack and dealt.

"You guys go ahead. We girls are gonna sit this one out." Tina glanced at Kaitlyn. They finished putting the dishes in the dishwasher and headed to the living room. Kaitlyn stretched out on her new red couch, one she had picked out for her birthday to replace the ugly, ripped, garage sale one.

Kaitlyn had been lucky to find this house with its 1920s wood windows. Above the door, framed in dark oak, was a lead cut glass window which shot rainbows when the sun shone. The massive stone fireplace stood on one side with the perfect mantle for hanging Christmas stockings. Still six months away. If anyone was counting. Which she might be accused of. Could this Perfect Match date last long enough to make it to Christmas?

"Well," Kaitlyn whispered. "What do you think?"

"He's a typical guy—two helpings!" Tina adjusted a pillow behind her back.

"He wants me to help him with his studies. Is that an okay thing to do?"

Tina shrugged. "Why wouldn't it be? You had a great date, or you wouldn't have invited him over."

"I did. He's interesting. I just don't want to get into anything that I'll wish I hadn't started. Just a little gun shy after my rush to the altar."

Tina rolled her eyes. "As you should be. Just see if you can meet him at Coffee Corner after work. Give it a try. If you don't like it, you can always back out." Tina pulled her auburn hair out of a sloppy bun and redid it.

"Yeah, I guess." So far, so good. He had paid for their dinner the other night. He was polite and unassuming. Not distracted.

She turned towards the kitchen as Peter let out a whoop. Tina shook her head and grinned.

"But those green eyes! They're mesmerizing. I might not get any tutoring done cuz I'm sidetracked gazing at him!"

"True that. I say go for it! Just make sure you fill me in on every detail."

A loud shout arose from the kitchen from all three guys. Peter crowed his win and strutted into the living room, followed by the others.

"This is nice house!" Francisco let his eyes roam the room. "My house where I am from is very small. Is made of mud and branches. I like America. Es muy bueno."

"Well, I for one am glad you're here." Kaitlyn smiled. "Do you want to meet me at Coffee Corner Saturday around five o'clock?" Francisco nodded. "Oh, wait. I forgot I'm going on a bike meet-up. How about Monday?"

Francisco shrugged.

"Unless you like to ride." She cocked her eyebrow.

"I ride only motorbikes." Francisco shrugged.

"Well, bring your homework Monday and we'll see whatcha got."

Francisco repeated, "Whatcha got?" Kaitlyn just patted him on the shoulder. *She could teach him a few idioms along the way.*

Peter pulled Kaitlyn aside. "Maybe this is Mr. Right!" he whispered and winked.

Kaitlyn blushed and grabbed her keys to take Francisco home. She was beginning to hope Peter was right.

Chapter Seven

The sky couldn't have been any bluer for Luke's bike trip. He checked the air in his tires and made sure all the fix-it supplies were in his pack. Invariably someone would have a breakdown of one sort or another. It was just part of the gig. He didn't mind. He loved riding so much he wanted others to feel the thrill of the wind on your face and see what grew on the sides of the road up close and personal.

He grabbed a handful of healthy bars and cheese sticks in his pack. He looked around. He'd throw in a brownie for later. A little chocolate never hurt anyone. Star Wars sounded on his phone.

"Hey Dad, how's it going?' Luke filled his water bottle.

"Just checking in."

"I'm getting all my gear together to lead the bike ride."

"Sounds fun! It's a great day for it. Say, just wanted to let you know I'm taking GrandpaWilliam in for some tests. Hope it's nothing serious."

"You'll let me know what you find out, right?" His stomach

tightened. He loved that man. He really hoped it wasn't something serious. Grandpa had been the one to teach him how to ride a bike.

He remembered his seventh birthday. Grandpa William had shown up late. He said he had run out of gas and had to make a few stops. When Luke saw him get out of his car, he ran down the sidewalk and threw his arms around him. He'd never forget the twinkle in his eyes.

He had asked Grandpa where his present was. Grandpa had pretended that he had forgotten it. Luke had slumped his shoulders and walked off. Grandpa had called out to him and told him to look in the back of his pickup. And there was his red Schwinn, just the right size. Grandpa had taught him how to ride, telling him he didn't need training wheels, he was a big boy. He would run along beside him and tell him to keep peddling until Luke finally got the hang of it. The memory brought a smile to his face. Then a flash of pain. He couldn't think of anything worse than something happening to Grandpa William.

His dad cut into his thoughts. "Absolutely. You know I will. Love you, son. Oh, and maybe you'll meet some cute girl on your ride." Luke could see him winking.

Why was everyone so worried about his love life? He wasn't even thirty. He had lots of time. And he definitely didn't want to just jump into anything. He already had friends who had married and divorced. That was not something on his bucket list.

The Meetup spot was at one of Portland's beautiful parks on the east side. He arrived early and took out his list. Eight guys, five gals. Ten had been on prior trips. Newbies? Juan

Martinez, Guan-yin Lee and Kaitlyn Monroe. It would be fun to show them the ropes.

The group arrived, introduced each other, checked water bottles and tires. Luke made sure they all had reflector tape.

"Okay, friends," he said. "Let's review the route. This is a twenty-five-mile loop. It has a few hills, so I hope you're in good shape. We'll cross the Willamette River on the Canby Ferry, which is free for bikers. Then we'll finish through Historic, Oregon City. Any questions?"

Kaitlyn raised her hand so eagerly her curly brown hair bounced. "Are there any coffee shops along the way?"

Luke chuckled with the rest of them. She'll be fun to have on this trip. Was it her quirky smile? Or the animated way her eyes crinkled?

"I'm sure we'll pass one." He winked.

Everyone mounted their bikes and followed Luke's lead. The day was the type you saw in travel brochures. The August fields had turned brown, but the orchards were green and ripe with apples and pears.

Luke was clearly in his element. Wind in his face, sun on his back. Lots of time to reflect. He said a prayer for each of the participants.

Luke looked back to check on his troupes. All good. A fruit stand came into view. He motioned to them and pulled over to take a break. They parked their bikes, removed their helmets, and looked through the stands. Golden peaches, shiny purple plums and pears had been arranged in an inviting pattern. Luke watched as Kaitlyn purchased a peach and sat down at a picnic table with several others.

"Is this your first bike ride?" she asked Juan.

"Yeah. I bike to work and take my nephews for rides to the park. This is the longest I've gone."

"I've never done a ride this long. It's so pretty out here." Kaitlyn slid over as Luke joined them.

"Having fun?" he asked. Nods all around.

"It's so gorgeous here!" Guan-Yin said. She removed her U of O sweatshirt. "And getting a little warm!"

"Wait till we get to the river. The water is so beautiful. It sparkles in the sun and sometimes you can see fish jump. You might even see the family of swans. We definitely live in a wonderful state." The excitement in Luke's eyes said it all.

"We better head out now, so we stay on schedule. We don't want to miss the ferry." Luke watched Kaitlyn pull her helmet over her curly brown hair.

They started out and not ten minutes later, Kaitlyn let out an ear-piercing scream as her tire blew. Luke turned around as she stood by her bike. Kaitlyn frowned, hands on hips, and let out a long, slow exhale.

"Dang. Now what do I do?" She palmed her forehead.

"Not to worry," Luke said. He pulled out his repair kit, turned her bike upside down, pulled off the tire and repaired the tube. He felt Kaitlyn's eyes on him, and he flexed despite himself. Kaitlyn's look of admiration warmed him. He watched as she tucked a strand of hair under her helmet, wishing she had left it dangle.

Kaitlyn crossed her arms over her chest. "Where did you learn to do all this stuff?"

"I worked in a bike shop for a while, and I love to ride. Knowing how to fix bikes comes in handy when you take long trips." He grinned. In short order, they were on their way.

"How long have you been leading bike trips?"

"Not long, about a year. I love it and like to share the experience."

"Have you been on many trips?"

"No, this is actually the first time. I might have to make this a habit." Luke wouldn't mind that. He hoped she didn't notice the blood rush to his cheeks.

"It sure is beautiful." Kaitlyn scanned the countryside.

"Where do you work?" Luke asked.

"I'm a nurse at Mercy Hospital. I just graduated last June and fortunately got a job right away. My roommate, Tina, got a job with me. She keeps me sane. I never knew nursing could be so challenging."

"In what way?"

"There are so many patients with more than just physical problems. It's been an eye opener, for sure."

"I work at Healthy Kids. I see the same kind of things. We work in third world countries providing schools, job training and medical needs. We also serve refugees here in Portland. Hey, you wouldn't be interested in helping, would you? We've got a clinic set up for next weekend to give immunizations and could use some more RN's."

"I think I could do that." Kaitlyn's smile made its way from his eyes to his heart.

"Hey, there's the ferry up ahead. We better push to make sure we get there in time. Race you!"

Luke matched Kaitlyn's pace. A smirk played on his lips as she pushed hard against the pedals, the wind rushing through the strand of hair that slipped below her helmet. She moved in front of him. Should he let her win? She turned her head to glance around, and he shot past her with an easy grin.

The others, trailing along behind her, were shouting

encouragement and hoots of laughter. Kaitlyn pushed harder, the roars of victory spurring her on.

Another few yards, and they coasted in together. Kaitlyn started to laugh and held her belly. Hoots of fellow cyclers championed them. When had he had this much fun?

Chapter Eight

Luke's fingers fumbled as he locked his bike and headed to the office. He took the stairs two at a time. There wasn't time to wait for an elevator. He burst through the office door. Brianna walked towards him with a stack of newly copied papers. He shrank back. Slipping in unnoticed would not be an option.

She set the pile on her desk, glanced at the clock and back at him. "Nice of you to join us today, Mr. McCarthy."

"I know, I'm so sorry." She's going to think I'm a flake. "There was this single mom with three kids in her car with a flat tire. I stopped to fix it for her. It took a lot longer than I thought it would. I'll stay late tonight to make up for it."

"Aw, you're such a nice guy!" Brianna said. "Really, though, that's exactly why we hired you. We needed someone with that caring help-a-person-in-need outlook on life."

Luke breathed a sigh of relief.

"We need to get together," she said. "I'm developing a plan for outreach, and I need you in on it."

"How about I take you to lunch?" Luke asked. "We can talk then."

And maybe there would be a chance to get to know her on a more personal level. He didn't think she'd agree, but it was worth a try.

"I guess I could do that. Somewhere close by, though. I've got a lot to do today."

Luke leaned on the side of her desk and casually crossed his legs.

"We could go to Huber's for a burger or Masu Sushi. They're both within walking distance." Luke wasn't sure whether she was one of those *cool* vegetarian kids.

"Let's do sushi. I don't eat meat."

Yep, one of *those* people.

His desk phone rang. He sauntered over to it.

"Hello, Healthy Kids International." Pause. "Yes." He picked up his pen and started writing. "Yep, I'd love to. Okay, I'll be here. Ten o'clock it is." Luke stared at the floor and whooshed out a breath. That was weird.

He checked the time. Got an hour to get stuff organized. But first things first. Coffee. He headed toward the break room. There was invariably a flurry of activity in this office. Some staffers were making donor phone calls. Computer keyboards were clicking. Piles of newsletters were ka-chunking out of the copy machine.

He found his mug in the drainer where he left it. He poured the black roast into his cup and turned, nearly dousing Gracie with it.

"Oh, so sorry," Luke said.

"We need traffic signals here." Gracie smiled. "Say, who just called you?"

"Oh, so now you're eavesdropping on my conversations?" He cocked an eyebrow.

"Maaayyyybeee, just a little." She gathered her long blond hair and tossed it off her shoulder.

"So, who?"

"Well, if you must know, it was Mr. Steinberg himself." Luke straightened his shoulders.

"He's going to meet with you? Man, you must be pretty important."

Luke closed his hand and blew on his fingernails. "Yep, that's me. Mr. Important."

"Isn't he the CEO of Healthy Kids?"

"Yeah, I've seen his name on all the brochures. I'm not sure what he wants, but I hope it's good." Luke's eyes travelled to the floor. There's no way he's found out about what happened in Mexico, right?

His face grew warm as thoughts flooding in. He had worked at another NGO in Mexico — a birthday present to himself when he turned twenty-one. Go on an adventure. Save the world. It all sounded great. But when he got in the thick of things, he realized that the fishing trips his boss had been going on for parties had been for his own pleasure, funded with donor contributions.

He ignored it. Until the day when he met Zach—he could still see his dark eyes and pencil thin arms and legs. This little boy stole his heart. When Luke found out he needed a heart transplant or he wouldn't see his eighth birthday, Luke had to figure out a way to provide the funding he needed for that to happen.

The problem was his idea landed him in the Mexican jail. Turns out they don't think much of someone who embezzles.

Luke cleared his throat. "Gotta get back to work."

He logged into his computer and looked over the new website mockup. Being part of the marketing department was the most energizing job Luke had ever had. He thought he had a pretty good idea what it should look like, but the glitch was he needed video clips. Real clips. Not some cheesy stock photos from the internet.

When they went to lunch today, he'd talk to Brianna about it. He glanced at her. Now wasn't a good time to interrupt her. She was focused on her work. And he was still trying to figure out his place.

What could Mr. Steinberg possibly want? Luke had only been working at Healthy Kids a few months. Guess he'd find out soon. He checked his cell again. Ten till ten. He tidied up his workspace— loose pens into the cup, straightened his papers, put some files in the cabinet.

Gracie accompanied a distinguished-looking man dressed in an expensive Italian suit to Luke. His thick grey hair was neatly cut. Mr. Steinberg smoothed his fingers over his short mustache.

"I'll introduce you to him, Mr. Steinberg. This is Luke," Gracie said. She stepped back, caught Luke's eye, and did a silent, happy dance. Luke tried to ignore her but found his lips turning up in a grin. He held out his hand.

"Mr. Steinberg. How nice to meet you! To what do I owe this honor, sir?" Luke's palms were getting sweaty. He almost felt like he should bow.

"Mr. McCarthy, the pleasure is mine."

"Would you like to sit down?" Luke motioned to a lounge chair.

Mr. Steinberg sat and crossed his legs. "So, why you? Why

Luke McCarthy? I'll tell you why. You, my friend, have written an outstanding piece for the Oregonian, which was picked up by papers all over the United States. Your description and the manner in which you presented Healthy Kids was superb. That article has led to an increase in donors by fifty percent! I must say I am proud to have you as part of our team. And I wanted to come here personally and thank you."

Luke let out a slow breath. He tried hard not to let his jaw drop. Yes, he had written a great article, but outstanding? Did Mr. Steinberg, the Mr. Steinberg, founder of Healthy Kids, just say he had done something outstanding?

A flash of red was coming his way. Brianna sauntered up. Her red jean jacket covered a stylish navy blouse.

"Mr. Steinberg, what a surprise to see you!"

He looked up and smiled. "Brianna." He held out his hand.

"What brings you here? We're so privileged to have you. Gracie, did you offer Mr. Steinberg something to drink?"

He waved her off. "I'm fine, thank you. You know Brianna, how I enjoy honoring those who deserve it. I've come to let Luke know that I'll be presenting an award to him at the next general staff meeting in Chicago."

Luke's eyes grew large. He opened his mouth to respond. Closed it. Tried again.

"Not sure what to say," he finally blurted.

"Say you'll join us in September," said Mr. Steinberg. "I'll arrange for your plane ticket."

"Well, alrighty then," Luke said. "Yes, and thank you, Mr. Steinberg. A pleasure." Mr. Steinberg shook his hand and Brianna gave Luke a congratulatory pat on the back.

"He's a keeper, this one." Pride written on her face.

＊ ＊ ＊

The clock struck twelve, and Luke's stomach involuntarily growled. He looked over at Brianna—head bent over her work.

"Time for lunch," he said as he sauntered to her desk.

Brianna looked up, taking a moment to leave her deep thoughts and focus on Luke.

"Oh! Already? Okay. Let me get my bag."

They took the elevator and walked into the bright sunlight. Brianna put on her red-rimmed sunglasses. Apparently, she had a pair to match each outfit.

"Pretty impressive to have Mr. Steinberg visit you today. Wow!"

"Yeah, I was not expecting that. I thought it was just an article. I didn't realize the ramifications. So glad I could help." And obviously Mr. Steinberg hadn't known about. . .

Luke pushed open the glass door to the restaurant. The hostess took them to a low table. They kneeled down on mats and looked over the menu.

Luke admired the intricate design of her kimono as they ordered the special salmon sushi with tempura shrimp.

"So, what's on your mind for outreach?" Luke returned his attention to Brianna.

"Okay, so I have this idea. I'd like to get feet on the ground in our projects to see what's going on. I particularly want to look at San Pedro, Honduras." The server brought their drinks. Brianna twirled the stem of her glass between her fingers.

"We have a fairly extensive project there. A medical facility, a large farm where we grow vegetables, parks development for physical activity, clean water projects, counseling, mom's groups." Brianna took a sip of her margarita.

They looked up as the server brought the plates of sushi.

"That's a pretty wide impact. What would you like me to do?"

"Ideally, I would like to send you down to visit each aspect and give me a report." Luke's mind started to whirr. Was God giving him another opportunity? One to redeem himself?

"I can't get down there myself, and I think you'd be the best choice."

"Will I go alone? When were you thinking?" Luke did a quick calculation of the things on his calendar. Paint grandpa's house, bike ride to Silver Springs, counselor at the upcoming youth camp.

"At this point, I'm thinking October. That would be after your event with Mr. Steinberg in September. Which by the way, I was quite surprised that he came. You need to know how proud I am of you."

Luke beamed. He had never experienced this type of appreciation.

Brianna took a bite of sushi. "This is delicious. I was contemplating sending Gracie. You two seem to be a good fit." Gracie? She'd be fun.

"Alright. I need to dig out my passport. I guess I better get on that. Let me ask you this. You know I've been working on a new website. Would it be possible for me to take video clips while I'm there? I need genuine stuff."

"That would be perfect. I'd like to have footage of the different projects anyway to see what's happening." Brianna looked at her watch. "Wow, we need to get back." She signaled for the check. Luke dug out his wallet. Brianna waved him off.

"Don't worry about it. I'll put it on the company credit card." she dug out her wallet.

He smiled. He could get used to the perks of this job. Just as quickly, he shook his head. Nope, not going down that road again.

Chapter Nine

L uke listened to the chime of the Seth Thomas pendulum wall clock. Five o'clock came around quickly when you got sucked into the vortex of the computer world. He'd lost track of time.

Luke closed his laptop and glanced at Brianna, who was deep in a pile of papers. He was sure she was the kind of gal who knew where everything was in her piles. Sticky notes covered the bulletin board in her cubicle. A scripture posted along the top of her monitor read: *Whatever your hand finds to do, do it with all your might.* That would be Brianna—driven.

"See you tomorrow," he called. "Don't work too late!"

She nodded and gave a quick salute. Luke loved his job, but he was not interested in being married to it. He hoped Brianna wouldn't be requiring him to put in the kind of hours that she held. He started for the door, then turned. "Do you want me to pick up something to eat from the food cart?"

"Nah, I've got the other half of my lunch in the fridge. Thanks, though." She didn't as much as glance up.

He took the stairs down and opened the front door to the

brilliant sunlight. He rummaged in his pocket for his sunglasses and placed his helmet on. As he unlatched the bike lock, a man approached him, his long, grey hair wisped around his unshaven face.

"Hey mister, can you spare a dollar?" One hand grasped the handle of his shopping cart, full of tattered paperbacks, a chipped cup, utensils and who knew what else lay under a worn blanket.

Luke patted him on the shoulder. "John, how's it going?"

Luke reached into his pocket and gave him a five. John held it gingerly between his thumbs and forefingers of both hands. He studied it, raised his eyebrows, and said, "Thanks, man!"

Luke held his gaze. He didn't get it. John saw Luke every day. Luke had had entire conversations with him. Even introduced himself. But John always acted as if he'd never seen him before in his life. Just in his own little world? Or the victim of drugs and street life. He shrugged his shoulders.

This could have been him after his stint in jail. If it hadn't been for... He wasn't going to let his mind go back to that. Focus on something positive. Like the bike Meetup. And Kaitlyn. He wondered if she had a guy in her life. How could he find out?

He hopped on his bike and eased out into the bike lane. This bike was his pride and joy. He had spent a lot of time researching and finally decided on a Trek FX Sport bike. It had cost him a whole paycheck but had all the features he craved. A lightweight frame, twenty-speed drivetrain, shift, and brake cables that were routed through the frame. It was clean and slick. He also relished the fact that it had a Bluetooth antenna built into the frame that logged his routes and tracked fitness.

Last week he'd ridden two hundred miles. That, of course,

included his ride to Silver Creek Falls. He had clocked in at fifty-eight miles each way. What a beautiful ride that was. A gorgeous sunny day. Spectacular scenery. Mt. Hood, a majestic backdrop, still had a little snow on it, not unusual for summer. He'd checked out the route to make sure it would work for the next Meet Up.

He pedaled past the high school where some boys were playing a pickup game of basketball. In high school, Luke hadn't been the best student. The fact was nothing high school offered motivated him. He liked to fool around with basketball but wasn't on the team. He enjoyed receiving a bit part in a play but wasn't sure he was actor material. He had a few friends, but he wasn't in the "in" crowd, and frankly, didn't want to be. He never liked the idea of joining them for drinking parties or smoking pot.

The truth was, he always lived in his younger brother Ryan's shadow. It was as if Ryan knew where he was going in life the day he was born. His name was on the gym wall for the most valuable player. He had awards in Honor Society and Debate and every other thing you could think of. But Luke? Not so much.

His parents figured Luke would grow up at some point and settle into something worthwhile. Well, they were right. Again. His non-profit degree had led him to what he loved and felt a vital part of. Changing lives. Now that was rewarding. Changing kids' lives was even more so. Like Zach. That had been good, right? Worth the cost?

He turned down 12th Street and waved at Hong, who was organizing guavas and pineapples on a rack. He arrived home and guided his bike down the sidewalk, hopped off and walked it into his apartment.

Blinking red from the message machine reflected on the chrome of the toaster.

"Hey, Luke. It's dad. Just wanted to tell you we missed you. Just checking in. Grandpa would love a visit with you sometime. I know you're busy, but we're getting together for a barbecue at his place tonight. Give me a call. I love you!"

It hadn't been that long, had it? He should make spending family time more of a priority. And considering his grandpa's health was failing. He shook his head.

When he was younger, Luke would go to his grandpa's workshop learning to use his woodworking tools. Back in the day, Grandpa William had made fine furniture. He would carefully craft mortis and tenon joints in the specialty woods like black walnut and mahogany. Luke loved the reds of mahogany, especially once it was sanded and waxed smooth. Although people begged him to, his grandpa never sold his furniture,

"Luke," he'd say, "There are a lot of things worth value in the world, but the best is the love you show by doing a job with integrity."

Luke didn't understand what he was talking about then. But now, at HK he felt he was finally moving forward.

He opened the fridge and searched the near empty shelves. Maybe going to a barbecue at Grandpa William's wouldn't be such a bad idea. Ever since his grandma had died, he tried to call with him more often. He knew he was lonely. And besides, Luke really liked spending time with him.

Luke picked up the phone and dialed his dad. An hour later, he cycled up to Grandpa William's house. It was a long ride to where he lived, a rural farming community on the outskirts of Portland. His house, a 1950s craftsman, was in an older neighborhood. As he walked up the long driveway, Luke noticed the yellow paint peeling. Maybe he should offer to paint the house this summer. He'd ask his dad what he thought. Luke parked his bike on the covered porch.

"Hey, you made it!" his mom said through the screen door. "Come in here and give me a hug!" Luke gave her a grin. He rested his chin on top of her head and wrapped his long arms around her.

She would hate if he told her this, but he loved that she was round and huggable. She held him by the shoulders. "Look at you!"

"It hasn't been that long," Luke said. Had it?

"Six months! You haven't been around since Christmas." She looked up at him and cocked her eyebrow.

"Okay, well, it has been a little while." He ran his hand over the stubble on his chin. "Whatcha got going for dinner? I'm famished!" He eyed the peach pie on the kitchen counter as he followed his nose.

"Dad's in the backyard barbecuing pork."

Luscious aromas of barbecued pork rose through the air. Grandpa William sat in an Adirondack chair, a tall glass of iced tea in his hand. He looked pretty good for a guy of seventy-five. He'd gotten a little round in the middle. More of him to love. His full head of silver hair showed around the edges of his plaid cap. Twinkly eyes set in his round Irish face greeted him.

He got up. "Lukey!"

Luke moved to sit beside him. "No, don't get up. You're fine there."

"What have you been up to, my boy?"

"I've been working for Healthy Kids International."

"Do you like it?"

"Yes, I do. I never realized how many kids live in poverty all over the world. I guess I was always in my own little space without looking outward."

"What do you do there?"

"I'm in charge of the community relations and making our presence known so we can get funding. It's a non-profit faith-based organization, so funding is by donations. We have a few grants, but mostly it's just a lot of generous folks that fund us."

"What's their primary purpose?"

"They focus on kids and families. Provide fresh food, vitamins, immunizations, and exercise programs for families. Social workers work with mothers to provide education about their pregnancies and teach them about good nutrition." Luke leaned forward. He could talk about this all day.

"They also educate men in their role of nurturing and providing for their families. There are a lot of single moms trying to make their way." Luke watched some robins land in the garden. "There's a lot more, but I'm not sure about all of it yet."

"Well, now that's wonderful."

"And I get to go to Honduras to visit one of the locations."

Pretty excited about that." His grandpa leaned over and patted Luke's leg.

"Met any cute young ladies?" Here it goes.

"Nah. I date now and then, but nothing serious. I'm sure Ms. Right will appear someday." He looked out over the neighboring peach orchard.

His mom handed him a beer. He didn't drink much, but on a hot day like today, it hit the spot.

"What about that one girl? What was her name? Brenda, Barbara?"

"Benita ." He shook his head. That was one relationship that he was glad had ended.

"I knew it started with a B." His mom leaned against the railing. "Anyway, what happened to her?"

"Just not a good fit. She spent too much time in front of the mirror and going shopping." Lots of time spent on Instagram worrying about what other people thought of her.

His mom put her hand on Luke's arm.

"Well, honey, your ship will come in one day. And that beautiful girl, inside and out, that I've been praying for all these years, will appear and there will be no question that she's the one."

About now, Luke would be fine moving on to another subject. He stood up and stretched. It's not like he needed a woman in his life. He was plenty fine doing things alone. Or was he? He looked at the blooming Camellia bush his grandma had planted. He remembered what a magnificent pair she and grandpa had been.

A few dandelions popped up between the daisies. Maybe he should get over here and help his grandpa do a little weeding.

His dad rounded the corner and put an arm around Luke's shoulder. "Luke, you're here! didn't see you slip in. Why don't you come help me pull the pork off the barbecue?"

They moved to the side of the house where a smoke drifted up from the grill. Luke breathed in the rich fragrance.

"I see you got a new bike! Pretty swell!"

"Yeah, finally broke down and got a good one. It's pretty slick. Makes the Meet Ups smoother."

"That sounds like a heck of a lot of fun. Wish I was in as good a shape as you." His dad patted his belly.

"You're not bad, for an old guy." Luke grinned and

squeezed his dad's bicep. "You could use a bit of a work-out, though. Not feeling the muscle you used to have. Where's that old Bowflex?"

"Getting lonely in the garage, I'm afraid." His dad stirred the coals. "I'm glad you're here. Just wanted you to know your mom and I are getting a little worried about your grandpa."

"What's going on? He looks fine. What did the doctor say when you took him in for tests?" Lines furrowed Luke's forehead.

"Don't be alarmed. He wasn't too worried. I don't think it's anything that can't be managed, but just wanted to keep you in the loop."

Grandpa's my rock. Please don't let anything happen to him.

Chapter Ten

Kaitlyn stopped by the nurse's station where Peter was sitting backwards on the rolling desk chair. Delores must not be close by. The call light blinked incessantly. She ignored it. That wasn't her responsibility at the moment. Neither was the ringing phone.

"I finally got all my people tucked in. They should be happy little campers for the next hour, so I can get a bite to eat. Who wants to watch my people so I can go to lunch?" Kaitlyn asked.

"Nurse, nurse, help me," the patient in room 9 hollered. Again. So much for lunch.

"I was just in there," Kaitlyn said, letting out a heavy sigh. "As soon as I get in there, all she wants is for me to straighten her blanket. Or turn her light on. Or off. Or the TV on. Or off. Nothing she couldn't do by herself. It's just so darn infuriating! There are actually people here who need my help."

"I know," Peter said. "I was just in Room six. I feel for the roommate. He has to listen to that bozo all day. You can't believe the foul language that comes out of his mouth. You'd think he was in a gang or something." He paused. "Maybe he is

54

in a gang. He looks like he could be. Evil tattoos all over his body. Even has them on his bald head. And there's no space left on his face for any more rings or studs." He looked at Kaitlyn. "Should I be worried?"

Dan joined them. "About what?"

"Crazy people on this floor!" Peter scooted the wheeled chair across the floor.

Peter continued. "I just came out of room 6. The patient was watching TV and I was checking his chart, not really paying attention. He says, 'I've been there.' I just mumbled, 'Oh, what were you doing there?' and he says, 'What do you think I was doing there?' Then he says, 'Hey, I know that guy!' I looked up at the TV and it was a documentary about a prison and there was a guard!"

Kaitlyn started wheenking and Dan doubled over in laughter.

Tina popped in. "Kaitlyn, your patient is leaving AMA!"

Kaitlyn wiped the tears from her eyes. No rest for the weary. She ran out in hot pursuit of a man wearing clothes that looked like he's slept in a pigpen. The loose strap on his backpack dangled, hitting him on the leg with each stride.

"Wait, you can't leave. You're on a medical hold. Wait! Wait!" Kaitlyn ran after him through the double doors.

Arnold was heading to the stairs. The sound of Kaitlyn's Danskos echoed down the hall.

How could he possibly be that quick? Kaitlyn wasn't sure she could catch up to him. And there go her brownie points with Delores. As if she had any.

The elevator doors opened. Kaitlyn slipped inside and pushed floor one. As it reached the bottom, she ran out and headed to the stairs. Arnold tottered his way to the bottom step.

Kaitlyn held her arms out to stop him from getting through the door. Arnold pushed her aside, jumped from the bottom step, and ran outside.

Kaitlyn shot daggers at him. Feet of Jesus. Feet of Jesus. He never promised this would be easy.

Kaitlyn took a deep breath and held her hand to her aching side.

"Wait!"

Kaitlyn fought to catch her breath as she gained on him.

"No, not the parking lot! He can't possibly have a car." Could someone be meeting him for the getaway?

Arnold caught his breath as he leaned against a pole, eyeing her warily. Keeping a distance, Kaitlyn stopped beside a car.

"Arnold, let me take you back," Kaitlyn said, barely above a whisper. She held eye contact. Why did this feel like taming a wild animal?

"I'm not going back to that frickin' place." He clenched his hands and let out a snarl like a trapped bobcat.

"Come on, it's not that bad," Kaitlyn coaxed. Sometimes a person had to tell a white lie.

"That's what you think. You're not the one getting needles stuck in you," he said.

"Look, I'll give you a turkey lunchbox. With some of your favorite cookies." Kaitlyn had his attention now. "The ones with the chocolate frosting." His eyes darted towards the exit.

"Come on, let's see what we can find," Kaitlyn said and took a step towards him.

He took a small step and ran his hand through his tousled beard.

"Could you toss in some of those chocolate pudding cups?"

Kaitlyn eased herself beside him. "Yep, I'm sure I can get you some of those."

"And curly fries." He took a few steps forward.

Kaitlyn moved her hand to his shoulder. "That's it. You're okay. You can make it through just a few more days. We've got to make sure the meds are doing their magic for you before you go home."

Wherever that may be.

"And you know, you're not gonna get those pudding cups there." She guided Mr. Crazy Pants to the elevator and back to the unit.

What had she gotten herself into? Was it too soon to ask for a transfer to a different floor?

As they returned, Sahid rounded the corner.

"Arnold, going for a walk I see." Kaitlyn gave him a quizzical look.

"Yeah, he's a frequent flyer. He pulls that crap on all the newbies." Sahid laid a gentle hand on Arnold's back and guided him to his room.

Kaitlyn placed her hands on her hips, narrowed her eyes, and frowned at Arnold.

Not cool. She stomped towards the nurse's station.

"Having fun yet?" Tina laughed.

♥ ♥ ♥

Was this the right profession for her? She was confident about giving meds. Most of the time, she was compassionate. Employee relations? Not so much. Learning to get along with

Delores. Hadn't that been one of her worries? A boss that was more difficult than learning to place a catheter. And just as stress inducing.

Breathe Kaitlyn. Breathe. She drew a square in the air. Breathe in. Breathe out. Breathe in. Breathe out.

Maybe she should have followed her dad's suggestion and become an engineer. That would have been interesting.... Not. Math wasn't exactly her forte.

And after she had returned from her mission trips to Peru and then to Guatemala, her parents had suggested international studies. It had turned out that nursing could lead to medical missions and exploring other countries—the best of both worlds.

But when Tina's mom developed cancer, she and her best friend cemented their decision to go into the medical field. Helping people was what they felt God called to do.

Even the daily dose of crazies.

"You have a new admit," Delores snapped. She clapped her hands. "Chop, chop! You're on the clock."

Peter looked at Dan, a glint in his eye. Tina locked eyes with Kaitlyn. Four hands reached out for a quick rock, paper, scissors. Kaitlyn pouted as she saw her scissors to their rocks.

"I guess it's me." Kaitlyn's shoulders slumped and she drug her feet in mock rebellion. She reluctantly grabbed her laptop and began the new admit.

Chapter Eleven

A few minutes passed, and Kaitlyn followed the gurney holding an elderly gentleman. White, tousled hair framed his face.

"Good afternoon, Bodashka. I'm Kaitlyn. I'll be your nurse today." She stood out of the way as transport hoisted him onto the hospital bed.

"Kaitlyn, what a nice name." Bodashka's grey eyes gleamed.

"I like it. My mom's name is Kate, and she's a peach. She's someone to live up to." She filled in spaces on his chart. "Bodashka—never heard that name before. Can I ask where you're from?"

"Originally from Ukraine. I've been in the States since I was ten."

Kaitlyn helped him sit up. "Are you able to walk?"

"Yeah, I'm fine. My kids just got a little worried because I was out of breath."

"Let's get you on the scale." Kaitlyn wheeled his oxygen tank behind him. She logged his weight on the white board—

one hundred fifty pounds. Not overweight. She helped him back to bed.

Kaitlyn held a thermometer to his forehead. 98.9. Normal. She removed the blood pressure cuff from the hook.

"What were you doing when you got out of breath?" Blood pressure seemed a little high. "Are you taking any blood pressure meds?"

"Yeah, I take that hydro something or other. I don't know what it's called. My wife, Yana, she keeps track of all that." He's old, Kaitlyn thought. That's probably normal. She checked his heart rate. It looked fine.

"You're so healthy for a man your age."

"That's what I told my kids. We were out clam digging on the coast. I had my daughter, her husband, and my two grandkids. Timmy is five and Carolyn is eight. We were close to getting our limit, and I just got winded." He shrugged his shoulders.

Kaitlyn checked his oxygen saturation and respiration.

"Timmy and Carolyn? Not Ukrainian names?"

"No, they are all-American. Yana and I immigrated in the sixties. My daughter Katya was born here. She married an American and wanted her kids' names to reflect this wonderful nation."

"I bet they all had a great time at the beach. I wish I could have done that when I was small."

"They had a blast. But then I was huffing and puffing, and they said I should see my doctor. I told them I was okay. But then this morning after my shower, I was putting on my socks and noticed my leg was swollen and red. They insisted I go straight to the ER. My kids, they can be pushy sometimes. Treat me like I'm an old man. I'm only seventy-five. That is not old."

Kaitlyn hid a smile. Her grandpa would say the same thing.

"They were right to bring you in. The CT scan shows the clots in your leg traveled to your lungs. I'm starting a heparin drip to break them up." She hooked up his IV and went through his belongings.

Deep lines formed in his forehead, and he looked as if he would come after her.

"Don't worry. I need to make sure we account everything," she said.

"Wait, that doesn't mean you have to take my Swiss army knife, right? My sweet Yana gave that to me for a birthday present."

"No worries, just making sure we get everything back to you when you go home."

A family of four entered the room.

"Is it okay for us to visit? We're his family." Kaitlyn assumed the woman with long salt and pepper hair was Yana.

"Absolutely." Kaitlyn turned to the kids. "You must be Timmy and Carolyn."

"Yeah, we want to see Grandpa!" Timmy's blue eyes sparkled as he jumped up and down. "Is he okay?" Carolyn asked. Her worried eyes contrasted with the curls cascading down her back.

"I'm sure he'll be fine. We take good care of people here. Don't you even worry about a thing." Kaitlyn put her hand on Carolyn's curly haired head and locked eyes.

"I'm going to check in on my other patients. I'll look in on him in a while. Meanwhile, you're in charge of keeping him out of trouble." Kaitlyn winked.

Finally, all her rounds were through. Kaitlyn checked her

phone. It was already two, and she hadn't eaten any lunch yet. No wonder her stomach was rumbling.

She checked in at the desk and let them know she was headed to the break room. When she walked in, her pals were just finishing their lunches. They must not have had full schedules too.

"Hey, we thought you'd never make it," Peter said. He chugged down a carton of milk.

"I know—seems like you can't get everyone situated and satisfied before there's another fire to put out," Kaitlyn said. She took out her Tupperware container of enchiladas—leftovers Francisco made for last night's dinner and popped it in the microwave.

"So, how are things going with Fran-cis-co?" Dan said. "Are you two," he double raised his eyebrows, "you know, dating?"

Kaitlyn could feel her cheeks burn. "Yes" She didn't need to reveal any more than that.

The microwave beeped. She took her food to the table.

Kaitlyn scooped her steaming food onto a plate.

"We were just telling Tina she should sign up for a dating app," Dan said. "She's been lonely far too long."

"It worked for me." Kaitlyn grinned.

"I'm perfectly fine being single." Tina looked down and pulled in her lips.

"Come on, let us fix you up," Peter said. "We know everything about you." Peter held up his phone. "Look up." He snapped a pic.

"Wait! What are you doing?"

Peter scrolled through the internet.

"Okay, I found it. I know your name, I know your birthday,

I know your email address. I know what you like. And I have a great picture." He started filling in blanks.

"Give that thing to me," Tina reached for it. Peter held it over his shoulder.

"Nope, too late, I already pushed send." She crossed her arms and sat back, glaring at him.

Delores walked in.

"Whach y'all doing in here? Lunch time is over. This hospital isn't going to run itself!"

Kaitlyn finished a quick bite and hustled to clean up her lunch.

"Don't forget—my house for game night," Peter said.

Kaitlyn nodded. Peter was always dropping things or spilling something. He was cute. And he had that crooked smile. And the way his eyes lit up when he told a quirky joke. He would have made her a good brother. Some goober girl was going to fall head over heels in love with him some day. Just like falling in love with a scraggly puppy.

Kaitlyn gloved up and looked in on Bodashka. He and his family sat around his bed playing cards. Bodashka laid down his cards and threw his hands up in triumph.

"Grandpa, that's no fair! I was just about to go out. You always win," Carolyn squealed.

He put his large hand on hers and gently squeezed. The girl looked at him and gave him a peck on his scruffy cheek.

"I love you, Grandpa. It's okay if you win. I want you to get well."

She rested her head on his chest. Kaitlyn smiled at the two of them. So sweet together.

Carolyn looked up at Kaitlyn. "He's gonna get well, right?"

"Of course, he is. We're gonna get your grandpa all fixed up and out of here before you know it."

Kaitlyn reached for his arm and checked his blood pressure. It was still high. She checked his leg—still swollen. His heparin drip needed to be changed. She walked into the med supply room to retrieve a fresh bag. Peter, Dan, and Tina were sitting on the floor, looking as if the world was coming to an end.

"Woah now, what's going on?" Kaitlyn said. They looked at each other. "Well?"

Peter's eyes went to the floor. He shook his head. Tina placed her hand on his arm.

"I screwed up," he said. "I knew this would happen. They're going to put me on probation or send me home, or I don't know what. I was never meant to be a nurse. You guys are smart. You don't make dumb mistakes."

"Maybe no one will find out," Daniel said. Tina looked up at Kaitlyn.

"What did you even do?" Kaitlyn said. "How bad was it?"

"I gave my patient his oxycodone too early. He was yelling at me and calling me all sorts of names—words I never knew existed. He just wouldn't quit, so I gave him the oxy to shut him up. But what if he OD's? What if he sues?"

"Did you fill out the PSI?" Daniel said. Peter gave him a blank stare.

"You know, the Patient Safety Incidence."

"Where do I even find those?" Peter's shoulders slumped. They looked at each other. No one had filled one out yet. And they hoped they never would need to.

"Guys, we need to have a secret code word or phrase, so when something like this happens, we know we'll meet here to debrief," Tina said.

"Like what?" Dan said.

"Pickles!" Kaitlyn said.

"Pickles?" Peter scrunched up his face. "Are you serious?"

"How about stretcher," Dan said.

"Naw. Let's just make it bandage. I'm wounded. I need a bandage."

They nodded and put their hands in the center of them like they were in a football huddle. "Count of three—one, two, three—bandage!"

Peter and Dan left—Peter to the charge nurse and Dan to resume his rounds.

Kaitlyn stood in the center of the med supply room.

"What did I even come in here for?" She looked around. "Oh yeah, the IV bag of heparin." She checked it out and asked Tina to co-sign for her.

Working with these guys was like having family around. Closer than family. It wasn't like she didn't love her own. Her parents were always supportive. But these guys. They were the bees' knees.

When Kaitlyn returned to Bodashka's room, she replaced the heparin bag and checked his vitals. They looked fine.

She left and changed the bedding for the woman in room 5. It hadn't been easy to move her more than bulky body. Folding all the linens inside her bundle, she carried them to the laundry room. She was just placing them in the bin when Sahid burst in.

"Kaitlyn, your patient is coding. Hurry!"

"Which patient?" Who could be coding? She had just checked them all. They were fine. "Code Blue, 5C, Room 7. Code Blue, 5C, Room 7," belted out of the intercom.

"The Ukrainian." They ran down the hall. Sahid had already called the code. Kaitlyn ran into Bodashka's room. The ding of the continuous pulse ox seemed as loud as a siren. Kaitlyn checked his pulse. Non-responsive. This couldn't be happening. He was fine a minute ago. She knocked over his lunch tray as she reached for the blood pressure cuff. Her shaking hands could hardly place it around his arm. Think Kaitlyn. Think!

Dan started compressions. Tina grabbed the ambu bag as Kaitlyn removed the oxygen tubes from his nose. Tina tilted his head back and held the rubber face mask in place with both hands. Kaitlyn took the bag and began pumping.

"Breathe," Kaitlyn said. "You have to breathe!"

Sahid took over the compressions. Minutes later, the code team arrived with their cart. Doctors, pharmacists, respiratory therapists, social workers, internists and Delores. The doctor orchestrated from the foot of the bed.

"Tell me what is the situation?" the doctor said.

"He had blood clots in his leg that went to his lungs," Kaitlyn said. The respiratory therapist started the mechanical ventilation.

Yana rounded the corner of the room. She screamed and dropped her coffee.

"What's wrong with Grandpa?" Carolyn said. She began to cry and push in through the crowd.

"Get the family out of here." Delores shooed them out.

The chaplain quickly ushered them out with Carolyn kicking and screaming. The chaplain picked her up.

Yana reached out her arm towards her husband. "Bodashka! My sweet Bodashka!" Kaitlyn blinked back tears, hearing Yana's gut-wrenching cry.

Carolyn wrestled herself free and ran back into the room. She squeezed between the crowd to get to Kaitlyn. Small fists pounded Kaitlyn's leg.

"You said he'd be okay! You said you'd take good care of him! You lied!"

Kaitlyn wiped her cheeks with the back of her gloved hand. How was she supposed to revive someone and minister to the emotional needs of the family at the same time?

The doctor shouted out, "If you're not actively doing something, get out of the room!"

Several interns left, guiding Carolyn to the hall.

"Push one milligram of epinephrine." Peter handed Kaitlyn the syringe. Her hand trembled as she inserted the needle. Peter put his hand on hers to steady it.

"It's in." Kaitlyn reached down aimlessly and cleaned up the spilled tray. Everything morphed into slow mo. She fixated on the heart monitor. It was flat. If only she could share her racing heart with Bodashka.

"We need to intubate!" the respiratory therapist shouted. Kaitlyn stepped in to do compressions. She laced her fingers, pushed, counted, pushed again.

"Come on, Bodashka. Come on. You can do this." She pushed again. This can't end like Janey.

The doctor looked at everyone. "We've done compressions, ventilated, intubated. We've given epinephrine. Does anyone have any more suggestions?" He looked around.

"Okay then, we're going to do one more round of compressions and call time of death."

Kaitlyn couldn't give up. She had to do this for Carolyn. For Timmy and Yana. She pushed, counted, pushed. For Janey.

No response. She checked his pulse. Flat. She checked his pupils. No sign of life.

The room went silent.

"Time of death," the doctor said. He looked at the clock.

Kaitlyn reluctantly looked at the clock. "Nineteen thirty-two," she said. Her hands went limp by her sides. Her shoulders shook as Tina hugged her.

"Go ahead and cry, baby girl," Tina said. She gently tucked a damp tendril behind Kaitlyn's ear.

Kaitlyn swallowed thickly. "I need a bandage."

♥ ♥ ♥

Peter ducked his head into the patient fridge and grabbed four sippy cups of apple juice and followed the others into the dirty linens room. They slid down the wall onto the floor.

Kaitlyn fixated on the corner. Peter handed out the juice and said,

"I thought nursing was supposed to be fun."

"There have been way better days than this," Tina said.

"He shouldn't have died! He was doing great. Everything looked fine. How did this even happen?"

Dan shook his head. "We've got a lot to learn. Apparently, he had a pulmonary embolism. You couldn't have stopped that."

"I kept doing dumb things! I dropped his dinner tray and then picked it up. What the heck was I doing? I should have been helping him, not worrying about a spilled tray!"

"You were in shock. It's hard to think when there's so much going on." Peter rested his hand on hers.

"Why does God let bad things happen to good people? It's not fair!" Didn't the Bible say God cared for everyone? Even sparrows? Bodashka was worth more than a sparrow."

Tina put an arm around her.

"Didn't God let his own son die? And Jesus was a good person. I guess we have to believe He has a better plan."

"It's hard to trust Him when I don't understand." She didn't have the energy to wipe away the tears streaming down her cheeks.

The door swung open. Delores entered—arms full of dirty laundry. Her eyes scanned the four.

"You guys aren't looking so invincible today." She leaned against the wall.

"I remember the first time I ever lost a patient. It was a beautiful teenage girl. She was in the wrong place at the wrong time. So much life left to live and here she was, dying at sixteen." She shook her head. "It was rough. I thought I was just going to quit nursing right then and there. It was the most devastating day of my life up to that point. I never knew what nursing would look like or how much pain and suffering there was in the world until I became a nurse. You guys are gonna make it." She turned to place the linens in the bin.

"Was she just acting human?" Kaitlyn mouthed.

"Okay troops, mope time is over! You're getting another admit. Don't let your other patients fail because you're having a bad day. Kaitlyn—the patient in room 9 just crapped his pants. Get in there and clean him up."

Chapter Twelve

Kaitlyn stumbled down the stairs in her pajamas. She'd start the coffee. Who doesn't need a little caffeine first thing in the morning? She turned on the radio softly so as not to wake up Tina and measured the grounds.

When was she going to get over Bodashka? A cloud of grief had surrounded her. That sweet man shouldn't have died. She hoped little Carolyn could forgive her for a promise unkept.

She searched in the cupboard for her favorite mug and filled it. She held it up to her face and breathed in the aroma. Ah. She swirled in caramel creamer, trying to create a heart design. It more resembled a cloud. She'd take a photo. Maybe that could be a new thing to go viral. Hearts turned to clouds. Which would turn to rain. Yana's scream echoed in her ears.

The sun shone through the window, casting light on the kitchen table. Beauty for ashes.

Kaitlyn carried her mug to the back deck, where she intended to snuggle on the padded porch swing and read. The sun highlighted the steam rising from her coffee. A perfect morning.

Until she heard Tina shouting and stomping through the living room and onto the deck.

"What the heck is Francisco doing on our couch in our living room?"

Kaitlyn set down her Bible and looked up. It took a second to make a transition from Psalms to an angry roommate.

"I come down the stairs, the stairs in my house, not expecting to see my quilt that my mom made for me covering a lump on the couch! A lump with curly black hair and a hairy leg. And who should it be but Francisco stinkin' Hernandez!"

Kaitlyn set her Bible down. "Yeah?" She stretched out the word and raised her eyebrows. *This was a little overkill, wasn't it?*

"I thought we agreed no guys were going to sleep over," said Tina.

"We didn't get done studying until one, and I didn't want to drive him home that late."

"I shouldn't have to worry about going downstairs in my footy pajamas with no bra on in my own house and see a male on our couch," Tina said. She clenched her hands at her sides and her eyes became angry emojis. Forehead furrowed; eyebrows slanted. "Get him out of here. Now!"

Kaitlyn gave Tina a blank look. "It's not that big a deal," she said.

"It *is* a big deal! That's my quilt! And we weren't going to have guys spend the night." Tina turned and stormed back into the house.

Kaitlyn watched as Tina snatched her quilt and yanked it off a very confused and sleepy Francisco. Tina sniffed it, pulled a look of disgust and stomped upstairs. The door of the washing machine slammed, and the sound of water echoed.

Kaitlyn sat on the coffee table next to Francisco. He turned over and immediately started snoring. She shook him. "Hey, we gotta go."

He grunted.

She shook him again. "I need to take you home," she said.

He sat up and yawned. "What, why? I can eat some breakfast first? Have a cup of coffee?"

"Nope, up you go. Shoes on."

He ran his hands through his tousled hair and rubbed his bleary eyes. "You are mad at me?"

"Nope, but Tina is. Let's book it outta here," she said. "We'll talk in the car." She grabbed her bag and his backpack and headed out. She should have at least loaned him her toothbrush to get rid of the dragon breath. Kaitlyn watched the neighbor's cat ran out from under her car. That cat was going to get killed one of these days.

Francisco fastened his seatbelt and reached to turn on the radio.

Kaitlyn put her hand out to stop him. "Francisco, you can't spend the night anymore."

"Why not? I was just on the couch. What's wrong with that?"

"I know, but I'm sharing this house with Tina. And we agreed, no guys sleeping over. And Tina is my best friend. I don't intend to jeopardize our friendship."

"Okay, I am sorry." He touched her arm.

Kaitlyn into his eyes—the green of moss on a forest trail.

"It's okay, I'll work it out with her."

"Well, since we're up, do you want to stop somewhere for breakfast?"

"Um, sure. We can go to that cute little place in the Pearl District. They've got amazing waffles and eggs and home cut potatoes and excellent coffee and cinnamon rolls and..." She put her hand to the corner of her lips, expecting some drool.

"Woah there, amiga. I get the picture!"

Kaitlyn circled the Pearl District several times before she found a parking spot close to the restaurant. Beautiful Victorian houses with cut glass windows lined the street. The moldings and rails on the porches were intricate and finely made. Beautifully landscaped yards exploded with summer color. Azaleas, hydrangeas, heather, and Japanese Maples. Monkey Puzzle trees and old growth cedar towered over them.

Portland was the perfect place for people watching. It provided a variety pack. A pug was pulling on his leash attached to turbaned man. They followed an Asian couple, hand in hand, with matching shoes. A couple of teens were jostling about, dressed in tie-dyed shirts.

"A line is forming," said Kaitlyn. "Let's hurry."

Once inside, a Latino server seated them. Kaitlyn scanned her menu.

"Que recomiendas?" Francisco asked.

"Los huevos con tomate, queso, y pimientos. Muy sabroso!" the server said.

"Gracias, quisiere ese," Francisco said.

"Um, yeah, whatever that was." Kaitlyn frowned, feeling the odd girl out.

"Miss? What would you like?"

"Coffee. Lots of coffee. And Belgian Waffles. With strawberries. And whip cream. Lots of whip cream."

He nodded and took their menus.

"I receive a letter from mi mama," Francisco said. "It say things are no so good there."

Kaitlyn wondered if correcting his English was hopeless. She'd just ignore it and focus on the conversation.

"What's going on?"

"She say has some stomach problems and can no afford go to the doctor."

"Did she say what type of problems? Like what is actually happening? Maybe we could send some meds to her." She looked up as the server set down their coffees.

"No, she no say. Didn't say," he corrected. Kaitlyn nodded and smiled. "But," he reached for her hand, "Do you think is possible you can go with me to check on her? You're a nurse. You can help her."

"I don't know," she said. "Let me think about it. I'd have to get time off. When were you thinking?"

"Soon. Don't you have a week off coming up? We can go then."

Kaitlyn pulled out her phone and checked her calendar. "Yeah, okay. Let's check tickets and see." Francisco moved closer to her as she checked for flights. The warmth of his shoulder on her bare arm made it hard to concentrate.

Did she really want to travel to Honduras with him? She felt more and more drawn to him. And they had been spending a lot of time together. But a whole week? Doubts made their way to her stomach.

Kaitlyn inhaled deeply and took a bite of her waffle. "How much money do you have?"

"Only one hundred dollars," he said.

"Well, honey, that's not gonna be enough."

"I know." His shoulders slumped as he aimlessly stirred his food.

"I guess I can loan you some money."

Might as well just give it to him. The chances of him paying her back were slim to none. Other than their first date, she had paid for their meals. She had given him rides everywhere. She even paid for his summer term books. She seemed to be spending a lot on him, but he didn't have anyone else to help him. Was that why God put him in her path?

He looked up. "You would do that for me?"

"Yeah, I could do that. You'll need to pay me back." Kaitlyn searched his deep green eyes.

"Oh yes! Of course. Thank you!" He leaned over to kiss her cheek.

Kaitlyn's heart raced. Was his kiss just a thank you? Or was it something more? A trip to Honduras was sure to make or break their friendship.

♥ ♥ ♥

Kaitlyn stepped off the plane in San Pedro, Honduras. They were greeted by Francisco's friend Marco, who roared up on his motorcycle. Kaitlyn eyed it skeptically. Were they both expected to ride on that thing with its bald tires and covered in dust?

And where were the helmets?

Ultimately, she was glad that she had packed light—only her red backpack instead of a suitcase. Francisco carried a satchel. Apparently, he still had clothes at his mama's house.

Francisco took Kaitlyn's backpack and hoisted it on.

Kaitlyn climbed onto the frayed black seat—glad she didn't have to sit on the peeling duct tape. Where should she put her hands? Not around Marco's waist, that's for sure. He was cute and all, but that would be a little too familiar with someone she just met. And would Francisco be jealous? He had side-eyed Peter when he flirted with her.

As it was, squished into a Kaitlyn sandwich, she didn't need to hold on to anyone. Francisco put his hands around her waist. She gladly rested her hands on his.

How did this trip even come about? Had she really agreed to pay for Francisco's ticket? Maybe she could write it off as a donation.

Was her motivation to help his mom? She had thought about medical missions. Or did she just want to spend more time with Francisco? She liked spending time with him. And he was becoming more than just a friend.

Kaitlyn's entire body tensed as Marco zoomed in and out of vehicles. Weren't there driving rules around here? Everyone seemed to stop and go whenever they pleased, regardless of who was surrounding them. There didn't seem to be any logic to it. Her heart was racing so fast, she felt as if she could use a dose of a beta-blocker. She hoped her guardian angel was watching over her. She didn't want her parents to receive a phone call saying she gotten killed in Honduras.

Kaitlyn gasped as Marco made a turn, the motorcycle tilted to such an angle that her feet nearly scraped the dirt road. The houses had become sparse, and the only stores were small, sitting in sectioned off fronts of houses. Not only did Marco have to swerve around dogs, but he sent chickens squawking across the roads. Kaitlyn's tightly clenched hands tingled.

Several more turns put them at a stop in front of a house.

Kaitlyn breathed a sigh of relief. Francisco dismounted and helped Kaitlyn off. Marco waved goodbye and sped off.

"We're here?" Kaitlyn asked.

"No, we still have to walk up this path," Francisco said.

Kaitlyn's eyes followed his pointing finger up a steep hill. Bushes and shrubs were dense. She hoped they wouldn't be full of bugs. She had heard that the beetles were as big as her hand. And spiders. Enormous spiders. Wait, was that in Honduras or somewhere else? *Please tell me it's somewhere else.*

They trudged up the path. Wearing her nursing clogs hadn't been the best choice. Everywhere she looked there was garbage. Plastic bags, papers, containers. "No tires basura aqui" was plastered on a trash can.

"Don't throw garbage here. A lot of good that sign does," Francisco laughed.

Obviously, the garbage truck didn't make rounds here.

Kaitlyn looked at the houses, if that's what you wanted to call them. Mud and sticks. Rusty tin roofs. Branches tied together with rope to form fences. A woman dressed in a faded skirt was washing her laundry in a bucket and hanging it on the fence. Kaitlyn was afraid to comment. She didn't want to embarrass Francisco. These, after all, were the neighbors he grew up with. His people.

Just when she thought she couldn't manage one more step, they reached the house. The sun reflected off the new metal roof. Kaitlyn was glad to see that her "donation" had been put to good use. Inside, her eyes adjusted to the dimness.

"Mamá?" Francisco said. He set their bags down.

"Mamá?" De donde vas?"

"Francisco, hijo mío. I am here, Son. Laying down." She

held her arms out to him. A thread-bare woven blanket covered her. He ran to her bedside.

"Mamá, I've brought my friend Kaitlyn with me. She will help you get well." He spoke in Spanish, then switched to English.

"Kaitlyn, this is my mamá, Miguelita."

"Mucho gusto," Kaitlyn said, proud that she knew that much. "How are you feeling?"

"Not so good. I have ache in my stomach and no energy." Miguelita looked back and forth from Kaitlyn to Francisco as he translated.

"Have you eaten anything today?" Francisco asked.

She might be hungry, Kaitlyn thought. She looked around. Calling her place a mess was an understatement. Clothes on the dirt floor, which could use a good sweeping. A crusted ceramic bowl and dirty glass of water sat beside her bed. Or perhaps it was dirty water she'd been drinking.

"No, I haven't gotten out of bed today." Francisco looked around the small room. There was no sight of fresh fruits or vegetables. He found a bag with a few beans and rice.

"Here, let me make you something. We'll go to the market in a while and get you some groceries."

"What can I do to help?" Kaitlyn asked. Where should she begin?

"There should be some sticks outside next to the stove. You could start a fire. Wait. Look on the table for some matches."

As Kaitlyn wandered out, a gaunt chicken squawked as she shooed it out the door. Next to the weathered brick wall was a small stack of sticks. This would be a bit like camping. She looked around for something that resembled a stove.

The house had no electricity, so she didn't expect to see a

conventional stove. In a corner she saw bricks stacked up into a square with a shelf to contain the fire and topped with a rusty grill. A dented aluminum pan rested on the grill.

Alrighty then. She rubbed her hands together. She stacked the wood on the shelf and searched for paper to start the fire. Evidently that was a wrong expectation. She noticed a bundle of straw and placed some in between the sticks. Finally what she had learned as a Girl Scout came in handy. She lit the match and watched it kindle to a start. Next, she carried the pan inside.

"Where do I get clean water?" she asked.

"There is a bucket outside that catches rainwater. Dip out of it." *That was a snippy response. Does he imagine I know how to survive in his world? Give me credit for trying.*

Kaitlyn found the black plastic barrel outside. It was full of water alright, but a layer of dirt and bugs floated on top. Ew. There was an obvious reason his mama wasn't feeling so well.

She scooped some water into the pan. She hesitated, working up courage to skim off the few dead bugs and dirt. *Just breathe. You're acting as if you didn't grow up on a farm.*

She placed the pan on the grill. Hopefully, boiling would kill anything deadly. She shook her hands to dry them and unclipped her hand sanitizer from her backpack.

Francisco brought out the rice and beans. He'd found a few shriveled tomatoes and some peppers to add to the concoction.

"Francisco, isn't there anyone to help your mama? This place needs to be cleaned up, and she needs fruits and vegetables. And this water has to be the root of her stomach problems."

"I know, I know. That's why I brought you here. When my pápa died, things went downhill. My brother moved to the city and now she is all alone. Do you see why I wanted to go to the

United States? Is a dead end here. I love my mamá, but I cannot stay here and help her. The best way to help her is for me to get citizenship and send her money until I can bring her up to the States."

"That's a long way off, my friend. We need to get something in place now. Aren't there any social services in Honduras? Anything to help the poor?"

"There is nothing. That's the problem."

Kaitlyn was determined to research what could be available to help. This was way bigger than her. What she wouldn't give for.wifi.

"Where is the nearest doctor's office? Or hospital?" Kaitlyn asked.

"You have to go back into town," Francisco said.

"Well, that will be the first thing on our list for tomorrow. How are we going to get your mama to town? I don't think Marco's motorcycle would be a good option."

"We can probably borrow the neighbor's donkey and you and I can walk beside it."

"Walk? All the way to town? That's a long way!" Kaitlyn said.

"My people are used to long walks." Kaitlyn shook her head. A Lyft would come in handy about now. She searched around the room. There was only one bed, and his mama was in it. No couch. No dresser. A few boxes with clothing and some food.

"So, I hate to ask this, but what were your plans for where I'll sleep?"

Francisco gave her a deer in the headlights look. He obviously hadn't given that a thought.

"Um...."

Kaitlyn put her hands on her hips. "You can't possibly think I'm staying here. I'm not sleeping on the dirt floor if that's what you're thinking."

She stomped out to check on the beans, which had finally come to a boil. She took a spoon and ladled off more specks of dirt, then put a few more sticks on the fire. The chickens were squawking and pecking at the dirt, somehow thinking they were going to find food. She scooted one away with her foot.

What had she gotten herself into? This. It was too much. Her sister Maggie would have laughed and called her naïve. Well, she would be right. What had she expected to find? Not dirt floors. Not such poverty. She'd been overwhelmed at situations before, but this was way beyond her pay grade.

Francisco came from behind and placed his arms around her waist. Startled, Kaitlyn turned. He leaned in close to her. Close enough to kiss. But did she want to kiss him?

She took a step back.

He placed his hands on her shoulders. "Don't be mad. I will stay here. You could go back into town and find a nice place to stay. Then you can find out what I can do for my mama."

"I just think you should have thought this through. I know nothing about this country or your community." Her hand found her hip.

"I'm sorry." His hands moved to cup her face. "Kaitlyn, thank you."

He kissed her lightly on the lips. She pulled back and sucked in a breath. Was that kiss supposed to make things better? Because in the mood she was in, it wasn't working.

"Okay, point me in the right direction. It's a good thing it's only mid-day." She picked up her backpack and struggled into it. "I'll text you when I figure out where I'm staying." Francisco nodded and attended to his mama. *As if he'll be able to receive a text.*

♥ ♥ ♥

Kaitlyn trudged down the path, trying to estimate how far it was to town. She saw women with babies swaddled on their backs, held in place by woven fabric. Some carried baskets on their heads. It looked like a recipe for a headache. How could they do that? Then she saw one woman roll up a scarf and form it into a circle first, so the basket rested on it. These ingenious women had strenuous lives. Kaitlyn wasn't sure she was made of the stuff necessary to live here. And if she were to marry Francisco, would that be her future?

A small boy lugged a five-gallon bucket with both hands. Water slopped out of the top. An older boy came to the rescue to share the handle and share the load. How far must they carry it? Was it clean? Where did they get it from, anyway? Was there a stream nearby?

Men with colorful scarves tied on their heads labored on the steep hill, hoeing weeds. Long rows of purple grapes hung along fenced netting. Were they for eating or for wine? She wouldn't mind having a bunch to munch on. It hadn't occurred to her to bring some food. Then again, it wasn't exactly like she could have grabbed something from Miguelita's. This was Francisco's territory. What kind of guy wouldn't have looked out for her comforts?

She arrived at an intersection where a colorful bus passed.

There wasn't room for one more person. satWere those chickens in their arms? What would she see next?

A truck sped past, kicking up the dirt. A blue tarp covered the rack on the back under which sat or stood about ten people. No DMV regulations here. She crossed to the far side of the road. She wasn't ready to be roadkill.

And what about Francisco? That kiss. She licked her lips, still feeling the gentle touch of his to hers. She couldn't deny she was starting to like him, and it hadn't gone unnoticed that girls always gave him a second look.

But were good looks enough? It seemed like she was doing all the giving in this relationship. Kaitlyn helped him study. She bought him groceries. She paid for his mom's new roof. Heck, she paid his way down here.

It wasn't like she never got anything out of the relationship. But he was giving what he had to her. He cooked dinner, was totally fun on game nights, even brought her coffee at work one day along with a flower he'd picked just for her.

Taking things one day at a time seemed to be the path forward. She really needed to find some Wi-Fi so she could text Tina. She could count on her to put things into perspective.

Once in town, Kaitlyn asked for a pharmacy. She explained that her friend's mother was having stomach problems, which she suspected was from drinking the water. The pharmacist gave her a knowing look and handed her some water purification tablets and a medication. She pulled out several pesos and was surprised to receive change. Cheaper meds. Now that was one thing better here than in the States.

The sun was getting low in the sky. She needed to search out a place to stay, and soon. She tried the Wi-Fi on her phone. No luck. She'd walk around a bit and hopefully run into somewhere to stay. What she wouldn't give to use Yelp right about now.

A few boys were playing in a vacant lot, kicking a couple of new soccer balls with their bare feet. Yelling, screaming, laughing. *Where did they get new balls?*

Her feet were killing her. Another pair of shoes would have been a better choice had she known she was going to walk several miles. She sat down on a bench, kicked them off and rubbed her feet.

"You don't look like you're from around here," a voice said in perfect English.

Kaitlyn looked up. She smiled at the petite woman with cropped black hair.

"Oh, hi. No, I'm from the States. I came with a friend from here to see if I could help his mom."

"I'm Maria." The woman held out her hand.

"Kaitlyn."

"What kind of help does she need?" Maria asked.

Kaitlyn explained.

"How fortuitous. I'm just the person you need!" Maria said. "I'm the director of Healthy Kids International. We have all sorts of resources."

"Yeah, but she's not a kid."

"That's okay. We help families and elderly as well. We have a health clinic that she could access. It's free."

"That's a good start. But she needs someone to help her around the house and make sure she's eating well, and ensure she has clean water," Kaitlyn said.

"I'm sure we can arrange something," said Maria.

Kaitlyn breathed a sigh of relief, looked to the sky and whispered thank you Jesus.

"Say, do you know somewhere I could spend the night? I'm feeling a little lost here."

"I'd say you could stay at our compound, but we have people from our headquarters in the States staying with us and there's no extra room." She placed her finger to her lips. "There's a nice bed-and-breakfast around the corner. I'll take you there and introduce you."

"Any chance there's Wi-Fi?" Kaitlyn asked.

Maria gave her a smile. "Of course. Honduras isn't completely backwards."

Chapter Thirteen

The Portland airport was calm as Luke and Gracie climbed out of their Lyft. Naturally, considering it was four in the morning. Their baggage bulged with enough clothes and essentials to last two weeks. Luke hoisted a large box, crammed with bandages, vitamins, syringes, stethoscopes, thermometers, and other medical supplies from the SUV. Another held markers, colored pencils, pads of paper, children's books and Bibles in Spanish, pencils and sharpeners. And don't forget the case of soccer balls.

It had occurred to Luke to bring his bike, but then figured he'd have to take his all-terrain, knowing the streets were possibly not that great. And let's face it, he could get along without it for a couple of weeks. Then again, if the itch got too great, he could always find a bike to borrow in Honduras.

"Let's check in curbside," Gracie said. "We've got a lot of luggage and I don't want to pay for a cart."

Luke nodded. They lugged the heavy boxes out and slid them to the counter.

"Now aren't you glad you didn't bring your bike?" Gracie said.

"I see what you mean." Luke handed over the HK credit card to pay for the extra luggage. He paused. "Gracie, would you mind keeping the credit card?" She shrugged and took it. He didn't even want to be tempted to pay for things that would cause questions.

"Listo?" Luke said.

Gracie screwed up her face. "What in the heck does that mean?"

"Ready," said Luke. He adjusted his backpack. "I spent some time in Mexico. I know enough Spanish to get me into trouble."

"You mean besides, como estás? And buenos días?" Luke nodded. A small smile played on his lips.

"I downloaded the Duolingo app on my phone," Gracie said. "My dad's been trying to learn Spanish on it for over a year. I'll see if I can get a few words figured out before we get there."

They made their way through security and found a coffee shop. Luke ordered his usual, a twelve-ounce hot mocha, no whipped cream. He checked his watch. Two hours till boarding. "Add a muffin," he said. Gracie took her large berry smoothie and oatmeal and paid.

"Shouldn't we be using our own money to pay for this instead of donor funds?" Luke said.

"Brianna said we had a daily food allowance. But maybe you're right. That money should go towards the kids," she said. "I'm sure they need it more than we do."

He shrugged. Straight and narrow. Just stay on the straight and narrow.

They found a table near the window. Gracie leaned back and stretched.

"Tired?" Luke asked. She nodded. "So am I. We'll be able to sleep on the plane once we board. Have you flown much?"

"No," she said. "This is my first flight."

"No kidding." Luke said. He held a napkin under his chin to catch his muffin crumbs.

"I've always lived in Oregon and all my family lives here. My parents used to take me camping, but we never flew anywhere."

"Sheltered life, I see," Luke smiled. "I guess you're gonna have to show me the ropes." She playfully punched him in the shoulder.

Luke wondered exactly what ropes she was thinking of. She was kind of cute. Long blonde hair, unusual brown eyes, long thick lashes. But it was her amiable smile and sense of humor that made her a pleasant companion. He pulled out the itinerary Brianna had given him.

"Looks like we'll be staying in a compound near the health center," he said.

"I wonder what it will be like. You've got your camera, right? Or are you taking all your pics on your phone? There will be so much to see."

"I was going to bring my Canon, but it's so heavy. I'll just use my phone. I need to take shots for a new website I'm building. I need footage of people and the programs. Some interviews."

"That sounds cool. I did a little of that when I was in college. Maybe I could help you."

"That would be great. I can always use help." Especially from an intelligent woman. He finished his coffee and tossed the cup in the trash. "I'm looking forward to going down there. I'm eager to see the work we represent."

"Hands and feet of Jesus, baby," Gracie said.

"Now boarding for Copa flight 624, Portland to San Pedro at gate twelve."

They picked up their backpacks and pulled out their boarding passes and passports.

♥ ♥ ♥

After a six-hour flight and waiting through the excruciatingly long line of customs, they got a cart, collected their luggage and scanned the crowd until they saw a woman holding a sign with their names on it.

"That must be Maria," Luke said. He smiled and waved at the petite woman.

"You're here!" she said. "You must be exhausted. We'll load up and take you to our favorite coffee shop and get you revived. You've got a long day ahead."

"That sounds amazing. We caught up on a few movies and got a little snooze in," Luke said. He smiled as he thought about how he had allowed Gracie to fall asleep on his shoulder.

She only drooled a little.

"We're anxious to see the monumental work you're doing and dig in to help." Luke spotted the van with the Healthy Kids logo on the side.

"There is plenty to do, don't you worry about that!" Maria started for the luggage, but Luke beat her to it.

"I've got that," he said and hoisted the first box into the van. Gracie grabbed her small bag and climbed in.

Maria noticed the label on the other box. "You brought soccer balls?" she said. Her dark eyes widened.

Luke curved his hand and blew on his fingernails. "Yep, that was my idea. I played in high school and I know how much kids enjoy a pickup game."

They passed buildings and streets that could have been any big city in America. It surprised him to see all the familiar fast-food places and big box stores.

They quickly came to a neighborhood with buildings several stories high and painted in a variety of bright colors. Murals of Garifuna families covered a few walls, giving a history lesson. He would make a point to read up on them.

The van stopped near a café where a couple were dancing tango on the sidewalk. Luke tapped Gracie on the shoulder and nodded towards them.

She smiled. He grabbed his phone and took a video.

"Let's try to fit in some tango lessons while we're here," she said. "You must be an excellent dancer, right?"

"There's always room for improvement," Luke said. He had taken tango lessons when he had dated Corina. Dancing with that red-headed girl had turned out to be the only enjoyable part of their relationship.

"That would be fun." They were so mesmerized by the fluid moves and music they didn't hear Maria until she tapped them on the shoulder.

"Okay, here we are," Maria said. She ushered them inside. Luke inhaled the fresh coffee bean fragrance. They sat at a round, rustic table where Maria ordered buñuelos and café con leche. A look of heaven crossed Luke's face as the donut melted in his mouth. He licked the sugar off his fingers.

Gracie's lips turned up as she handed him a napkin.

"I can't take you anywhere!" she said.

"Right? I may want to move here if this is how they feed us," he said. He took a few more photos. Gracie leaned over and planted her face in the middle of one of them. She laughed as Luke playfully slapped her away.

Maria set her napkin on her plate and drank the last of her coffee. "Okay, so here's the plan. You're only going to be here for two weeks, and we've got a lot to see and talk about. I'm very glad you're here, so someone from the States sees what we do. We'll visit the schools, the community farm, the health center, and join in on some family groups. Okay troops, vamanos!"

"Small but mighty," Gracie whispered. Luke nodded and headed out.

♥ ♥ ♥

Sitting at a rustic wooden desk, Luke's eyes travelled from the stucco walls to the open window of his room. The courtyard had several palm trees laden with dates. Lizards skittered up the trunks, camouflaged, showing themselves only when they moved. The magenta flowers of the bougainvillea were an optical overload.

The people seemed so friendly. It was nice to know that a smile was a universal language. Their weathered faces and calloused hands revealed that life was tougher than what he was used to.

His phone chimed. Brianna.

"Just checking in. What's the word?"

"We visited the community farm—it was pretty amazing to see the PVC greenhouses full of tomatoes, peppers, lettuce—all sorts of vegetables. They've been able to create a sustainable subsistence for their community. They also market them to bring in income to continue the venture."

"Have you visited any homes?"

"Yes. That was an eye opener. Makes our poverty look like mansions. Dirt floors, daub and wattle houses with rusty metal sheets for roofs. They're lucky if they have one bed for six people!"

Luke wondered how they had privacy for intimacy—it had to happen because there were always more kids.

"You're taking photos and videos, right?"

"You bet."

"Okay, say hi to Gracie and Maria for me."

"Will do."

Luke stood, stretched, closed his journal and walked out. The temperature was similar to Portland—cool in the morning and warming up in the afternoon. He held his face to the sun, closed his eyes and let the rays radiate. It was so quiet here. No traffic. The hoo hoo of the doves made his heart sing.

Gracie and Maria were sipping coffee on the veranda. Luke took a candid photo and sauntered over to join them.

"We've been able to see a vast improvement in the health of the kids since we began vaccinating. There had been measles epidemics and a lot of kids died. It was very tragic," Maria said.

"What about the women—what have you done to improve their health?" Gracie asked.

"First, we've trained midwives in current practices. We've

given them supplies. Here, the women are used to having their mothers attend to them during their births. They generally have their babies at home."

"That doesn't seem to be a very sanitary solution. Those homes have dirt floors and no bathrooms. And only a fire pit for a kitchen," Gracie said. Her eyes were wide, trying to take in the reality of life here.

"We have to work with what they have. At least when we train the midwives, they know what to look for and how to proceed if, say, a woman hemorrhages or if it's a breach birth." Gracie had a hard time imagining a home birth after having seen her niece being delivered in the hospital. Thankfully, it had gone smoothly, but what happens here if it doesn't? Hospitals are few and far between.

"Let's not leave out the men," Luke said. "What have you got going on with them?"

"Several things," Maria said. "As you know, men have traditionally been the head of the families. They are given a higher status than women. They are always served meals first. The women don't eat until after they're done. Sometimes there's not enough left for them. Another example: if a family has both boys and girls, and they can only afford to send one child to school, it will always be the boy. If girls go, they traditionally drop out by sixth grade since they believe they don't need any more skills than that to become a mother."

"Woah, woah woah," Gracie said. "That's just wrong!"

"Back to Luke's question," Maria said. "One thing we are trying is a men's class where they learn to recognize the value and feelings of the women in their lives. Remarkably, since the class has begun, several men have given testimonies of how when they changed their perspective. They have begun to help around the house and with the children. They have been surprised by how their relationships improved."

"Seems elementary," Luke said, "treating others with respect. But I guess men can kinda be dopes when it comes to women." Gracie cocked an eyebrow.

"It's a cultural thing. We don't want to be the "white guys" who come down here and try to "fix" or turn their lives into our "better" way. We just want to expose them to some different ways of thinking and let them decide if that's what they want to incorporate into their way of life."

Maria looked at her phone. "Time to head out. We're going to the marketplace so I can show you some of the family businesses that have started with the help of micro-loans."

Maria hailed a three-wheeled vehicle with a blue canvas roof tied to the sides and only two doors. Gracie squeezed into the back. Luke groaned as he ducked his head and squeezed into the tuc tuc. Definitely not made for people that were six feet two.

The driver zoomed down streets successfully avoiding most potholes. Passing motorcycles held three or four riders hanging onto bags of groceries. Clearly, there were fewer driving regulations here.

They turned down a dirt road, avoiding chickens and mangy stray dogs. The vehicle stopped in front of a lean-to built of wooden poles with a worn tarp tied to the poles. A woman, two small girls and a boy who was, perhaps, ten, stood cooking. The boy and older girl were husking corn. The mom patted her youngest on the head when she ran to her mom and clung to her skirt.

Luke asked if it was alright to take photos. That little girl would be great to add to the promo video.

Maria got out and embraced the woman with a cheek-to-cheek air kiss. She turned and introduced Luke and Gracie.

Luke held out his hand and said, "Mucho gusto." The woman's dark eyes sparkled. She looked him in the eye and rattled off something in Spanish. It felt good to converse in their language. Learning the language had been one of the few good things that had come from his stint in Mexico.

She took the husked corn from the kids and placed the cobs into a large pot of boiling water, which sat on what appeared to be a new propane stove. Maria explained Bianca was a single mom who had been evicted from her home. The owners had wanted to move their children in.

She had only recently found a modest place—one room, dirt floor, corrugated tin roof and a wood cooking stove outside.

"Did Healthy Kids donors fund the stove?" Gracie asked.

"That's part of the micro-loan that we offer to start small businesses. It may not seem like much, but this will bring in enough to meet nearly all their needs each month."

"What they live on before?" Luke asked the woman.

She explained that her husband worked in the fields, but he was in a tragic accident. They sold corn, but when they would take the corn to market with their pot, would have to build a fire on the bare ground. Because of all the smoke, they had to move away from the market. The smoke was also getting in the family's faces causing them to have lung issues.

"Where do they get the corn?" Gracie asked.

"Remember the HK community farm?" Maria said. "It's a cyclical solution. We support the farm that in turn gives income to both the farmers and those who sell the produce. It's a suitable model. You took photos, right? Brianna will want to see this in action."

Bianca took her tongs and fished out several corn cobs. The boy handed her some husks to hold them, steam rising. She held them out to Gracie and Luke, her mouth forming a huge grin, revealing more than a few missing teeth.

As they left, Gracie said, "How do people who are in such poor circumstances manage to be so grateful and happy? If we lived like her, we'd all be whining and complaining."

"She seems happy. Maybe she's learned how to be content in any circumstance,"

Luke said. "We could all take lessons."

They waved goodbye with "gracias" all around.

Crammed once again in the three wheeled tuc tuc, Luke held his phone out the window to take videos as he passed. They soon stopped in front of an artisan market. Vendors had their wares stacked to the ceiling, hanging from the ceiling, and covering all but a narrow walkway. It was amazing how much they could cram in eight-foot cubbies.

Maria hustled them along to a hipster style sandwich shop. The refurbished buildings in this neighborhood were inviting. People dressed like Portlanders, not in traditional indigenous clothing. How could all this be such a contrast only a few short blocks away from where they had just come? Luke listened carefully, trying to discern between the different languages of the tourists.

They found a spot on the veranda. Bougainvillea clung to the trellis, creating much needed shade. They ordered traditional carne asada with chimichurri and handmade tortillas.

As they waited, Luke watched the couple sitting across the way. The girl, her curly brown hair hung down her back, talked wildly with her hands. The guy, facing Luke, had dark hair, a trimmed beard and was clearly Latino. Something about that girl looked familiar. He thought he'd search out the men's room and sneak a peek at her face. He excused himself and skirted the edge of the veranda, past the bar and into the building. When he returned, he sauntered towards her table.

"Kaitlyn?" He never expected to see anyone he knew this far from home.

She looked up, startled. "Luke? What are you doing here?"

"I came down with my job to check out the programs they administer. You?"

Luke looked at the guy, who was clearly wondering what the connection was. "Luke, this is Francisco. We came down here to visit his mom. She's got some type of illness and we thought that me, being a nurse, might be able to help her."

Francisco shook his head. "She is very sick. I think Kaitlyn will be a miracle worker." He reached over and put his hand on hers.

Kaitlyn moved her hand away ever so slightly.

"Well, good luck to you. Great to see you. Hope everything works out." Unbelievable.

He went all the way to a remote part of Honduras and sees someone he knows. But that Francisco. There's something unsettling about him. He wasn't sure what it was, but it was cause for pause.

Chapter Fourteen

The sun was just breaking through the few puffs of clouds, casting a golden glow on the tiled roof of the Community Garden. Luke donned his running shoes. Gracie sat on the steps beside him and pulled on her own shoes.

"What do you think of the projects so far?" Luke asked.

Luke took off with Gracie matching his stride. It felt good to be getting some exercise. The air was so clean and refreshing. People here may live in poverty, but beauty surrounded them. Maybe their wealth lay inside rather than in material things.

"They're certainly doing a lot of things—the garden, the health center, the parent groups. We still need to see the school."

"That's true. Maria seems to be an excellent director. I'm looking forward to giving a report to Brianna. She'll be pleased." Gracie matched Luke's easy stride.

"Is Maria from here? Her English is so perfect."

"She said she had been an exchange student in the States, but yeah, she's a native," Luke said.

"Brianna seems very focused. She does a good job running HK, don't you think?"

"Yeah. I actually thought about asking her out, but the most I could get was a business lunch," Luke said. "Maybe I'm just not her type."

Gracie laughed. "Or maybe she's just married to her job."

"What about you? Are you seeing someone?" Luke asked.

"Why? You thinking I'm your type?" She made a show of flipping her long blonde hair over her shoulder. Luke laughed.

"The answer to that question is yes. I've been seeing Eric, a guy I've known since high school. He's an engineer."

"Choo choooooo," Luke said. He pumped his arm up and down. Gracie punched him on the arm.

"No, silly. He's an electrical engineer with a renewable energy program."

They passed fields of ripe sugarcane. Men with scarves tied around their heads used their machetes to chop down the stalks.

"What kind of girl is your type?" Gracie asked.

Luke slowed his pace. "I don't know." He hadn't really thought about it. He tried to visualize that woman by his side. "I guess I want someone who's devoted to their faith. But can have fun too. Someone who stands up for what she believes in. Someone who has a good relationship with her family. It wouldn't hurt if she was cute."

Luke checked the time. "Better get a move on or we'll miss coffee and those amazing rolls." They ran through town where vendors were setting up their wares. Women were patting out tortillas and cooking them on small propane griddles. Luke's stomach was rumbling.

"I'll race you," Gracie said. Peddle to the metal, she beat him by inches. They collapsed in chairs, laughing.

♥ ♥ ♥

As the HK van drew up to the school, rows of children dressed in uniforms welcomed them. They held colorful balloons and were singing, accompanied by a few students playing instruments and keeping time with the rhythm of a big bass drum. It was the perfect video op.

Luke followed Gracie into the office, where Maria introduced them to the principal, Mr. Ortega. He wore white pants and shirt, His long black mustache reminded Luke of a cartoon character.

He told them how grateful the community was to HK for funding their school. In the past, there had only been an elementary school with classes from kindergarten to grade six. The school used to be worn down—broken windows, non-functioning toilets and had few learning materials. Now, because of their funding, they had hired teachers from their village and bought new books and supplies.

"How many students attend this school?" Luke asked. "The building is beautiful! I bet the kids love the playground."

"About one hundred fifty. I say about because some students have to walk over a mile to get here and attendance is irregular. Others may stay home to help their mothers with younger siblings, or help their fathers in the fields," Mr. Ortega said. "Come. Let's take a look around."

They followed him to the classrooms. Luke supposed that the metal bars on the windows were to keep vandals out.

Small hands waved in the air for attention from their teachers. Colorful drawings covered the walls. Outside, children kicked a ball made of plastic bags wrapped with tape. The sound of laughter was universal.

"They're gonna love what I brought them," Luke said and threw them a couple of brand-new soccer balls. Two boys squealed, ran, and kicked them into the field.

A couple of girls ran over and threw their arms around Gracie, nearly knocking her down. Gracie laughed and patted their heads.

"Small treasures of life," Gracie said. Her wide grin was like sunshine.

♥ ♥ ♥

Back at the center, Luke and Gracie reviewed the photos and videos he had taken. Tango dancers, street scenes, steaming coffee, a woman with her baby snuggled in her woven wrap, men hoeing in the fields.

"Wait," Gracie said. "Look at this video of the kids in the playground."

"The girls with their soccer balls seem happy," Luke said.

"Right, but," Gracie pointed. "Look over here in the corner. Stop the video. Look at this girl."

"Ohhhh," Luke said. "I never noticed her." A girl crouched at the corner of the building. Her dark eyes were wary and desperate.

"What's going on here?"

"I don't know. Does she want to go to school?"

"Maybe. But she looks so afraid," Luke said.

"What would she be afraid of?" Gracie asked.

"I don't know."

"How old do you think she is?"

"Maybe nine? Ten?"

"Let's show this to Maria. Maybe there's a way we can help her," Luke said. He took his tablet and found Maria in the office.

"Look at this girl," Luke said. "Is this something you should be concerned about?"

"Let me see." Maria studied the photo. "I think I know what this is—she's probably one of the girls forced into human trafficking."

"Whoa, seriously?" Color drained from Gracie's face.

"Yes, unfortunately, there is a lot of that going on. There's a ring of men who kidnap girls and force them to work in the fields, then force them into prostitution."

"They're kidnapped?" said Luke. This was a horror beyond his imagination.

"Sometimes," said Maria. "But sometimes they are just presented as a way out of poverty by working in the fields. They're promised a good income and because they are so poor, they buy into the lie that they can help their families. They soon find out the labor is backbreaking, and their bodies are required of them as well."

"Can't they get out?" Gracie asked.

"The girls are told that if they report them, they will kill their families. The girls have no way of knowing if this is true or not, and since they themselves have often been beaten, they believe it. Honduras has laws against it. But often, the police have been bribed and are part of the problem."

"Unbelievable," Luke said. His stomach roiled just thinking about it. "If we contact the school, could we ask them to look out for her and offer her protection?"

"I'll look into it," Maria said, "but don't get too hopeful."

Luke thought of his small world growing up. The rural community outside of Portland had been safe. Kidnapping was something in movies, not a reality. He shook his head. He couldn't even imagine the desperation of these girls to think that they would leave home, hoping to support their families, especially at such a young age.

He didn't have a sister. But he was sure if he had and anything were ever to happen to her, he'd do everything in his power to bring her home and keep her protected.

Chapter Fifteen

Kaitlyn unlocked the front door. Tina was preparing a late breakfast—steam wafted up from the waffle maker.

"Tina!" Kaitlyn dropped her bags and flew into her best friend's open arms. "I can't tell you how glad I am to be home!"

Tina squeezed her tight. "Why? Did more things happen? Are you okay?"

Kaitlyn's entire body sagged. "I just need a hug."

Tina pulled back, her hands on Kaitlyn's shoulders. "Okay, girl, sit down. You want coffee?"

Kaitlyn nodded. Tina put Kaitlyn's favorite mug in front of her, filled it with coffee, added pumpkin creamer, and sat down at the kitchen table across from her.

"Talk."

"I've never seen anything so desolate before. His mom. She's frail and just lays there on a thin, dirty mattress. Her house is a disaster and there's no clean water to drink and..." Kaitlyn looked out the window and swallowed thickly.

Bentley came running in and jumped up on Kaitlyn's lap. She stroked his head. "Hey Bentley, I missed you."

"Okay, start from the beginning. Did you find out what's wrong with her?"

"I think she's drinking—no, I know she's drinking filthy water. She has this rain barrel I scooped water from. It was filled with dead bugs! So gross. I wouldn't have given it to Bentley." She stroked his head.

"I went to the pharmacy and got meds for her and water purification tablets. But she needs help. A lot of help."

"Isn't there anyone to help her? Other family members? How was Francisco with her?" Tina asked.

"I ran into a woman from Healthy Kids—it's an organization that helps families."

"Wait, don't they have an office in Portland? It's in the Pearl District," Tina said.

"Yeah, maybe. Anyway, she's going to look into Miguelita's situation and see what they can do to help. Francisco? He totally loves his mom. I think he would do anything for her. His only brother moved away. Francisco feels obligated to take care of her."

"Okay, so I'm confused here." Tina extended her hand, palm up, to Kaitlyn. "It sounds like you helped get things under control. What's the real issue?"

Kaitlyn took it. "It's Francisco. I told you he kissed me."

"Yeah, in your text. This isn't something new."

Kaitlyn looked away. Tina took Kaitlyn's face in her hands. She locked eyes with her.

"I thought we talked about that, and you were alright with it."

"That's just it, I'm not sure. Is a relationship with someone who is from a third world country a great idea? I mean, after I saw what his background is and the hard conditions. How would that affect us? I didn't grow up rich, but by those standards, I certainly did. I don't know," Kaitlyn said. "And what if we got married and he wanted me to move there? That would be a huge adjustment. I don't think I could do it."

Tina held her palm up like a traffic cop. "Slow down here, kiddo. First off, if God wants you to follow someone to another country, He'll move in your heart, and it will be the right thing. Second, you can't think about marriage yet. Do you like him? Like, are you thinking he could be marriage material?"

"Yeah, I do. But is it because I like him or because I just like feeling needed?"

Tina said, "It's probably a little of both. He has some good qualities. He's focused—he seems determined to get his degree."

"That's because he wants to get a good job and bring his mom to the States. He's determined to get a visa and citizenship," Kaitlyn said.

"I'd say just give it some time and let it play out. Either you're going to build your relationship or you're not. It's going to happen naturally. And if it does, roll with it. Breathe, girl, breathe." Tina drew a square in the air.

Kaitlyn took a deep breath and let it out. Talking to Tina was like talking to her mom. She always knew the right things to say. And let's face it, Tina probably knew her even better than her mom.

"I'm so glad you're my friend," Kaitlyn said. "You know how to set a girl straight." She gave Tina a hug. "I'm going to go upstairs and take a nap. That red-eye flight took it out of me. And I've got to go to work tomorrow. Come on, Bentley."

The November air was crisp. There were fewer sunny days as grey clouds became the norm. Kaitlyn parked her car and followed the sidewalk to the hospital. Scalloped fan-like Ginko leaves scattered the ground. Brilliant red and orange maple leaves floated into piles. Kaitlyn smiled as she remembered how her sister Maggie and she would run and jump in the piles when they were kids, ending in peals of laughter. Kaitlyn pulled out her phone, snapped a photo of the burst of color piled high under the tree and sent it to her.

What was on her agenda today? It was always a surprise. She might have some new patients or be stuck with some of the chronic ones. Kaitlyn never knew. She threw up a brief prayer for her co-workers and those who needed healing before she walked through the front doors. She rolled her shoulders and shook the tension out of her hands.

The elevator door opened on the fifth floor. It struck her how bland and ordinary it looked. She thought someone would have taken the lead to decorate while she was gone. Well, she'd soon fix that. She put her things in her locker.

Peter followed her in.

"Mornin' Kaitlyn."

"Mornin' Peter. What's the word of the day?"

"I just made coffee."

"Good job! I'm glad there's someone here I can count on." Kaitlyn said. She patted him on the shoulder.

"Nice scrubs! Cute little squirrels with acorns. Fall-ish," Peter said.

"Like 'em? My mom made them for me. She could make some for you too if you want!"

Peter put his hand on his chin. His blue eyes twinkled. "Yeah, I'll think on that."

"Better see about my patients," Kaitlyn said. "Ready to face the day?"

She checked in at the front desk and got her assignments. Joe. He'd been here for over a month. Cute little old guy. Jin-lu. Eighteen. Problems with her pacemaker. Awfully young for that. River. Nineteen. IV drug user. Only three patients—she'd probably get the new admit. Didn't sound too bad.

Kaitlyn rounded the corner, nearly bumping into a cart.

"Woah, we need crossing lights here," she said.

Daniel laughed. "Hey, you got a minute? I could use help with my patient. I'm having a hard time getting the IV in. Veins are not my forte."

Kaitlyn blew on her fingernails.

"Super Nurse at your service." She bowed with a flourish.

"Do I get to choose which size needle to put in?" Daniel grinned. He put his open hand to the side of his mouth and whispered, "You might want the big one!" He winked.

They entered the room where a considerably large middle-aged man was lying on the bed. Clyde hadn't shaved for several days and had a severe case of halitosis.

"Hey Clyde, this is Nurse Kaitlyn. She's an expert at needles. Can you hold out your arm for her so we can get your IV put in?"

Clyde sniggered. "Expert at needles, eh? I'm pretty good at needles, too." His eyebrows waggled.

Kaitlyn examined his forearm. She snuck a peek at Daniel. Track marks made a path along the inside of his arm.

"Maybe I should just let you put in your own IV," Kaitlyn said. Clyde chuckled.

Kaitlyn tapped his arm with two fingers, trying to find a good vein.

"What's your other arm look like?" she asked. He held it out. It was clean. Kaitlyn let out the breath she hadn't realized she was holding. Daniel handed her a blue elastic band that she wrapped and tied around his upper arm. She tapped, trying to find the vein.

"I just came from the University Hospital. I had that guy, Dr. Bryson. Do you know him?" Daniel shook his head.

"He took care of me, and I had the biggest poop of my life. I tell ya, it was the size of a baby!" Clyde lifted his hands to show how big. Kaitlyn intercepted and held his arm as she inserted the IV. She removed the elastic band.

"And it had the shape of one too." He put on a wide grin, like he was proud of himself.

Daniel pretended to adjust the curtain so they couldn't see him hold in a laugh. Kaitlyn hooked the bag to the pole and taped the tube to Clyde's arm.

"We laughed so hard we didn't know what to do!" Clyde continued. "He'll remember me, believe you me, and he'll remember the poop." He slapped his thigh. "Could you tell him hi for me?"

"If I see him, I'll sure do that," Kaitlyn said and hustled out of the room.

Kaitlyn burst out laughing. Daniel pushed her down the hall so everyone wouldn't hear her guinea pig-like wheenk. Peter couldn't help but join her. He doubled over. Out of the corner of his eye, he saw sensible white nursing shoes. He elbowed Kaitlyn.

Delores said, "I hope you are not laughing at some poor patient's expense! Back to work. This isn't a playground."

Kaitlyn shoved Daniel with her shoulder and whispered, "Yeah, Daniel, back to work!" He swallowed down a chortle.

Kaitlyn held her palms towards her face and breathed out as she lowered her hands to her side. Okay, I can do this.

She grabbed her laptop and walked into her next patient's room.

"Good morning, River. I'm Kaitlyn. I'll be your nurse today. I've got a few questions for you. They're just a list that we ask everyone when they get admitted."

River looked at her through tired eyes, dark circles under them. Her hair could use a good wash. A wan smile formed on her lips.

"Do you use any drugs other than the ones that are prescribed?" Kaitlyn asked.

"I have my medical marijuana card, so I use that," River said. She looked at the ceiling.

"Oh, and I use heroin."

Kaitlyn typed.

"How much alcohol do you drink?"

River gave her a puzzled look. "None! You can't drink until you're twenty-one!"

Kaitlyn took River's blood pressure, trying not to let her eyes reveal how appalled she was at the bruises on the inside of her arm. How could nurses possibly help people like this?

Kaitlyn shook away the thought. *Can't drink till you're twenty-one, but you can do heroin.*

"Okay, my friend, I'll be back later to check on you. Get some rest." Add another one to the prayer list.

♥ ♥ ♥

Kaitlyn sat in the break room, grateful for a relatively quiet morning. She'd snagged some paper from the printer, pulled out her colored pencils, and began creating fall decorations. The door opened and the rest of her friends came in. Tina passed around fresh made chocolate chip pumpkin bread.

"What's the plan for Thanksgiving? Everyone going home?" Kaitlyn asked.

They all nodded. "Okay, let's set a dinner date at my house."

"Dude! More food!" Peter said. He raised his fist in triumph.

"Tina can make the turkey—she's good at that. I'll make a pumpkin cheesecake. Dan?"

"I'll peel potatoes. And bring drinks."

"I actually make a pretty good pumpkin soup," Peter said. They all looked at him.

"You cook?" they said in unison.

Peter shrugged and held his hands up.

"I've been known to a time or two."

"Don't underestimate this man of many hidden talents," Daniel said, and smiled.

It seemed this month was racing by. Kaitlyn dug in her closet for all her fall decorations—ceramic pumpkins, which she placed on the end table; a leaf garland wound through the stair railing, of course, with little twinkle lights.

Small scarecrows and baby pumpkins she'd made from old socks sat on the maple leaves she had gathered from the lawn. Several pumpkin spice candles were lit. The windows in Kaitlyn's kitchen steamed up and fabulous smells came from the oven.

But that wasn't all that was steamy.

Francisco came up behind Kaitlyn and put his arms around her. She leaned back on him and gave him a side kiss. He turned her around and returned the favor. His lips were soft. She gazed into those green eyes, still mesmerized after this many months. He moved his hands down and put them in her rear pockets. Kaitlyn stepped back and took his hands.

"Woah now. Let's not get carried away there, friend."

"I love being with you," Francisco whispered. "All I ever think about is you." He put his face in her hair and breathed in.

Kaitlyn wrapped her arms around him. The attraction had been deepening, but today seemed out of control. She moved her hands to his face and kissed him again.

Ever since the trip, they'd seen each other every day. And when they weren't together, they were texting or Snap chatting. She found herself constantly smiling. She was hopelessly drawn to him. And when she was away from him, she couldn't think of anything else.

"Hey lovebirds, I think the turkey's done," Tina said. "I could use some help to get it to the table."

Francisco gave her one more kiss and took her hand as they headed for the kitchen.

Chapter Sixteen

Luke looked out his kitchen window. Kids wearing new coats were waiting for the school bus to arrive. They threw their backpacks down and jumped into a pile of leaves. They jostled and laughed as they landed in a dogpile. Luke couldn't help but smile. Maybe someday those would be his kids. That is, if he ever found the perfect gal.

He thought back to his conversation with Gracie. What exactly was his perfect girl? He knew what she wasn't— someone who complained all the time like Amanda, his high school fling. He'd been drawn in by her soccer skills and confidence. But it always seemed as if she had a chip on her shoulder. Never satisfied with the coach. Or the team. Or her parents. It became toxic.

He poured himself a bowl of cereal. Then there was Benita. Too concerned about her looks and wearing the latest designer clothes and makeup.

What about Brianna? He shook his head. No—he didn't think he could break through to her inner "girl". Well, God knows what I need. He looked up. *You do, don't you?*

The Star Wars ringtone played on his phone.

"Hey Dad! How's it going?"

"Hi, everything's going fine." It was good to hear his father's voice. Deep. Constant. Reliable.

"Just checking to see if you're coming for Thanksgiving."

"Of course! I wouldn't miss it. What should I bring?" Holidays—getting together with family. Grandpa William would be there. Good smells, good flavors, loving people.

"Your mom was hoping you'd bring some of those great chanterelle mushrooms—have you gone hunting for them lately?"

"It's been wet and mild. There should be some. I'll check and see. Wouldn't want to disappoint m om." Or himself. Luke salivated at the thought of her chanterelle stuffing. And the pumpkin pie.

"Grandpa, okay?"

"He's slowing down. The doctor says he's got diabetes. He's got to change his diet, so we're trying to keep on top of that."

"I guess Mom will have to make sure there's sugar free pumpkin pie!" Luke didn't want to think about his grandpa failing. At least diabetes wasn't fatal.

Luke checked the time.

"Sorry to cut you off, Dad, gotta head to work. I'll see you next Thursday."

Luke made his way up the front steps to the home he grew up in, opened the front door as he had done hundreds of times before. He set his bucket of chanterelles on the kitchen counter. The succulent fragrance of the turkey wafted from the oven.

Two pies sat on the counter—pumpkin and peach. His mom knew what he liked. Ryan stood at the sink, rinsing potatoes.

"Hey bro, need some help?" Luke hung his coat on the hall rack, the one he had given his mom for Christmas one year. Wasn't that what every mom wanted? Heck, she had been glad to have gotten anything from her teenage boy.

He looked around. "Where's Jessica?" Luke dug through the drawer and found the peeler.

"Not here." Ryan scrubbed the potato harder.

"Everything okay?"

Ryan stopped and held his gaze. He shook his head. "Tell me about your work—you like it?" Okay, so much for that conversation.

"Um, yeah." Luke told him about the trip to Honduras and the trafficking. Rachel, their mom, joined them and reached for a stack of plates.

"Oh, you're here Luke." She gave him a peck on his cheek. "Thanks for helping, boys. As soon as these potatoes boil, we'll be ready to eat." She handed the plates to Luke. "And you brought the chanterelles. Just what I needed to top off the dressing. Set these on the table for me and then go join your dad and Grandpa William for a game of cribbage."

What was Ryan not telling him? Surely the golden boy wasn't breaking up with his fiancé. They'd been together for three years. His parents thought she was the bee's knees. Of course they would. Everything about his little brother was always great in their eyes.

After Ryan won the final round of cribbage, Rachel called them to the table. She had gone all out with her fall décor—orange pumpkin spice candles, a tablecloth with gold lamé leaves. She served the bird on a platter with an imprint of a turkey. Luke figured she couldn't have too many fall decorations to suit her taste.

"Joe, would you say grace?" Rachel held her hand out for his dad to take.

"Thank you, Lord, for giving me a wife who can cook amazing meals and sons who are the light of my life. Bless this meal." He kissed Rachel's hand.

Luke wanted that. A wife he loved for more than thirty years. Who still appreciated him after all that time. Not just appreciated, but adored him. Would that ever happen to him? He dished up some cranberry sauce and mashed potatoes.

"You're awfully quiet Ryan. Anything going on, son?" Joe said.

Ryan cleared his throat and set his fork down. He took a sip of wine. "I guess I need to tell you why Jessica's not here." He wiped his mouth with his cloth napkin. "She's uh," he began and looked down. Both parents set their forks down and gave him their attention. "She's pregnant." Ryan looked at each of them in turn.

Hooboy.

Their dad placed his arm around Ryan's shoulder. "These things happen, son. It's not the end of the world."

Rachel took a long gulp of water and set her glass down. "So that's why Jessica's not here? Is she embarrassed? Ryan, we love that girl."

"What's your plan?" Joe said. He scooted his chair back.

"That's just it. Jessica wants an abortion. I told her I didn't want her to do it. That she would regret it. And it's my decision too. My kid." Ryan's face was heating as his voice became more forceful.

Luke was the only one eating. He sliced his turkey into

small bites and mixed them in with the gravy and mashed potatoes. He looked up and saw his dad lock eyes with his mom.

"Your mom got pregnant with Luke before we married." Luke set his fork down. Now this was new information. "And look how great he turned out." Joe nodded at Luke.

Rachel glanced at Joe and let out a breath. "I didn't want to be pregnant. I had another year of college to finish and had my eye on my dream job. I couldn't see how I could raise a baby and follow my dreams. And I would be mortified to tell my parents."

Luke looked from his mom to his dad. This was supposed to be about Ryan and Jessica. How had it suddenly turned into how he had ruined his mom's life?

"Rachel thought the only way to go on was to have an abortion. I took her to the clinic, but when she got in the room with the doctor, she started crying so hard they sent her home and told her to rethink her decision."

Rachel reached for Luke's hand. It was all he could do to keep it there. She hadn't wanted him? No wonder they gave Ryan all the attention. He had been planned. Ryan hadn't been the one to ruin their lives.

Ryan rested his arms on the table and leaned in. "But mom, you guys made it work, didn't you? It was probably hard, but you figured out how you could finish your degree, even with a baby. I told Jessica I would be there for her. I'd even stay home and parent the baby while she finished school."

"Your mom was brave," Grandpa William said. "She faced us. We were mad at first, but when I held my grandson and looked into his eyes for the first time," he looked at Luke, "You melted my heart."

Ryan scanned their faces. "I don't know what to do here, d ad. Mom. I need your help."

Luke couldn't listen to another word of this conversation. They hadn't wanted him. He pushed his chair back and threw his napkin on the table.

"Luke?" He didn't respond but grabbed his coat and slammed his way out the door. He ran to his truck, started the engine, and squealed out of the driveway. He hadn't been wanted? His heart pounded in his ears. What the heck was his purpose for being on earth? Why hadn't his dad stood up for him? No one made him go to the clinic with his mom. At least Ryan wanted his baby. It all made sense now. Ryan always being in the limelight.

When they were in grade school, they both had been on the same baseball team. Luke couldn't hit the ball for the life of him. But Ryan? Yep. Star player.

And what about his soccer trophy? Luke loved soccer, but he never received an award.

Ryan was always on the honor roll. Luke always had at least one mediocre grade. It all added up now.

He pulled onto the highway and shoved his foot down on the accelerator. So much for Thanksgiving. At this moment, he couldn't think of anything to be thankful for.

Chapter Seventeen

L uke gobbled down his granola, threw a quick PBNJ together, and grabbed an apple. He tugged on his beanie, put on his helmet, and headed to the door.

He soon arrived at his building and locked his bike, took a dollar out of his pocket and placed it in John's open hand.

"How's it going, friend?" Luke asked.

John pulled his army blanket closer around him. "Gettin' colder."

Luke noticed John's red cracking fingers. He pulled off his gloves and held them out. "Here. Take these," Luke said.

John gave him a salute. Luke returned the gesture.

Gracie met Luke at the door.

"Hey," she said. He admired her burnt orange sweater, brown pencil skirt and leggings accented with a mottled colorful scarf.

"You look fall-ish," said Luke. "Are you trying to show me up by getting here early?"

"Sure am. I want Brianna to know who's the best!" Gracie grinned.

Luke shook his head. "What's on the agenda for today?"

"I was wondering if you wanted me to help you with your video. I've got some time," Gracie said.

"That'd be awesome. Another set of eyes would be great." Gracie was so easy to be around. Yeah, someone like her would be on his perfect list. Too bad she was taken. Maybe she has a friend who wants a perfect guy like me. Then again, I'm not so sure I'm worthy of a girl like that.

Luke hung up his coat and helmet and followed Gracie to the lounge chairs. He logged on—the desktop background of him biking up a steep mountain trail.

Gracie pulled a chair up next to him. Luke brought up the photos and videos from the Honduras trip. That was such an enlightening experience. He didn't mind reliving it. At least this was something to take his mind off of that *enlightening* thanksgiving dinner.

He scrolled through photos—the HK van, a candid shot of Maria, overloaded motorcycles with kids hanging off the sides and bundles of sticks strapped to the sides. The video of the Tango dancers at the restaurant. Gracie leaned over and pointed at the screen.

"Hey, we were going to take some Tango lessons!" Gracie said and leaned into him.

"Yeah, we were. That might make a fun staff get together sometime," Luke said. "Maybe I'll see what Brianna thinks." He stole a glance at Brianna. Her now ruby hair hung around her face as she focused on piles of paperwork.

He continued to scroll through the screen. Excited kids with their new soccer balls.

Scraggly kids outside of their daub and wattle homes.

"Wait a minute," Luke said. He switched pages to pull up

the story board he had created before the trip. Gracie looked it over.

"I like the concept, but do we have the photos that will fit that?" she asked.

"We might have to tweak my plan a bit," he said.

Luke returned to the photos. He tagged some. Luke stopped on the clip at the school with the girl desperately looking around the corner of the building.

"That video is really alarming," Luke said. Gracie stared at it. She pointed to the girl.

"Slow it down. Can you enlarge that area so we can see her face better?" she asked. He cropped the section and enlarged it.

"She's definitely afraid of something," Luke said.

"Or someone," Gracie said. "Play the whole scene again."

Luke replayed it. "Wait, see there towards the end? She turns and looks behind her like she thinks someone is watching her."

"Let's get Brianna. I think she should see this," Gracie said.

Luke nodded. Gracie walked to Brianna's desk and waited for her to look up.

"Luke and I have been going over the photos and videos from Honduras. We've got one we'd like you to see. We're a little concerned about what might be a dangerous situation."

Brianna followed her to Luke's desk. He replayed the video, slowing it down when it came to the girl. Brianna grew rigid. Her fists clenched at her side.

"Brianna?" Luke said. He looked at her with furrowed brows. She plopped down in Gracie's empty chair. "Do you want to see it again?"

"No!" she said, a little too forcefully. She shook her head like she was trying to dislodge it from her mind.

"Maria said that girl might be part of a human trafficking ring," Gracie said. Brianna glanced at her. "She said that it's a real problem down there and she didn't think they could do anything about it."

Brianna rose from her seat as if propelled by an explosive force.

"I will call her right now. If this is happening even remotely near our center, something has to be done!" She strode back to her desk and picked up her phone.

Gracie looked at Luke.

"Woah now, there's something here more than meets the eye. She was pretty upset."

"Well, I hope she can do something about it," Luke said. "But the way Maria talked, it didn't seem hopeful."

"Lunch time already. Let's take a break and come back to this later," Gracie said.

Luke nodded. He wasn't sure what was going on in Honduras, but Brianna's reaction seemed over the edge. Despite that, he was sure she could get to the bottom of it.

♥ ♥ ♥

In the lunchroom, Luke pulled out his peanut butter sandwich and apple. Fall had the best apples. He took a bite and juice dribbled down his scruffy chin. Gracie handed him a napkin and smiled.

"Can't take you anywhere!" she said.

"I know. A guy's got to have some faults you know."

"Christmas is just around the corner. Do you have anything planned for HK?" Gracie asked.

"Like a party? Or what?"

"Of course, we'll have a party, but maybe a fundraiser of some sort?"

"Already on it—I've found a tree farm that will donate a bunch of U-cuts and wreaths to sell," Luke said.

"Gonna make it fun and special?" Gracie said. Luke gave her a deer-in-the-headlights look.

"You know, pictures with Santa, maybe a reindeer painting on plywood with holes for people to put their faces in and take photos."

"You could dress up as an elf!" he said. "You've got that perfect sweet smile and sparkly eyes. They'd love you."

"Aw. Hey, you could be Santa!" she said.

Luke patted his slim, sculpted belly. "I'm not exactly built like him."

"Nothing a pillow can't fix. And we could have hot chocolate and cookies..."

Brianna came in and poured a cup of coffee.

"You okay? Your hands are shaking," Luke said.

She sat down and stared at the floor. Luke placed his hand on her shoulder.

"What's going on? Talk to us," he said.

Brianna looked up. "I talked to Maria. It's worse than you could possibly imagine. There's a whole ring of human trafficking and they've been kidnapping girls and forcing them to work on the neighboring farms. Maria went to the police, but apparently, they are a part of the problem." She shook her head.

A frown creased Gracie's forehead.

"That's horrible!" she said. "I can't even imagine what those girls are going through."

"Is there any way to protect the local girls from becoming a part of it?" Luke asked.

"Maria said they've started a new educational campaign in the community. But she's afraid she may have some backlash from the mob."

"Woah, this is more serious than we knew. Is there anything we can do?" Luke asked.

Brianna looked each of them in the eye. "Pray. God's plan is bigger than this."

Chapter Eighteen

Kaitlyn's arm plopped over her pillow, and she grappled for her phone. She opened her bleary eyes just enough to punch stop on her annoying alarm. *I have got to change that alarm tone.* She snuggled back into her covers, hoping to gain another ten minutes of shuteye.

Her mind drifted to thoughts of Francisco. She almost wished he was here snuggling with her. Now that was a thought she needed to keep to herself.

It was so nice to have a man in her life. Someone to go places with. To talk over the day. Someone to make her feel needed. And besides, he was an amazing cook.

She fumbled for her cell phone. Kaitlyn may as well shut the alarm off before she had to hear that annoying beep again. She eased herself up. A bemused smile crossed her lips. A message from Francisco.

I love you. Hope you sleep well.

Slept. He was hopeless. She shook her head as her smile turned to a chuckle. She let out a yawn, stretched, and stumbled into the bathroom to take a shower.

Tina pounded on the door.

"Okay if I come in?" she asked.

"Yeah."

"You got home kinda late last night," Tina said.

"Yeah, we went to a movie. Then stopped at the brewery."

"I waited up for you," Tina said. Her voice held a challenge. She crossed her arms.

"You didn't have to do that," Kaitlyn said. She shut off the shower and grabbed her towel.

"I just wanted to talk to you. You're never around anymore. It's like you don't even care about me." Tina gave an exaggerated pouty face.

Kaitlyn put on her robe and gave Tina a hug. "Better?"

"Yeah, but really, when are we going to have a girl's night? You're always around that guy."

Kaitlyn ran her brush through her hair. "Okay, okay, you're right. Let's do something Sunday afternoon. Just you and me." She put her brush down and looked at her. "I know. Francisco and I are going to get a Christmas tree. We'll set it up and decorate then."

"Decorate without him?" Tina lifted one eyebrow.

"Sure, I'll just leave a few ornaments out for him, so he gets the experience of it."

"Alright. Don't stand me up or I'll never be your friend again."

Kaitlyn held out her pinky to Tina, where they linked. "Pinky promise!"

♥ ♥ ♥

The sky was the kind of blue you saw in travel brochures. It was refreshing after the past stormy wind and constant downpour. The streets had rivers of water flowing down, threatening to overflow the gutters. School busses splashed waves of water on passing cars and pedestrians. The wind had taken most of the fall leaves and scattered them on lawns, in gutters and filled the drains.

But today. This was gorgeous. Kaitlyn adjusted her scarf, knit by her bestie Tina, and tucked it into her jacket. She started her car, watching for the neighbor's cat, and pulled out.

Tina was right. She had been spending a lot of time with Francisco. Kaitlyn had even made the bold move to take him to her parent's house for Thanksgiving dinner. He had made himself at home in her mom's kitchen. Her mom was impressed.

It was her dad, however, that she was getting uncomfortable vibes from. He was pleasant, all right, but there was just some-thing about him—a little reserved, perhaps? She didn't know. Her dad didn't just come right out and say anything bad or embarrassing. Maybe that was it. He hadn't said anything to embarrass her like he had when she had high school dates. She shook her head. Her cell rang, taking her out of her reverie.

"Hi Babe," she said.

"Where are you?" Francisco said.

"On my way, I'm just around the corner. Love you." A warmth travelled through her.

She pulled up to his house, well, not his house, and parked. He boarded with a woman who sponsored him to move to the states. She could see why he thought this house was beautiful. It was, compared to where he grew up.

Kaitlyn checked herself in the mirror. She fluffed up her curly hair and got out.

The sidewalk still sparkled with frost. She walked gingerly up to the front porch and looked in the window. Francisco was lying on the couch, snugged in a blanket, engrossed in a video game. Kaitlyn tried the door—it was unlocked. She walked in and sat on the couch by him.

He glanced up at her but kept playing.

"Hey," she said and ran her hand through his thick black hair. "Just a minute, I need to finish this level. So close." He shrugged her hand off.

She shook her head and sauntered into the kitchen and helped herself to a glass of water. She stood in the doorway watching him. A small thought niggled her. Did he really care about her? Was she really important to him? At times like this, she had to wonder.

"Come on, my love. Put that thing down." She reached for the tablet. He held it away. "I guess I'll just have to leave without you, then." She headed to the door.

Francisco put it down. "Where?"

Kaitlyn put her hand on her hip. "Don't you remember we were going to get a Christmas tree?"

"Oh, yeah. Okay, give me a minute and I'll be ready." He laid the tablet down, glanced at it before he threw on a sweatshirt, and they headed to her car.

Why was she feeling jealous of a video game?

"There's a place about a mile from here that's selling trees. I can't wait! I loooove Christmas." She remembered when she was a little girl how her dad had always taken them to cut a tree. He let her try the saw, even though he knew she'd never be able to do it. Then he'd set her on his shoulders and drag the tree, her mom carrying the treetop, to the truck.

"December in Honduras is the middle of the summer. It's always hot," Francisco said.

"Not here. Does that mean you don't put up Christmas trees?"

"No, I only see a Christmas tree one time when we went to the big city. I no think it was real though," he said. "Don't" he corrected himself.

She drove down a long dirt road and parked next to a large sign that read Christmas Trees-—Support Healthy Kids!

Rows of Christmas trees lined the lot, lights strung above them between poles. An old, weathered barn stood to the right, trimmed with twinkling Christmas lights. Someone dressed in a Santa suit was seated in a fancy painted sleigh. His fake beard and white hair were classic. His enormous belly obviously a pillow. A girl dressed as an elf stood beside him, ushering kids to his lap while she took photos.

"Come on," Kaitlyn said and pulled Francisco's sleeve. "Let's get our picture with Santa!" He drug his feet as he followed her into the barn. A plate of sugar cookies decorated as stars, snowmen and presents was on the table . Francisco grabbed one and followed her to the sleigh.

"Here for a photo?" Santa asked.

"Could we?" Kaitlyn asked shyly, shrinking into her shoulders. The little girl inside of her suddenly shy.

"Sure, hop on up." He held out his hand to her. She took it and climbed up. Those eyes. He looked familiar.

Francisco climbed up beside her and wrapped his arm around her shoulders.

"Do you want me to use your phone?" the elf asked.

"Yes please." Kaitlyn handed it to her.

"Smile. Say candy cane!" Francisco grinned and Kaitlyn laid her head on his shoulder.

"One more." Francisco kissed her. Snap. They jumped down and looked at the photos. Satisfied, Kaitlyn sent it to Tina.

"What do we use to cut a tree?" Kaitlyn asked.

"I've got a chain saw," Santa said. "Show me which one." His voice was deep and smooth. Somehow familiar. They walked down the row carefully judging which would fit in her house and was just the right shape.

"Let's get this one," she said. Santa started towards the tree, belly wobbling.

"Here, let me cut it," Francisco said, holding out his hand for the chain saw. Santa raised his eyebrows and handed it over. Francisco set it on the ground and pulled the string. It didn't start. He yanked on it again. Still didn't start. He scowled and backed away.

Kaitlyn watched as Santa stood back, crossed his arms and watched, a smug look filling his face.

Who was that guy? She knew she had seen him before.

"Here, let me get that," Santa said, straightening his shoulders. He took the saw from Francisco. One pull and the saw hummed to life. He set it next to the trunk, and it sliced like butter. The tree toppled over.

Kaitlyn gave Santa an admiring look. He winked at her.

Francisco glared at him. "Grab the top of the tree," Francisco said to Kaitlyn. "And I'll get the trunk." Kaitlyn took her end and followed him to the car.

"Will you need some rope to tie that on?" Santa called.

Francisco didn't turn around. Santa smirked, went to the barn and gathered some nylon twine and followed them. Francisco and Kaitlyn hoisted it on top of her car, where Santa deftly tied it down. Kaitlyn dug in her purse and pulled out the money.

"Here," she said, handing it to Santa. "You look really familiar. Don't I know you from somewhere?" She squinted her eyes and tilted her head.

He pulled down his beard and smiled. "Was that supposed to be a pickup line?"

"Luke?" She laughed. "How do I keep running into you?"

"Come on, Kaitlyn, we need to get going." Francisco opened the car door and gestured her in.

Kaitlyn rolled down the window. "Great to see you again, Luke!"

Chapter Nineteen

K aitlyn wheeled a cart out to the nurse's station with a large tub filled to the brim with Christmas decorations. If no one else was going to get this place in the Christmas spirit, she would take it on.

Working with constant illness, whiny patients and a bunch of crazies was enough to infuse Scrooge into the atmosphere. Kaitlyn started humming Deck the Halls.

What wasn't to like about Christmas? She got to wear her scrubs with gingerbread men and candy canes. Garland, lights, snuggling under Christmas quilts watching cheesy Hallmark movies with Francisco.

Don't forget the cookies. Or hot cocoa. And those homemade caramels her mom always made. She was going to have to get the recipe for those and make some for Francisco. She could just imagine his dreamy look when he bit into one.

The recipe always made a big batch. Maybe she could bring some here and win points with Delores. Kaitlyn broke into a wide, open smile and pulled out a long shiny garland from the giant red Christmas tub.

"Hey, need some help with that?" Sahid asked as he rounded the corner. "There's some packing tape in the supply room. I'll get some."

"That'd be great." See, there are other things besides MRSA that are contagious.

Sahid returned with tape, scissors and a step stool.

"OSHA standards. Gotta be safe!" he said. He grabbed one end of the garland and held it in place while Kaitlyn strung it in scallops along the top of the wall.

Peter heard the commotion and returned with a box of rubber gloves. He began blowing them up and tying them. It didn't take long until he had formed a goofy looking tree.

Tina walked out of her patient's room. "Whatcha up to here? Decorations! I know what you need." She pulled her phone out of her pocket and streamed some Christmas tunes. Tina sang along as she hung paper snowflakes from the garland.

"Baby it's cooollld out- side."

Kaitlyn took Tina's hands and twirled her around. They sidled up and fell into a little tap dance routine.

"Ladies!" Delores clapped her hands. Kaitlyn and Tina froze and backed up to the wall. "There's work to do— bandages to change, meds to give, and that man in room 8 needs an enema." She glared at them. "Don't just stand there, let's go! And turn that blasted music off. People tryin' to rest." She shook her head and stomped down the hall.

Kaitlyn and Tina suppressed a giggle and headed to their patient's rooms.

♥ ♥ ♥

The ninety-year-old man in room 10 was moaning.

"Hey there Mr. Miller. What's going on?" Kaitlyn asked.

"I can't get any sleep. It's too noisy." He wasn't referring to the Christmas music, was he?

"And there's lights on. And just when I get to sleep, some nurse comes in and starts poking me. I. Just. Want. To. Sleep."

"What do you usually do to get to sleep at home?" she asked. She adjusted his pillow.

"My great granddaughter gave me these gummy bears. You know those marijuana ones? I just take one a night. Do you have any of those?" he asked, hopeful.

"Sorry, none here. I'll put your request in the notes for the night nurse," she said. "She'll take good care of you." She patted him on the shoulder. "Would you like your door open or closed?" she asked.

"Just close it," he snarled.

Kaitlyn tiptoed out, tempted to wave, but thought better of it.

She checked on her other patients. All okay. She should head to the break room for a cup of coffee while she had the chance.

A few feet before she got to the door, she heard her pals talking.

"What do you think of Kaitlyn and Francisco?" Daniel said.

Kaitlyn stopped behind the open door.

"I don't know. They seem okay together," Peter said.

"They are not okay," Tina said. "Do you realize that she paid for his trip to Honduras? And she paid for his mom to get a new roof?"

"That was nice of her." Peter said. "Wasn't it?"

Tina shook her head. "She pays for everything! He's finished with his degree and he's still not working," Tina said.

"Doesn't he have a work visa?" Daniel said.

"No, just a student visa, and that's almost up. I think he's using her. I wouldn't put it past him to ask her to marry him so he could get citizenship."

Wait, Kaitlyn thought, could he do that? Would he do that? She took a step back.

Hey, I thought these guys were my friends and now they're throwing me under the bus.

She turned to walk away. Her chest tightened.

Her phone buzzed in her pocket. She pulled it out. Francisco's face popped up.

> Do you want to go Christmas caroling
> tonight with the group?

That was tonight? See, it wasn't all about her giving to him. He cared about her and what she liked. What did they know?

> Yes, of course

She popped in on her next patient. Lola Gonzales was sixty-nine, with congestive heart failure. Her daughter had placed an image of Jesus on the cross next to her bed. A rosary sat on the table, made of clear crystal beads.

"Lola?" Kaitlyn said as she entered. "How are you feeling?"

Lola adjusted herself into an inclined position. Kaitlyn adjusted her pillows. Lola reached for Kaitlyn's hand.

"You are such a sweet nurse. I'm okay, I guess. I just get out of breath." Kaitlyn checked her oxygen tank. Looked good.

"Can I take your blood pressure?" she asked.

"Yes, of course." She held out her arm. Kaitlyn adjusted the cuff and put on her stethoscope. BP was a little high.

"I saw that your daughter was here earlier. Did you have a nice visit?"

"Oh yes. She is so good to me. She always prays with me."

Kaitlyn smiled. She could relate. The best time of day was when her mom called and prayed with her.

"Is she married? Does she have a family?" Kaitlyn asked.

"Oh yes, she has a very nice family. Her husband is an investment broker and she home schools. My grandkids are active in sports and little Johnny plays the saxophone. It's almost bigger than he is." She looked out the window and smiled. "I am so lucky to have them in my life."

"That must keep her pretty busy."

"Oh, it does. But her husband is so supportive. He cooks dinner when he gets home, reads stories to the kids, and gets them to bed. He knows she needs a break after being with them all day. I couldn't have a better son-in-law. Twelve years they've been married, and he's still so in love with her. Anticipates her every need. They make good companions."

Kaitlyn envisioned a life with Francisco. Would it be like

that? Would her parents think he was the best son-in-law possible?

"Here, I've got some meds for you. They should help with the swelling in your legs."

Kaitlyn finished charting. "I'll be back later to check on you before my shift is over."

She walked down to the nurse's station. A patient in a wheelchair sat with a smile on her face, admiring the Christmas decorations. But wait, someone had been there and added more. Kaitlyn burst out laughing. Strung up like garland were alternating plastic urinals and bed pans. She turned as she felt an arm around her shoulders.

"I thought it needed a little something to represent our floor," Peter said. "Dan and I did it. Cool, right?" Kaitlyn stepped back and gave him a high five. . "Going caroling tonight?" she asked.

"Yep, we'll see you there," Peter said.

She clocked out and sent a quick text to Francisco.

<Be there in about an hour. Gotta change out of these nasty scrubs.>

♥ ♥ ♥

A dozen cars were parked in the church parking lot when she pulled in. Kaitlyn got out, pulled her coat tighter around her.

"Look at those gorgeous stars! It's such a clear night." she said.

Francisco linked elbows. "Very beautiful. This will be a

perfect night," he said. He seemed unusually happy and gave her a wide smile.

Tables and chairs were set up. A cute little Christmas tree stood in the corner decorated with paper angels. The little kids must have made them. Small poinsettias sat in the middle of the tables.

They each filled their bowls with chili and took an orange and decorated cookie. Dan waved them over where they joined Tina and Peter.

Mark Evans, the pastor stood up.

"Welcome everyone. As soon as you're done eating, we'll run through a few of your favorite songs before we head out."

"God Rest Ye Merry Gentlemen," Kaitlyn said.

"Rudolf!" Peter chimed in.

"Feliz Navidad!" Francisco said.

Kaitlyn rolled her eyes and smiled.

Mark slung his guitar over his shoulder, and they followed him out. The neighborhood twinkled with lights hung from the gutters and along fences. The frosty ground reflected the colors. Windows framed Christmas trees decked in garland, lights, and shiny ornaments. A large blow up Frosty greeted them at the first house.

Kaitlyn tightened her scarf, adjusted her knit hat, and zipped her coat.

"Cold?" Francisco asked.

"Freezing!" she said.

"Here, let me warm you up," he said and slid his arm through hers. She snuggled close. This. She was in her happy place.

They knocked on the first door and were met by a man surrounded by several laughing children. Mark strummed, and the group began singing Frosty. Daniel handed the kids candy canes before they went on to the next house.

Now this is what Christmas is supposed to look like. Why had she ever doubted God's plan for her? Good friends, lots of fun, making smiles, and snug with my guy. Tina didn't know what she was talking about. Francisco was great.

After several houses, Francisco pulled her back. He turned her to him and slid both hands around her waist. The surrounding air seemed electrified. She studied his earnest expression. A crooked smile played on her lips.

"Kaitlyn," he said. He slid his hands down to hold hers. "I love you. I want you to marry me."

Kaitlyn leaned back as she took this in. Her heart hammered in her ears.

"Francisco, I- I don't know what to say."

"Say yes." His green eyes pleaded with her.

She stepped back and turned her face away.

"I like you. I really do." She met his gaze. "But we've only been dating a few months. That's not a very long time. Let's revisit this topic in about six more months and see how we feel about each other."

He frowned, his eyes grey under angry brows. He let go of her hands as if they were a hot iron. Without another word, he turned and stormed back towards the church.

"Francisco? Francisco!"

"Kaitlyn?" Tina came up behind her. "What's wrong?"

The chili in Kaitlyn's stomach roiled. "I don't know. But I don't think Francisco is coming back."

Chapter Twenty

The Tri Met came to a stop and Luke jumped out. The skies were the color of the sidewalk and getting darker by the minute. He brushed snowflakes off his knit cap and stomped his boots before he entered the bike shop. The dark skies and shorter days were affecting his mood, and he was sinking into depression. It didn't help that his mom kept texting and leaving messages. If she thought he was going to answer them. . .

"Anything I can help you with?" A fit twenty-something dressed in an REI fleece greeted him with a smile.

"Actually, yes. I'm planning a trip to somewhere sunny—Arizona or Southern Cal. Gotta get out of this dark and dreary place."

"I hear ya. What are you looking for?" she said.

"I don't know. I want to go someplace warmer. What do I need?"

"Do you have a hydration backpack? They're always nice. Or how about some Polaroid sunglasses?"

"Yeah, great ideas. I could actually use both of those." She held a backpack up for him.

"Even on sale. Sweet!" He pulled out his wallet and paid.

"Are you going alone?" she asked.

"I checked online and there are some Christmas Meetup groups."

"You're not staying here with your family?"

Luke looked out the window. "Nope. Not this year." Or any year in the near future.

"Oh. Well. Here you go. Have fun and let us know how your ride goes. We always like to share our customer's adventures. You can post photos on our Instagram. Good luck!"

Luke tucked the sunglasses in the pocket of his down jacket and threw a backpack strap over one arm. The bell tinkled over the door as he left.

Christmas decorations hung in every store window. A group of bundled up carolers were singing outside of Nordstrom's. It sounded nice. He caught himself humming along as he boarded the Tri Met. He figured the Christmas spirit was manufactured to bring cheer to those like him who got the winter doldrums. Well, it seemed to work. For some people.

Luke hopped off and stopped at a coffee kiosk a block from his work. He ordered a peppermint mocha, extra hot with whip cream, and watched the steam rise. John sat on the sidewalk, swaddled in several worn blankets. Luke offered him the drink. John held his hands out and wrapped his gloved fingers around it. He could use a shave, Luke thought. Next time, he'd bring him a razor.

When he entered the HK office, the season bombarded his senses, luring him into the spirit of Christmas. Cinnamon and cloves of hot spiced cider met him. He salivated over a plate of homemade fudge and admired the twinkly lights draped every-where—along the ceiling, around the desks, wrapped around the stair railings. Christmas carols played softly in the background.

"Woah now," he said. "Is this the work of Little Miss Christmas Elf?"

"You would accuse me of all this?" Gracie asked, spreading her arms.

"I love it!" he said. "It's enough to turn a grumpy guy into Mr. Sunshine." He took off his winter garb and hung them up on the rack. "Has Brianna said anything more about the girl?"

"No, but she wants to meet with us in fifteen minutes."

Luke powered on his computer and revisited the video promo he'd made. It was only two minutes long but had taken hours and hours to edit and add music to. He was glad to have it done, and all in all he was satisfied with it. He'd show the final copy to Brianna and launch it on the website.

Gracie gave Luke a thumb jerk towards Brianna, who was approaching from behind.

"Hey Brianna," Luke said. "I see you're in the Christmas spirit—nice green hair to go with your red sweater."

She smiled. "You should try a new color, Luke. There are other colors besides brown!"

"Uh yeah. . ."

"Okay, folks, have a seat."

Luke pulled a chair over for Gracie and motioned to it. She smiled and sat. He grabbed the plate of cookies and passed them around, and sat on the stool, his legs stretched out before him.

"I spent a long time talking to Maria. She's pleased with the effect the education campaign is having on the girls. It's been positive. At least she hasn't seen any of the girls in her project go missing. I wanted to let you know that I'll be traveling down there the first of January. I'll be gone a week, so I'll be depending on you guys to keep the place in shape. I'll let the rest of the staff know that you two are in charge while I'm gone."

Luke straightened his shoulders and gave Gracie a smug look. "Okay, that's good. I plan to be back from my bike trip by then."

"Gracie? You going anywhere?" Brianna asked.

"Just for Christmas with my folks in Denver. Shouldn't be a problem."

"Looks like the bases are covered. Gracie, finish up the Christmas Gift Guide and let's get that in the mail."

"I'm on it," Gracie said and headed to her workspace.

Luke, let's take a look at your promo video."

"Right. Do you want to come over to my laptop?" Brianna followed him. A tap and it was ready to view. Brianna studied each scene carefully.

"I love the music—it's the perfect fit. You did a superb job of keeping it snappy and the visuals are right to the point. Right to the heart. Perfect. Get it posted to the website right away."

"Thanks, Brianna. That means a lot." At least someone appreciated him.

"I need you to send out the year-end donation appeal, too."

Her sparkling white teeth showed through her beautiful smile. "You're a great fit for this organization, Luke. I'm glad I hired you."

He was glad too. Relieved. So relieved.

Luke's bike trip in Arizona had been refreshing. A whole sky full of sunshine. And the stars—so magnificent! What the locals called cold, he called comfortable. More like Oregon spring than winter.

He shook off the rain from his jacket and headed into the office. Brianna had Healthy Kids running like a well-oiled machine. She hadn't needed Luke or Gracie to be in charge. When respect and dignity were the rule, there were seldom any, as Grandma Alice would say, kerfluffles.

Luke opened his email. Over a hundred. He figured it would take a while to catch up. He deleted all the promotional non-profit ads, checked in with a few donors, and scrolled to the next page. *Hm, what's this?* He clicked on it.

<< From: Gabriela López
    To: Luke McCarthy >>

Dear Luke,

You might remember me from your trip to Honduras last fall. I work with Maria at the central office.

There are some things going on here that I think someone in the States needs to know about. Brianna, as you know, is here. I would prefer that she doesn't find out I'm sending this to you.

Please delete it after you've read it.

Brianna shared with us that you and Gracie know about the sex trafficking. It's a horrible, terrible thing. The girls are terrified. The parents don't want to let them go to school or out of the house for fear that they'll be kidnapped. We've begun the education campaign, and yes, that has helped a lot, but it hasn't eradicated the problem.

When we tried to include the polícia, we soon realized that the mob was paying them off to allow the traffickers to continue. When they nab the girls, they tell them they'll be able to get themselves and their family out of poverty. The girls believe them but then find that they are forced to hard labor in the fields, sometimes for sixteen hours a day. They're starving because they aren't given adequate food. They're told that if they *service* the men, they'll get better food.

The next thing they know, they're forced into having sex with the bosses and any number of other crazed men.

Here's the tricky part. As you can imagine, many of the girls end up pregnant. Brianna's solution was to hire doctors to do abortions. The traffickers send the girls to us because they don't want babies on their hands.

Luke stopped reading. He ran his hands through his hair. His heart hammered against his chest. He couldn't believe what he was reading. Was it possible that this faith-based organization he put his heart and soul into would compromise on this? What could she possibly be thinking? Didn't Brianna value life? Yes, they were in a difficult situation, but abortion?

Abortion wasn't the answer. Fear and anger knotted inside him.

Luke looked around, sure that everyone would know what he had just read. He shook his head. Not possible. He stared at the computer, unable to continue. He ran his hands through his hair and rubbed his neck.

He inhaled deeply and read.

Luke, you know as well as I do that abortion doesn't conform to our values. I'm not sure what to do about it. Maria and I want to keep our jobs, so we haven't confronted her about this. Brianna thinks she's doing the right thing. I just had to let someone in the States know.

I'm sorry to drop this bomb on you. But you seem level-headed, and I'm sure that my prayers for a solution will be answered. Please join me in this.

Gabriela

Luke unbuttoned the top button on his shirt. Beads of sweat formed on his forehead. He sat back in his chair and ran his hands through his hair, and stared vacantly at the ceiling.

He shoved back his chair, and closed the lid of his laptop. He grabbed his coat and beanie and headed to the door, passing Gracie's workspace.

"I'll be back."

She shot him a startled nod.

Luke bolted down the stairs. He just needed to walk this out. He bolted through the front door to the sidewalk where fliers from a Planned Parenthood event blew onto his feet. Luke kicked one away into the pouring rain. He broke into a run, pushing past people with umbrellas, barely stopping for lights.

What was Brianna thinking? She had to know how an abortion was performed—that the baby could feel pain by six weeks —that the doctor inserts a long clamp and basically tears the baby limb by limb and crushes the skull.

Luke grabbed his stomach and doubled over. This was what had been planned for him. Dizzy, he threw up. He leaned against the wall and looked up into the sky, letting the rain wash over his face and down over his soaked clothes.

What was he going to do? He should quit. How could he continue to promote HK? If the donors ever found out... he shook his head. If he quit, did he have enough money to tide him over until he found a new job? No, he couldn't let that be the determining factor.

He wouldn't want to tell everyone why he quit. Donors might stop their support. He couldn't work there anymore. He wasn't going to be a part of this. And what about Gracie? Should he tell her?

He started walking again. He felt like he was in a slo-mo movie in a thick fog.

No, he was going to have to let Gracie in on this. She could give him some perspective.

Luke found himself back at the door of the office. He put his hand on the door handle and paused. He climbed the three flights of stairs and entered the office. As he stood at the door, Gracie looked up.

"You look like a drowned puppy!" Gracie laughed.

Luke stood staring, shoulders bent.

"Hey, you okay?" She helped him out of his dripping coat and led him to a chair.

"Want a glass of water? Coffee?" she said. He nodded and pulled off his soaking beanie. She handed him a glass of water. Luke took a drink and looked at her.

"We've got trouble in River City," he said. "Big trouble." If he had thought that he had been in the winter doldrums before, this was enough to put him over the edge.

He got up and motioned her to his computer. He looked around to see who else was nearby.

They needed privacy. He took his laptop and headed into Brianna's office, where he shut the door.

"Look," he said. "I got an email that I was supposed to delete after I read it." He paced. "I'm so angry I could burst." He slammed his fist into his other palm.

"Slow down, show me the email." Gracie leaned in towards his computer.

"I'm gonna warn you, it's not pretty." He brought it up.

Gracie started reading. "Oh, I remember her."

She jerked back from the computer and put her hand over her open mouth, then moved her hand to her chest. Worry etched her face. She stopped and looked at Luke. Her shoulders dropped, her eyes bordered with tears.

"I know, right?" He let her sit and take it in.

"What are we going to do?" Gracie whispered.

"First, I'm going to delete this, like she asked. We don't want Gabriela getting in trouble." He held his finger over delete. Was he sure? Yes, he definitely was.

He turned in Brianna's lounge chair to face Gracie.

"We have to confront Brianna." This was not going to be easy.

"Have you prayed about this yet?" she asked. "Cuz now would be a good time to do that."

Chapter Twenty-One

Mud splashed Kaitlyn's Prius as she drove down the long dirt driveway to her family's home. A Blue Heron jumped from the field and flew off, its long wingspan helping it soar to the slough.

As she neared the house, she flashed the lights on her car to announce her arrival. Her dad, Dave, glanced up from stacking firewood and gave her a grin. He plugged in the Christmas lights to welcome her.

Dave held his arms out wide to engulf her in a hug. Kaitlyn didn't want to leave the strength and security of his arms. Just what a girl needed. A girl who had just been dumped.

"Hi Dad!"

"Hi you. We're so glad you could make it. We saved..."

"Auntie Kaitlyn!" Maggie's daughter Lizzie shrieked. She shot out and jumped on Kaitlyn's back.

"Auntie Kaitlyn! Auntie Kaitlyn!" Sophie and Liam, her brother Sam's twins clung onto her legs.

Kaitlyn took one slow step after another, laughing with the cling-ons. She made it through the front door where Riley and

Jackson perched on stools with her brother James, rolling out cookie dough.

"I see you've gotten the proper greeting," James said. He blew her an air kiss.

"Yes indeed. It's like a preschool in here!" Love. Her family knew how to make the season bright. Coming home was a healing balm.

"Come on!" Lizzie grabbed her hand. "We saved the decorating for you. Hurry!" Lizzie drug her to the living room where a fresh tree stood in the stand, the pine scent completing Christmas.

Maggie pulled the tub of decorations closer.

"Remember this one? I picked it out for you when you were born. I was so excited to have a baby to love and play with. You were so cute." Maggie scrunched up her nose.

Kaitlyn held the ornament, a mouse sitting on a bulb that read First Christmas.

"Did you get a real tree this year?" Maggie asked.

Kaitlyn started to smile at the memory of Francisco and her cutting the tree from Healthy Kids. But then shook it off when she thought of how jealous he had been of Luke. There had definitely been red flags. She should have paid attention to them.

"Yeah, just a small one. Tina helped me decorate it." She held up a paper gingerbread garland. It had been accordion pleated, the faces awkwardly drawn on with colored pencil.

"I remember you helping me make this—you cut, and I colored. A regular artist!" Kaitlyn smiled.

"How's everything going? I haven't heard from you in like, forever!" Maggie said.

"Okay, I guess."

"You guess? Work okay? Love life okay? Roommate okay?"

"Work's good, Tina's great."

"That leaves love life."

"As in, there isn't one." Kaitlyn said. She held Lizzie up to place an angel on a limb.

Their mom, Kate, came in, her arms full of gifts.

"Oh Kaitlyn—you're here! I heard commotion, but," she glanced around, "it's always noisy with kids running around." She gave Kaitlyn a peck on the cheek. Liam and Sophie ran in.

"Can we help?" Kate handed a box to each of them to place under the tree.

"What did I hear about 'love life'?" Kate said. Hope written in her eyes.

"Basically, there isn't one." Anymore. Kaitlyn looked down just in time to lift Liam out of the way of stepping on a bulb.

"I'm gonna go check on the cookies. They smell delicious!" Not exactly the time or place to talk about issues of the heart.

"Hey James, need any help?" She watched him take a tray out of the oven.

"Careful, they're hot!" Jackson moved a step back.

"I made these," Jackson said. That little boy had his dad's contagious smile.

"I can tell — I love the elongated body of the reindeer. And the crack in the snowman—it looks like it's trying to talk." She smiled. "Unique!"

"Be nice! Help Jackson with the icing." Kaitlyn scooped green and white icings into some bags. She snipped off a corner and handed one to Jackson, showing him how to hold it with both hands and squirt designs.

"When are you going to have some kids? You're good with them," James said.

"When I get good and ready. Don't hold your breath."
Maybe never at the rate I'm going.

♥ ♥ ♥

They had to add two extra folding tables to seat everyone. Kate had gone to simple settings— no placemats or tablecloths to get stained, mismatched plates in order to have enough, and plenty of sippy cups to preserve sanity.

No Martha Stewart here. Who needed it? Relationships came first. True, they may not always agree on everything, but there was no doubt they loved each other. If she ever did find Mr. Right, she wanted him to be from this kind of family— fun loving and caring.

Francisco was fun loving. And somewhat caring. He was just so darn needy.

"Mashed potatoes?" Sam said. Kaitlyn shook out of her reverie and nodded. Look at her mom and dad. They had different interests, but they filled their chosen roles like a well-oiled machine. And Sam and Kim? They were just sappy in love. Inseparable. And so into their kids.

"Auntie Kaitlyn, will you read us stories tonight?" Sophie asked.

"And do the voices!" Liam cried. Being an auntie put her in her happy place.

"Of course! Which would you like? Trolls? Or Polar Express?" Trolls was Kaitlyn's personal favorite.

"Trolls!" Lizzie chimed in.

"Okay, if I take them to the living room? They're done

153

eating. It will give you guys some adult time." They nodded.

"Bring the book. And a blanket. Can't read without snuggles."

The couch looked like piles of puppies. Riley and Lizzie were on her left, Jackson and Liam were on her right, and Sophie made herself at home, sitting on Kaitlyn's shoulders.

After putting on her best Troll voices, Kaitlyn got them all settled for bed. This was her absolute dream. Making cookies, reading stories, playing, giggling. She headed down the stairs with a smile on her face.

"Thanks, Kaitlyn. You're so good with them."

"You would be too, Maggie, if you only saw them once every five months!"

Kaitlyn went to the couch and laid her feet on her dad's lap. He started rubbing them. She gave a heavenly sigh. He always knew what she liked.

"How are things going with you, Katey-girl?"

"Oh, you know..."

"I need you to be a little more specific."

"Where should I start? Don't answer that. You'll say, at the beginning." Kaitlyn scrunched up her nose.

She took a breath. "So, remember Francisco? From Thanksgiving?"

"Yeah. And?"

"He was living with a host family. His mom's house had a leaky roof, so I bought a new roof. And then she got sick and so we flew down to see her."

"You went to Honduras? I never knew that. You should call more often. Email. Snapchat. Text. Something." He pulled on her toes. "How was it?"

It hadn't been that long since she'd called, had it? She talked to her mom every day. But it was true, she hadn't wanted to share the nitty gritty with her. Now that she thought about it, if she had trusted her, she might not have been in this mess.

"Poor. I guess I had a little culture shock. Anyway, after the trip, Francisco and I got close, and I was really starting to like him. But out of the blue, he asked me to marry him."

"And you said...."

"No! We'd only been dating for a couple of months." She pulled her knees up to her chest.

"A wise choice."

"Tina thinks so. She thinks he was just using me. To help his mom. And to get a green card."

"What do you think?"

"I don't know. You know me. I'm so naïve." She pulled on a ringlet. "It's all your fault, you know. You let everyone baby me." She stuck out her bottom lip.

Her dad laughed. "I'm sure not all Latinos are like that. Most are very hard-working people trying to better themselves. It sounds like you just happened to get a dud."

Kaitlyn laughed. "I think I'm going to take time off from guys."

Maggie came in. "Yeah, we'll see how long that lasts!"

Chapter Twenty-Two

Luke was supposed to be working on a giving campaign. He couldn't concentrate. Not on this. Not on anything. How was he going to talk to Brianna? He played a number of scenarios in his head. He could just go in and give her notice that he was quitting—make something up, like some family reason, or he's moving to the coast. Should he talk to her alone or bring Gracie? Maybe he should call Mr. Steinberg. But what if he's in on this too? Or what if he wasn't and it resulted in firing Brianna. And then there's Gabriella—he didn't want to risk her losing her job.

Luke sauntered into the boardroom for their annual review, yellow stencil pad under one arm, pencil slipped behind his ear and carried two cups of coffee. He set one down in front of Gracie and sat down in the comfortable upholstered chair.

"She asked me to prepare a list of local resources similar to what we do. Brianna's only been back a day. Plunging right back into the throw of things."

Luke glanced around the dozen chairs surrounding the mahogany table. A screen was pulled down. Croissants and muffins sat on a tray in the center of the table. He grabbed a napkin and a muffin. He lowered his voice. "I need to talk to her about the email. You coming with me or not? No judgment, just trying to figure out how I'm going to approach this."

Gracie locked eyes. "Oh, I'm with you alright. We'll just go in casually and ask her how her trip was. Then just bite the bullet." Luke nodded.

Brianna entered with a stack of newly printed and collated pages. John, the volunteer coordinator, took one and handed them to Julie, who continued them on around. Why did this remind him of school?

Luke glanced around the table at each of the faces. Gracie was like a sister. John kept donor retention up. Julie headed the education department. Assad, fluent in six languages, translated letters. He appreciated what a strong team they made and how blessed he was to be a part of it. Which might not be for much longer.

"Okay, friends. I know you all have a lot of important work to do, so let's get started." Brianna said. "I've started some pages going around. I thought of emailing them to you, but I think it's easier to have them in paper form." Someone moaned. "I know, sometimes I'm just old-fashioned. Take a few minutes to look them over." She tapped a pen on her lip.

Luke perused the report. The promotional materials he had generated and the fundraisers he'd done continued to bring an increase in donors and funding. He straightened his shoulders. Job security. Yet, he didn't want to get too comfortable. It was still possible for them to find out about his lack of integrity in Mexico. And after he confronted Brianna, well, who knew what would happen.

Brianna dunked a tea bag in her cup and took a sip before proceeding.

"Things are looking pretty good for Healthy Kids this year. I talked to Mr. Steinberg and we're looking at putting something together here for the local community. Gracie has done some leg work looking at what's already available here for folks and where the gaps are. I'm looking for input."

"Would you have the same type of services? Medical? Education? Family Services?" John asked. He rolled up his sleeves.

Luke leaned over and whispered to Gracie. "I hope not all the same services." Surely, she wouldn't want to provide abortions here. Would she? He couldn't stop the anxiety settled in his stomach. He rolled his shoulders, hoping to remove the tension.

"There are already schools in place— public, private, home-school. Even post-secondary. What type of education are we looking at?" Julia asked. She drummed her fingers on the table.

"What about parenting classes? Or English for non-English speakers?" Assad asked. He had been born in the States, but his parents were immigrants from Somalia.

"Parenting classes for grandparents raising their grandkids?" No surprise that question came from Philip. He had taken on his own grandchildren after his son and daughter-in-law had been killed in a car accident.

"All good ideas," Brianna said.

"What type of medical? There's pretty much everything already here," Julia asked.

Gracie caught Brianna's eye. "May I?"

Brianna nodded.

Gracie projected her findings. "Portland seems to be pretty

well covered with services." She showed a slide with a graph of medical facilities, schools, and daycares.

"The sizeable gap comes when we look at refugees. We have a vast population from countries all over the world. Where we could be an asset is having a department concentrating on helping them navigate the systems." She changed slides.

"There's a lot to know. Many of these people come from countries without social services. They don't have rental assistance or food stamps. Just going to the doctor with limited English is a tremendous burden. Many would rather not receive the medical care they need than to navigate the red tape. Which leads to health issues and ultimately more poverty."

"I would be willing to be a main cog in this process," Assad said.

"It would be powerful if we could train some refugees to be the mentors for others. There are some brilliant people in the mix. It would give them dignity and a purpose." Julie wrote a few notes on her page.

"Great ideas. Okay, thanks Gracie. I know you have a lot more to share," Brianna said. She looked at the time. "But let's take a break for lunch and resume at one o'clock."

Everyone gathered their things and left, conversation buzzing with ideas. Luke raised his eyebrows and looked at Gracie. He nodded towards Brianna.

"Come on." They followed her to her office.

"Hey, have time to tell us how things went in Honduras?" Luke said. She motioned for them to sit.

Luke tried to look casual and sat down. He crossed his legs. Brianna put her pen down.

"It was good. I think we're making a lot of progress down there."

"How was Maria?" Luke said.

"Great. She has such great leadership skills. She's seen a lot of progress with the safety education classes."

"Do you think there are fewer girls being trafficked?" Luke asked.

"It's hard to say, because we don't really know how many there are. Since the police are involved covering up, we don't really have a way to tell," Brianna said.

Luke looked at Gracie. She gave an imperceptible nod. Luke swallowed.

"Say, while you were gone, I got a disturbing email. It didn't seem like the information was right, so I wanted to confirm it." Brianna raised her eyebrows, confused.

"Who was it from?" she asked.

"I'd rather not say," he said.

"Well?"

Luke swallowed. "It said that many of the trafficked girls were getting pregnant and that HK was providing abortions." There, he'd said it. He let out a slow breath.

Brianna pulled back. She looked around the room, then walked over and shut the door and pulled the blinds on the window leading to the rest of the office. She sat back down, composed.

"It's true. We are." Her hands were folded on her desk.

Luke looked at her, puzzled.

"Look, I know it's a nasty business, but these girls are desperate. We're supposed to be compassionate. We can't just let them end up with babies that will be neglected and possibly end up being sex slaves as well." Brianna had gone from zero to three-sixty. Her body tightened and her face was strained.

Luke didn't know what to say. His mom had nearly aborted him. This atrocity had to stop.

"But Brianna, it's wrong. All life is sacred," Gracie said gently.

"It might be, but we have to do what we can to prevent any more hardship on them," she shot back.

"How do you know that those babies might be the one thing that they could actually love in their lives?" Luke said.

Brianna got up and walked to the window. It rattled as a wild wind with pelting rain pushed against it. When she turned back, her cheeks were wet.

"Brianna?" Gracie said.

She sat and shook her head. "When I was a teen, I was raped and got pregnant. My mom took me in for an abortion." She looked Luke in the eye. "I had a right to not have that baby! I would have had to think about that vile man every time I looked at it."

"You could have adopted it out," Luke said. There were other alternatives.

Brianna shook her head. "I just wanted it to go away." She let out a sob. Gracie knelt in front of her and held her hands.

"I can only imagine the pain you endured," Gracie said. "You must have been very angry."

"God abandoned me. I won't abandon those girls!" Brianna said. She shook her head.

"Brianna, you know God was there the whole time. He loves you. He didn't abandon you," Gracie said.

"I'm not so sure anymore," said Brianna. She reached for a tissue.

"Do you feel like God made it happen?" Luke said.

"He didn't make it happen, but he stood by and watched!" Brianna said.

"He watched, yes, and he grieved. It's people who choose to harm and hurt. God is there when that happens, to open his loving arms to you and comfort you," Gracie said.

"He can turn ashes to beauty. Have you forgiven the perpetrator?"

Brianna looked at her like she was crazy.

"It's not easy, I know, but until you do, you're going to continue living in bondage— tied to that one defining moment," Gracie said.

"I can't forgive him. He ruined my life," Brianna said.

"Forgiveness doesn't mean that he wasn't wrong. You don't have to confront him. But if you will allow yourself to forgive, you'll be set free. You've been holding this helium balloon called anger and resentment. Let it go, sweetie," Gracie put her hand on Brianna's shoulder. "You don't have to live with it anymore." Gracie said. "Let God's grace enfold you, sister."

Brianna let out a sob. Luke shifted in his seat. This was supposed to be about Brianna. Somehow, he felt it was as much for him.

"Brianna, I know it doesn't seem like it, but you gotta believe that God has a plan for you in all of this. He works things around for good," Gracie continued. "We're gonna be here, to stand beside you and help you work through this. You don't have to carry this burden alone."

Brianna looked up and gave a small nod.

"Can I get you anything? Water? Coffee? Chocolate?" Luke said.

Brianna gave a tear-streaked smile. "Get out of here." She

shooed them away. "Don't you have some kind of project to work on?"

Luke and Gracie stood and walked out. "Door open or shut?" Luke said.

"Open. Thanks— both of you." Brianna let out a big breath, relaxed her shoulders and nodded.

Chapter Twenty-Three

K aitlyn sat on the couch reading her romance, legs resting on the coffee table. If she couldn't be in a healthy relationship, she could at least fantasize about one.

She cradled her Best. Day. Ever. cup filled with coffee laced with left over peppermint white chocolate creamer. A half-eaten scone sat on a napkin.

She hadn't bothered to get dressed—Saturdays were for lazing around. She paused and looked through the window at the falling snow. Huge flakes drifted lazily, making the tree branches bow under the covering. A red-winged blackbird flicked its wings, contrasted with the white.

Bentley bounded up with his happy little doggy face and wagged his tail.

"Guess we're not taking you for a walk today, Bentley." She scratched him behind his ears.

"Maybe I should get my lazy butt off the couch and take down the Christmas tree." January was half over, for pity's sake. She just hadn't been motivated. And she hadn't been ready to face the fact that Francisco wasn't in her life anymore.

Why couldn't things just turn out like in her cheesy romance novels? Boy meets girl. They have some reason they'd don't get along. Next thing you know, they push past it, and Mr. Wonderful is taking her out for a walk. They have their first kiss, fireworks explode, and magic occurs...

Tina bounced down the stairs with a towel covering her wet hair. "Hey lazy bones, what're ya up to? You look deep in thought!"

"Yeah, well, um..." Kaitlyn set down her cup. "It's Saturday, okay? A girl needs a little recoup time."

"True that. Look at that snow! Let's go out and dance in it!" Tina said. She reached for Kaitlyn's hands.

Kaitlyn shook her head. "I'm all cozed up here." She drew her quilt tighter around her.

"Come on. It's not like we have this opportunity every day. Come on!" Tina yanked the quilt off and grabbed Kaitlyn's hands.

"Ugh, you almost made me spill my coffee!"

Tina headed to the closet and pulled out Kaitlyn's hat, scarf and down coat. She threw them at her. "Put these on. We're going!"

"But I'm still in my PJs!" Kaitlyn protested.

"That doesn't matter—put them on top. Let's go!" Tina clapped her hands together. She pulled the towel off her wet hair and donned a beanie.

Kaitlyn drug herself off the couch and let Tina tug on her hat and wrap her scarf around her neck. Sometimes she could be such a mom. Bentley ran over to her legs, wagging his tail. "Okay, pooch, you can come too," Kaitlyn said. "Where's your sweater?" She pulled it out of the closet and tugged it over his wiggling body. "Sit still, silly dog. I can't get your little sweater on you when you're yipping and jumping!" She laughed.

A blast of cold air hit her face as she opened the door. The thick downy flakes were falling faster now, a contrast against the dark clouds. Kaitlyn stood in the yard and held her face to the sky, letting them drift on her cheeks and eyelashes.

Tina grabbed her hands and swung her around. They fell back on the snow, laughing and sweeping their arms up in down to make angels. It took her back to when they were kids.

"Isn't it beautiful? It's so clean and magical." Tina propped her phone on the branch of the tree and pressed video. She started in on a dance, alternating her hands in the air, swirling her hips, boogying. Kaitlyn laughed and joined her, trying not to trip over Bentley, who was yipping and prancing around them.

"I'm sure that will be Instagram worthy," Kaitlyn laughed.

Tina put her forehead to Kaitlyn's. "It's good to see you laugh. You've been in a funk for far too long. There's relaxing on a Saturday morning, and then there's moping around."

"Thanks, friend." Kaitlyn pulled back. Tina always knew how to pull her out. Then again, Kaitlyn had done her share of holding Tina up through the lengthy battle of her mom's cancer. Turnabout was fair play, right?

"It's free-zing out here! I'm going back in. Come on, Bentley—you're shivering!"

Bentley ran through the door and shook. She removed his sweater and sent him to his bed. Kaitlyn paused and looked at the tree. That momentary diversion had not made it disappear.

"I'm just going to leave this stuff on and try to get to the grocery store before we can't get out," Tina said. She reached for her keys.

"Get coffee beans. And creamer. And popcorn. You know, the essentials!" Kaitlyn called out. "And cocoa. And whip cream."

"I'm lea-ving...." Tina said and closed the door.

Okay, that tree has got to go. Kaitlyn heaved a sigh. She dragged out the Christmas tubs from under the stairs and began pulling off ornaments one by one. Her mom had given her a special one each year, creating a train of memories.

That was something she planned to do for her kids. That is, if she ever had any. Of course, it would probably be good to have a husband first. She shook her head and snorted. Until then, she'd have to start the tradition for her niblings.

She unscrewed the bolts in the tree stand that now held only a drop of evaporated water and slime. The memory of Francisco trying to start the chain saw flashed through her mind. And then Luke adeptly cutting the tree. She chuckled. That *was* pretty funny. And what about Luke? It seemed she kept running into him. He was always with that cute blonde girl. They were probably an item. No sense wrapping her mind around that possibility.

Still, he was pretty darn handsome. That scrubby little beard. Twinkly eyes. Flannel shirt. And his muscular legs hadn't escaped her when they did the bike trip. She sighed. Okay, girl, enough of that.

Life would go on, with or without a guy. She'd just focus on being content in all things.

Chapter Twenty-Four

The bare arms of the peach orchard silhouetted against the drab sky didn't help the bleakness consuming Luke as he wheeled his silver Toyota Tacoma down Grandpa William's drive. The days were getting longer, bit by bit, but it was still dark at five. He calculated that at an increase in daylight by approximately a minute a day, things should be much better by the end of February. His trip to Arizona had been a refreshing change, blue skies, and t-shirt weather.

Still, spring was a long way off.

At least things had improved with Brianna. He still had some concerns to wrap his mind around, but the dark storm of doubt that overshadowed him at work had diminished.

Pouring rain pelted the truck. This was his first contact with his family since that fateful day. He parked and turned off the wipers. Luke zipped up his Carhart coat over his red flannel shirt, tugged down his baseball cap and headed to the front door, taking the steps to the wraparound porch two at a time.

"Hey, Grandpa, I'm here!" He peeled off his dripping coat and hung it near the fireplace.

"Lukey! You look like a drowned rat!" Grandpa William laughed. "Pull those muddy boots off and come sit where it's warm and comfy. I can open a jar of your mom's home pressed cider and heat it up for you if you like. It'll only take a minute."

"Sounds great! It ain't a fit night out," Luke began quoting W. C. Fields and was joined by Grandpa, "For maaaan nor beast!" He chuckled as he pulled off his boots and set them to dry by the fire. Watching old movies together had been a tradition. The reflection of the flames danced on the large picture window.

"Will you be able to stay the night?" Grandpa asked.

"Better than that—I've got three days off for President's Day. Thought I could do some chores for you," Luke said. He glanced around. It might be time to get Grandpa William a housekeeper—newspapers lying around. The floor looked like it hadn't been swept in a couple of weeks, cobwebs dangling from the windows and ceiling.

Grandpa William stepped into the living room from the kitchen, carrying two steamy cups of cider. "I threw in a cinnamon stick—hope that's okay."

Luke held it under his nose. He breathed in, closed his eyes and felt wrapped in his Grandma's love.

"This reminds me of Grandma Alice."

"Me too. Gotta keep some memories alive," Grandpa said and winked. He shoved another log into the wood stove. Luke looked up the length of the stovepipe and thought that cleaning the chimney should be a priority on the chore list.

The weather app on his phone said it was supposed to be sunny the next day and fifty degrees. He could work with that.

"How about a game of checkers?" Grandpa said. He nodded at what Luke thought was an end table. Business as usual. If Grandpa didn't bring up the dreaded conversation, he sure didn't intend to.

"Yeah, we haven't played that for years!" Luke said.

"And as I recall, I beat the snot outta you the last time," Grandpa chuckled. "Take that stack of newspapers to the garage to recycle." Luke stacked them up and realized the end table was, in fact, a checkerboard.

"You made this, didn't you?" Luke said.

"Yeah, it was supposed to be a school shop project for your dad. He started it and never completed it. It sat in my workshop for years. Then one day I said to myself, by golly, I should finish that!" He folded the throw and smoothed it on the back of the couch.

"It didn't need much. Nothing a little sanding and Varathane couldn't fix. There's a tin box sitting on the shelf with the checkers." He pointed.

Luke retrieved them. He set them up—chocolate on one side, blonde on the other. After the third game, Luke said, "You are a beast! You could have at least let me win one game." He shook his head and laughed. It felt good. Being in his presence.

Grandpa William patted him on the shoulder. "I may be getting older, grandson, but I still have a few tricks up my sleeve."

"So, what do we want to get done tomorrow?" Luke said.

"The gutters need cleaning. You could help me take down the Christmas lights and maybe, while you're on the roof, do a little moss control."

"Sounds like a plan. I'm bushed—okay if I head to bed?" Luke took his empty mug to the sink, washed it and put it in the drainer.

"Sure, see you in the morning. Still a coffee person?" Grandpa asked.

"You bet!" Folgers wasn't his favorite, but Luke knew he could count on Grandpa to add a splash of Bailey's. He smiled and headed upstairs.

♥ ♥ ♥

Luke climbed out of bed and stretched; a long yawn escaped. He pulled aside the curtains and looked outside. How could it already be seven? This was the latest he'd slept—the best he'd slept in as long as he could remember.

The sun was just coming up over the hills. Light glistened on the peach orchard, reflecting off droplets of rain. The way they stood in rows with long shadows in the morning lights would be a great photo op. He should have brought his Canon.

He jumped in the shower, threw on his flannel shirt and jeans, and followed his nose downstairs to the kitchen.

"What is that delicious smell?" Luke said.

"Thought you might like some pancakes. I threw some blueberries in too. Hope that's okay?"

"More than okay." Luke grabbed a plate from the 1940s white metal kitchen cupboard. The handles were worn. Vintage, he thought. People he knew actually tried to reproduce this stuff.

"Maple syrup is in that cupboard. Coffee on the counter," Grandpa William said.

"Sweet!" Luke carried both plates to the table. Grandpa carried the coffees.

"Well, grandson, where should we start?" *At the beginning. When you held me in your arms and first loved me.*

"I know you have a ladder. Let's start on the gutters and roof."

After breakfast, Luke followed his grandpa to the pole barn to his wood workshop. Luke walked around the table saw, the planer, the chop saw, and the sander, running his finger over each. He breathed in the smell of sawdust. He smiled as he remembered making a step stool for Grandma Alice for Christmas. That had to have been ten years ago. And then there were the toy race cars and train set they had made for Toys for Tots. Good times.

Luke grabbed one end of the extension ladder while his grandpa took the other. They moved to the back of the house, where they slid it up the wall. Luke strapped the leaf blower on his back and climbed up.

"You be careful up there, grandson. I don't want to have to answer to your mom!"

As if she'd care. He quickly had the gutters cleaned and blew off all the moss.

He sat on the roof and stared across the fields. What a glorious day. He wished he had brought his bike. It would have been a prefect day for a ride.

A vision of Kaitlyn riding her bike passed through his mind. He wondered what she was up to. Was there a reason their paths kept crossing? The ride, Honduras, Christmas trees. He didn't want to read anything into it. That could lead to confusing something that was just a coincidence with thinking it was a God thing.

He climbed back down the ladder and removed the leaf blower.

"Here, let me help you," Grandpa said. They carried the ladder back into the pole barn and set it on the rack. Luke leaned against the workbench and looked around.

"How are things going for you at work?" Grandpa William asked.

"Okay. I guess." Luke rolled his neck, trying to ease the tension.

"Just okay? Last time I talked to you, it was going terrific. What's going on?"

Luke stared at his boots. Anxiety, like ants, crawled up his chest.

"There was kind of an incident." He looked up. "I'm not sure if it's good or if it's bad," he said.

Grandpa William adjusted his plaid flat cap.

"Well, let's start with the bad and get that out of the way."

"You knew I took the trip to Honduras, right?"

Grandpa nodded.

"Well, when we were down there, I filmed a video that, on closer inspection, had a girl in it that looked scared. The more we studied it, we figured it must be a girl caught up in the sex trafficking ring."

"Is that prevalent there?"

"I guess so."

"I can see where that would be disturbing." Grandpa said.

"It's hard to imagine the anguish. Healthy Kids has started an education program for the girls and community to try to make them aware of it. The police are part of the ring, so that doesn't help," Luke said.

Grandpa shook his head. "That's awful! But there's something more, isn't there?"

Luke hopped up on the workbench and let his legs dangle. His straightened his arms and grasped the bench.

"Here's the thing. I told my boss, Brianna, and then she immediately took a trip to Honduras to see what was happening. While she was there, I got an email from one of the staff that said Brianna had set up a clinic where the trafficked girls could have abortions. I was livid. My first thought was to just quit. How could I work in a place that called itself Christian and yet provides abortions? The two do not go hand in hand."

"That was your first thought." Grandpa sat down on a stool. "What was your second?"

Luke looked out the wide door. "I knew I had to confront Brianna. My co-worker Gracie and I prayed before we went in and told Brianna about the email. I asked Brianna if it was true."

"What did she say?"

Luke shook his head. "She got really upset about it. She felt justified, like it was the only way to help these girls. Like it was the compassionate thing to do—save the girls from going through with the pregnancy and save the children from inevitable poverty and abuse."

"And you didn't think that was the right choice?"

"Heck, no! Killing babies is never the right choice." Luke removed his cap and ran his hand through his thick hair.

"And then," he paused, "Then she said that she had been raped as a teenager, gotten pregnant and had an abortion. She felt like she was justified in doing it."

"It's a complicated business, isn't it?" Grandpa said.

Luke felt the frustration rise to choke him. "You can say that again."

"How did you handle the conversation?"

"Gracie was better at it than me. She saw through to Brianna's hurting heart." Luke looked into Grandpa William's eyes. "We told her we would be there for her and help her through. That God had a plan for her and had not abandoned her."

"Sounds like this may be more than about your boss." Luke crossed his arms and stared at the floor where piles of sawdust remained from the last project. "I believe a seed of rejection was planted in your heart the moment your mom and dad went to the abortion clinic."

Luke shoved sawdust around with the toe of his boot.

"They may not have wanted you at the moment, but God said yes to you. He had a plan and a purpose."

Luke swallowed the lump in his throat. He wanted to believe this was true. But anger continued to well up in him. It was hard to reconcile the facts in front of him with faith. With a bigger picture.

Grandpa gave Luke a man hug and held him by the shoulders. "You're a good kid, Lukey. I can't imagine life without you. And someday, that pretty little gal I've been praying you would meet will walk into your life and you'll be the best thing that ever happened to her. She'll come out of the woodwork when you least expect it, and it will be the most natural thing in the world. I just think God is working on both of your hearts to groom you for each other."

Luke gave a little nod.

"Come on, grandson. I'll get some lunch started for you. You seem to have worked up a pretty good appetite!"

Chapter Twenty-Five

It had been a particularly crazy day at the hospital. Needy. That's what those patients were. Manipulative and needy. It was enough to drive Kaitlyn crazy.

"Can you bring me some water with ice? This isn't cold enough." *Sure, no problem, I don't have anything else to do. Like maybe help the patient with chest pain down the hall.*

"Nurse, I need my pain meds now!" *You aren't due for another two hours.*

"There you are. I've been hitting the call button for the last half hour! Where have you been?" *Ignoring you and trying to help someone who really needs help and, here's an original thought, someone who actually appreciates my help!*

Seriously, why had she become a nurse? Sometimes reality didn't match with what she imagined she had signed up for.

Kaitlyn grabbed her laptop and snuggled up onto the couch. She checked her Facebook. Aww, Megan's new baby! Precious! Olivia came in second in the marathon. Cool! I should train for that next year. Kaitlyn's cousin's prom photos.

Nice dress. Maybe I should have gone to a prom. She shook her head. Not that she hadn't wanted to, but she couldn't come up with a date.

She opened the classified tab and flipped through photos of furniture, vehicles, pets. Here was something. Wanted—Companion for an elderly gentleman with diabetes—three evenings a week. Pay negotiable.

Companion. The word stood out like a blinking neon light. Maybe she should look into that. She reached for her phone and tapped in the number.

"Hello?" The deep velvety voice on the other end was young—maybe her age.

"I was calling about the ad you had on Facebook. Can you tell me more about it?"

"Oh, sure. We need someone to stay with my seventy-five-year-old Grandpa William three nights a week. He's a really nice guy. My grandma died this year, so he's all alone. He's just found out he has diabetes, and we want to make sure he's checking his glucose and taking his shots each night. A family member will cover the other nights."

"That sounds great! I'm a registered nurse. I work three twelve-hour days at the hospital. It's fine, but, well, I'm single and want something to do in the evenings, so I just thought maybe being a companion would work for me."

"Sounds like just the person we've been looking for. Could you come over tomorrow night and we can see if this is a good fit?"

"One question. He's not crotchety, is he?" She didn't particularly want to go from crazies at the hospital to another when she didn't really need to do this."

He laughed. "My grandpa? Heavens no. He's the sweetest guy you'd ever meet."

"Okay then, sounds like a plan." Kaitlyn hung up.

"Who are you making plans with?" Tina asked. Her arms were full of laundry.

"Oh, some dreamy guy!" Kaitlyn said and fluttered her eyelids.

"Seriously?"

"I don't know. I just saw an ad for someone who has diabetes and needs a companion three nights a week. It'd get me out of the house."

"Where does Mr. Dreamy come in?" Tina said.

"Oh, the guy who answered the phone—he's the grandson. Deep voice. The kind of voice I could get used to hearing." She repressed a shiver. Trust, Kaitlyn. Just trust your Daddy.

♥ ♥ ♥

Kaitlyn got out of her Prius. She studied the buds forming on the peach trees. Soon pink blossoms would break out, filling the field with an array of beauty.

She glanced at the two-story house. Could William navigate stairs? No sign of an outdoor dog. She knocked on the screen door and tried to look through the front window without seeming like she was creeping.

The door creaked open. A middle-aged man wearing a base-ball cap and a flannel shirt met her.

"You must be Kaitlyn," he held out his hand. "Joe

McCarthy. Nice to meet you!" This isn't who she talked to on the phone. He ushered her through the mudroom and into the living room. Kaitlyn's eyes swept the room. Newspapers were in a heap on the floor. Several empty soda cans sat on the end table. A candy dish held Snickers wrappers. When was the last time someone had vacuumed?

"Dad, this is Kaitlyn Monroe. She's a nurse and will stay with you three nights a week while we get you into a routine with your diabetes."

"Kaitlyn, did you say?"

"Yes, nice to meet you Mr...."

"Mr. McCarthy. But you can call me William." He eased the recliner so that he was sitting up.

"Joe, can you switch off the TV? I can pick up on that baseball game later."

"Mr. McCarthy." Kaitlyn reached out and grasped his outstretched hand. It was soft and held a surprisingly firm grip. She met his twinkly blue eyes. "I'm so glad to meet you." William patted the couch beside his chair.

"Sit down here, young lady." She smiled and sat down. I think I'm gonna like this guy.

"Do you mind if I ask you a few questions?" Kaitlyn said.

"Not at all."

"How's your blood pressure?"

"A little high," William said, as he looked at Joe for confirmation.

"Are you on medication for that?"

"Yes"

"Your cholesterol?"

"Good."

"You look like you're fairly fit. What's your weight?"

"178 funds last week at the doctor's."

"How much exercise do you get?"

"Dad hasn't been feeling well lately, so I'd say he needs to get out for a walk now and then. Hopefully, you can encourage that!"

Kaitlyn nodded.

"Are you a smoker?"

"Heavens, no! I wouldn't let that disgusting stuff in my house!"

"Drinker?"

"Joe occasionally brings home a beer for me." He grinned, held his hand by his mouth conspiratorially, and whispered, "We better keep that on the down low."

Kaitlyn hid a smile and shook her head.

"Cataracts? Glaucoma?"

"Nope, and nope."

"Okay then, that gives me some idea of where we're at." Kaitlyn looked around the room. "You're gonna have to ditch the soda. Too much sugar."

William mocked a hurt frown. "I'm not sure I'm gonna like this girl."

Kaitlyn smiled and patted him on the shoulder. "We'll see what we can find that tastes as good or better. We're off on a new adventure."

She rose and Joe showed her to the door.

"He's had a bit of a hard time. Last week his blood sugar was forty-five. He was hallucinating and irritable. That's not like him at all. We got a shot of glucose in him right away. We keep all of his meds, glucose, and his glucometer here in this tote. There's OJ in the fridge. Oh, and the door's never locked. Just let yourself in."

"Sounds good. I'll come by tomorrow, then?"

"Perfect." Joe said.

Kaitlyn started her car and backed out. This was going to be the perfect gig. He seemed like someone who would appreciate her care. She already felt at home.

Chapter Twenty-Six

K aitlyn's eyes scanned the yard. The house looked much better—the gutters had been cleaned, no more moss on the roof. Someone was looking after her new charge.

"William, it's me, Kaitlyn." She stuck her head through the front door.

"Oh hi, honey. How's it going?" he called from the couch. A woven throw was wrapped around his shoulders.

Kaitlyn took off her coat and hung it on the hook by the door.

"I see you're watching some baseball. Who's playing? Not that I'd know if you told me." She grinned.

"Your family doesn't watch or play baseball? You're missing out! Whoa! He caught a fly!" William jumped out of his seat; fist raised.

"Looks like fun! How are you feeling tonight?"

"Pretty good. A little tired, maybe," William said.

"Well, let's just get your glucose test out of the way." She pulled out the monitor.

"Just a little prick."

"Yeah, I know. They're not bad. What's the reading?"

Kaitlyn looked at the tab and then showed it to him. One hundred.

"Looks pretty good. How about taking your shoes off and let's check your feet? Sometimes diabetics get neuropathy, a kind of nerve damage, and have no feeling in them so they don't realize they're getting infections."

William removed his shoes and socks. Kaitlyn pulled on some gloves and checked between each toe, his nails and the sole of his foot. She rubbed lotion on them.

"Boy, does that feel good!"

Kaitlyn smiled. "Did you have anything to eat for dinner?"

"No, I probably should do that. Say, why don't I fix something for the both of us?"

"You sure you feel up to it?"

"Feel up to it? A date with a pretty girl? Of course, I feel up to it!"

Kaitlyn laughed and followed him into the kitchen. William opened the fridge door and peered in. "Looks like our choices are left over meatloaf. There's a little pulled pork, and chicken noodle soup."

"Which option is the most recent?" Kaitlyn asked. She wasn't eager to get botulism.

"Well now, I made the meatloaf last night."

"Meatloaf it is. Grab a couple of potatoes from that basket over there and I'll stick them in the microwave."

She held them under the clean running water. She remembered cooking dinner for Miguelita. Wouldn't she have loved that? A far cry from the tainted water barrel outside.

"Those potatoes are from my garden. Can you believe

they're still good?" He took a cast iron pan from the hanging rack and placed it on the gas stove, sliced up the meatloaf, and put it in the pan.

"Get some cheese out of the fridge, would you now? And I think there are some chanterelles in the freezer. My grandson likes to go mushroom hunting."

Kaitlyn rummaged around and found them between some freezer burned chicken and a Ziplock bag of a mystery item. She ran some hot water in the sink and washed the pile of dishes.

"How many children do you have?" she asked.

"Just three. I have my son Joe—you met him. Then Amelia and Bill, my oldest."

"And you have at least one grandson." Kaitlyn's thoughts flew to her conversation with that guy and his silky-smooth voice on the phone. Should she ask what his name was or just wait and see? She felt certain she'd get to meet him sometime. That is, if she were lucky.

"Right. He's Joe's son, and then Amelia has three and Bill has six. It's a nice family."

"I bet it's fun when you all get together."

"Sure is. Noisy! But nothing compares to being surrounded by family."

"Mm—smells good. Shall I grab some plates?"

"Sure. Silverware is in the drawer. There's homemade apple cider in the fridge if you're thirsty."

Kaitlyn took the loaded plates and silverware to the table. William brought a canning jar of cider.

"Mind if we pray?" William asked.

Kaitlyn looked up, surprised. "Why, of course." She held her hand out to his.

"Dear Lord, thank you for answering our prayers and

184

bringing Kaitlyn to us. And bless this food to our bodies. Amen."

"Actually, God answered my prayers. I was looking for something more and he brought me here." Kaitlyn's eyes twinkled.

William patted her hand and smiled back. "God answers all our prayers."

❦ ❦ ❦

Dinner was through and she'd finished the dishes.

"What do you say I straighten up the living room?" she asked.

"That might not be a bad idea. Joe's a little busy and it's been harder for me to get around."

Kaitlyn took a duster and swiped cobwebs, gathered the pop cans, and started dusting the fireplace mantel. She picked up a photo of William. And who?

"William, was this your wife?"

"Yes, that's Alice. She died last year. She had Alzheimer's pretty bad. It was a very hard time. She was the love of my life. You know, we'd only been married eighteen years. Can you believe that?"

Kaitlyn studied the two of them. Alice was leaning into him, comfortably snuggled together. Her bright eyes showed an excitement about life. Or maybe it was satisfaction. "Is that right? Were you married before?"

Kaitlyn sat on the couch beside him.

"Well now," William replied. "That's a fun story. Yes, I was

185

married before. Unfortunately, Esther, my first wife, was not the love of my life. We got married way too young. I had just returned from the war and everyone was getting married when they came back. There was a shortage of men, so it was easy to find a bride."

"What was it about her you didn't like?" This seemed like a teachable moment. She wanted to learn all she could about relationships. What to do. You know, just in case she was ever in another one. Her track record hadn't been stellar.

"Oh, she was a dutiful housewife, something that was expected in those days, and she cooked good meat and potatoes. But she was never satisfied with life. She never wanted to have any kids, and she was always complaining."

"Did you get a divorce?" she asked.

"No, she died. She had breast cancer."

"Oh, I'm sorry."

"Don't be. It was for the best."

"So, how did you meet Alice? She has such a sweet, cheerful smile."

"Well now, this was when I was still married to Esther. I had taken up weaving as a hobby. One summer I went up to Maine to a craft school and there, sitting across from me at her loom, was Alice. She lived in Arizona and had just divorced. She was there with her three children. We started talking and didn't stop that whole week. When I left, I knew I was in love."

"Uh oh, that put you in a dilemma. What did you do?" Kaitlyn couldn't imagine being in love with someone besides her husband.

"It was only right that I should honor my wedding vows, and living with Esther wasn't intolerable. So, I just went on with life. But then, after she died, I decided I would try to find Alice."

"Did you look her up on the internet?"

"No, sweetheart," he patted her hand. "Remember, we didn't have the internet yet. No cell phones either." He chuckled. "I started calling people I knew in Weaver's Guilds. She had become well known in those circles as she had written numerous articles on fabric dying. I was told that she had gone to study weaving in Japan.

She had also taught at Denver University, so I contacted people there. I would have gone to the ends of the earth to find her. I had all but given up when, one day, I was watching the news and they mentioned Eugene, Oregon. I remembered she had lived there at one time, so on a whim, I called the operator to see if they might have a number for her. And lo-and-behold, there she was."

"I can't imagine how exciting that must have been for you. You're quite the detective!"

"Yes indeed. That was a special moment when I heard her voice on the end of the line." Was that a dreamy look on his face? "I was living in Florida at the time, so I had some finagling to do."

"What did you do? Did you go to Eugene?"

"Yes, I caught the next flight there. I didn't care how much it cost. All I wanted to do was to see my gal."

"What did she say when you saw her?" Kaitlyn imagined hearts floating up around Alice's face.

"She opened the door, and I presented her with an enormous bouquet. She started crying. Crying! Can you believe that? I thought maybe she didn't want to see me!"

"Well of course she wanted to see you. She was just so over-whelmed by her dream come true!"

He nodded. "We were married within the month."

Kaitlyn picked up the photo again. "That is some kinda love story."

"Yes, it's amazing how God has plans for our lives, even when we don't see them."

"Funny you should say that. My friend Tina and I were just talking about that." Kaitlyn set the photo back on the mantle.

"And are you married, young lady?"

"No, that's the problem. I don't even have a boyfriend. I keep praying about it. I just want to be satisfied. I know I should trust God and be content. But sometimes it's really hard."

"Let's just say that you met the perfect man. What would he be like?"

"Tall, dark, handsome, deep voice, flannel, a little scruff," she said. William's mustached mouth turned up. "Really, though, I'm more interested in who he is than what he looks like."

"Well then, what's he supposed to be like?"

"Kind, fun-loving, adventurous, giving, not afraid to admit if he's wrong."

"Sounds like my Alice."

The phone rang. Just when she was enjoying the story. William reached for it.

"Hello. Oh, hi!" He covered the mouthpiece and whispered, "It's my grandson."

"How've you been? For how long? Oh, be sure and come by and bring your fishing pole."

She walked into the kitchen. Kaitlyn wished he was on

speakerphone so she could listen in. Tina would have called it eavesdropping, and she'd be right.

She found a jar of peaches and opened them. She served out two bowls and set one on the end table by William.

"I know it's hard, but you just have to keep trusting. In due time, everything will work out. Keep your chin up. Yeah, we'll see you soon. Bye." William reached for the bowl.

"Thanks." He picked up a picture of his grandson from the end table and showed it to her. He was about eight years old, posed with his cleated foot on his ball and soccer uniform. Dark hair, sparkly eyes.

"He's cute," she said. Something about those eyes.

"This is when he was much younger. I don't have a recent picture of him. He's a great kid." Wait, was that the same grandson she talked to on the phone?

The pendulum clock on the wall struck eight. "I'd better get going. I've got a long day at the hospital tomorrow. We have a new set of interns on our floor, so there's lots to prepare for."

"Okay, we'll see you in a couple of days, then?"

"Sure will. Thanks for dinner. And the story of you and Alice." She put on her coat and grabbed her bag. If God could give William the desires of his heart, couldn't He do it for her, too?

She slid into her car and sat, staring absently out the window. God, you could answer my prayers for the perfect guy, right? And what if that perfect guy just happened to be asking for the perfect girl right now, too? Kaitlyn gave a little shiver and started the car.

Chapter Twenty-Seven

Luke drove the back roads to Grandpa William's. The lengthening days of April brought more sunshine. The fields were being plowed. He loved that fresh look and fragrance of the mounded rows of rich soil. He was already salivating at the thought of the corn on the cob dripping with melted butter and sweet red strawberries that would grow there.

He parked and hopped out of his truck. Grandpa William was outside and holding two fishing rods, wearing his beige fishing hat with a couple of flies stuck into it.

"Hey grandpa," Luke said. "Looks like you're all ready to go. Do you need me to grab anything?"

"Hey, grandson!" Grandpa William patted him on the shoulder. "Naw, I think I've got everything." He patted the pockets of his fishing vest.

They walked off through the peach orchard and down to the little stream. The rain had caused the river to swell, and the water rushed and sprayed over the rocks.

"Let's go down a little farther where it's calmer," Grandpa

William said. They climbed down the bank and found a boulder to sit on. There was an outcrop of trees bending over the water. They swatted away the swarms of insects that buzzed just above them.

"This should be perfect. Fish like to be under the shade of the trees." Grandpa tied a fly onto his string and whipped a cast out. Luke hopped a few rocks to a place near him, but not close enough to entangle their lines.

A light breeze rippled across the water, causing the sun to sparkle on it. He didn't care if they caught anything. He just enjoyed spending time with his grandpa. And one never knew how much time you might have together.

He wished he had spent more time with Grandma Alice. He had made plans to spend the day with her out in her garden, but then something came up that, at the time, seemed more important. That was the last opportunity he had. He wasn't going to let that happen again.

"Have you talked to your folks lately?"

"Nope."

Luke pulled down his sunglasses from the top of his head.

Grandpa William side-eyed him. Luke adjusted his cap.

"Woah now, what do we have here?" Grandpa William's line grew taut. Luke pulled out his phone. This would be a perfect video moment.

Grandpa began reeling in. A fish splashed and writhed. "I gotcha. Just settle down now." He snapped his rod, and the fish flew into the air. "Grab the net!"

Luke set his phone down and jumped over to him, holding out the net. But just as the fish got close, it wriggled free and land in the stream where it high tailed it away.

Grandpa let out a boisterous, contagious belly laugh and

slapped his knee. "Now that was fun. There's lots more fish where that came from."

Luke was sure he was right. Fishing wasn't just about catching the fish. It was the fun in pursuing it. Kind of like pursuing the right girl. Some get away, but there's always the hope that you'll get your catch sooner or later.

The sun was setting. They packed up and headed back to the house.

Someone had parked a Prius in the driveway and a woman was standing beside it, looking around.

"Whose car is that in the driveway?" Luke said.

"Oh no, I forgot she was coming today," Grandpa said. His palm hit his forehead. He waved at her. "We'll be there in a jiff, honey."

Kaitlyn set her backpack on the porch and started walking towards them. "Luke? What are you doing here?"

"Kaitlyn? Hold on. Are you the one that's been caring for my grandpa?"

"That would be me."

"How do you kids know each other?"

"Remember me telling you about leading a bike ride to Mt. Hood? Kaitlyn was on that bike ride."

Kaitlyn warmed at his smile. He remembered not being able to take his eyes off her curly hair as the sun shone on it.

"And then I saw you in Honduras," Kaitlyn said. "Don't forget that."

Luke remembered that. And that guy she had been with. Was he still in the picture? He sure hoped not.

"Listen, Kaitlyn, I'm sorry I made you come all the way here for nothing. I forgot that Luke and I had a fishing date and that he was going to cover your shift."

Luke stared at her—that inviting smile. Same luscious curly brown hair that he remembered.

"Oh, that's no problem. I brought some dinner for you—fried chicken and fresh blueberry pie. I hope you don't mind if I stay long enough to eat." That glint in her eyes—it was downright captivating.

William glanced at Luke. "Okay with you?"

"Yes, of course. Especially since we came up empty-handed from the stream," Luke grinned. They set their poles in the garage, tugged off their boots and went inside.

Kaitlyn had already set the table for three. Luke watched her bustle around the kitchen. Could she feel the intensity of his gaze?

"Need any help?" he asked. She turned around; hands held high, covered in flour. Luke let out a chuckle.

"I thought I'd make some biscuits. You like biscuits, right?"

He was pretty sure he'd like anything she made. "Here, may I?" he reached for her cheek. "You've got a bit of flour on it." Why hadn't he noticed before that she had freckles?

Her eyes widened, then she smiled and returned to the biscuits.

"Thanks! I can be a bit messy sometimes. Do you mind if I cut these out and you put them on a tray? The oven is already heating."

Luke reached for a biscuit, his finger lightly connecting with Kaitlyn's. How could one small touch ignite something in him? What was he thinking? Just because he'd run into her a couple of times didn't mean this chance encounter was going to turn into anything. He rubbed his fingertips.

"How are things working out with my grandpa?"

"He's so sweet! I'm enjoying coming over here. My job has

some pretty crazy patients, and it's nice to work for someone like William who shows some appreciation!"

"He is definitely a great guy. Tell me, what were you doing in Honduras?" He leaned against the counter and stretched his long legs out in front of him.

"Oh, I had this boyfriend who was from there and his mom was ill. He thought if I went down there, I could try to help her." Luke fixated on the word had.

"Were you able to?"

"Yeah. Seeing all the poverty was an eye opener. But I ran into someone from an organization called Healthy Kids, and they were going to provide her with the help she needed."

"You're kidding! Healthy Kids is the organization I work for. That's why I was down there, visiting one of the projects."

"Were you with your girlfriend? The blonde? At the restaurant? She had a cute smile."

Luke thought a minute. Girlfriend? "You must mean Gracie. No, she's engaged. She's just a co-worker." Luke placed the biscuits in the oven and set the timer.

Kaitlyn turned and studied him. "I just put this together. You were with her when Francisco and I got the Christmas tree. That was a Healthy Kids thing." She planted her palm on her forehead. He nodded, a slight smile forming, remembering how inept the guy had been trying to cut the tree.

"Okay, boss, what now?" he asked.

"I'll just get this mess cleaned up. I think there's some jam in the fridge. You find something to drink and napkins."

William looked around the table. "Well now, this is a mighty fine treat, Miss Kaitlyn. Let's hold hands and pray."

Luke put his hand out palm up and grinned at Kaitlyn. Her hands were so soft.

"Gracious Heavenly Father, thank you for all your gifts—another day of life, fine food, good friends, and family and for making our paths straight. Amen." Luke and Kaitlyn joined the amen.

"How have you been feeling, William?" Kaitlyn asked.

"Pretty swell. I had a good nap before Luke came over."

Kaitlyn looked at Luke. "Are you going to do his blood test? Or do you want me to?"

He set his fork down. "I think I'll take advantage of the professional tonight."

"Thank goodness. Nothing against you, grandson, but she's a little more gentle." Luke held his hands up in surrender.

"No offense taken."

Kaitlyn finished the dishes and put them away. She headed towards the coatrack.

"I'd better get a move on. I've got work tomorrow morning." Luke took a few steps towards her.

"Luke, why don't you walk her out? It's dark out there and I don't want her to trip on anything."

"Be glad to." Any chance to prolong her leaving.

"And Kaitlyn, give Luke your phone number so if he ever needs to contact you about me, he can." Awkward. Was that a little red creeping up her cheeks?

"Uh, sure. See you next week then?"

"Yes ma'am," Grandpa William said.

Luke helped Kaitlyn on with her coat and held the door for her. The stars twinkled in the inky sky. They stood mesmerized by them. Luke could have stood there forever next to her.

"Well, I guess I better get going," she said.

"Okay. Thanks for dinner. That was really kind of you."

"Text me if you need anything." A twinkle of moonlight caught her eyes.

Yes, maybe I just might do that. She must be a fisher of men because she just reeled me in.

***

Kaitlyn sat in her car. Okay, breathe, breathe, breathe, inhale, exhale, inhale, exhale. I can do this. She started the car. Her mind was a blur as she drove down the crazy long driveway.

Jesus, so, I just went to see William, who is a really sweet guy, and he's really great and he's really wonderful and then I found out he has a grandson, and his grandson is Luke? How on earth, of all the people is Luke his grandson?

She slowed way down and lifted her hands to the sky. Okay God, this is all in your hands now. Do whatever you're gonna do. I'm just gonna trust you. She let out a long sigh.

Chapter Twenty-Eight

Kaitlyn kept an eye out of her kitchen window, scanning for Luke. She grabbed the bottle of window cleaner and some newspaper and started washing the windows. When she was nervous, she cleaned. And right now, she was so nervous her windows shone.

She felt certain she didn't need to be. He was such a nice guy, right? She'd been around him before, and he was easy to talk to. But this was different from the other times. This was almost like a date. Well, not exactly a date, but he asked her to go somewhere, and she said yes.

Friends. That's what she was planning to be. Just a friend.

Luke drove up. She quickly threw away the paper and put away the cleaner.

"Have fu-un without me!" Tina called.

Kaitlyn finished tying the knot in her shoes as he tapped on the door. She took a deep breath and let it out and opened the door.

"Hey, ready to go?" he said. He looked good wearing a sports jersey and shorts. And dimples.

"Yeah. Well, I thought I was. Maybe I better get some shorts. You have to excuse me. I haven't played sports since high school. Come on in. I'll just be a minute." She hurried into her room and rummaged through her drawers, throwing things all over the floor.

Tina came in. "Here, wear these." She tossed her a pair of nylon shorts.

"You're a lifesaver. As usual!" Kaitlyn gave her a hurried hug and headed downstairs.

"Okay, let's do this!" she said.

Luke held the passenger door open for her and she climbed into his truck. She smiled. Had Francisco ever done that?

"Gorgeous day. I'm so glad it quit raining, and the weather is warming up," Luke said.

"I'm with you on that. It gets depressing. Tell me about the refugees," Kaitlyn said.

"I told you about where I work. It has locations in a lot of countries and works to educate, provide health services and strengthen families. We started looking into something we could do locally that wasn't being provided for.

Portland has had a big influx of refugees and so we thought we could begin working with English classes, helping them navigate the systems. Since soccer was my forte in high school, I started a little pickup game on Sundays. A lot of kids know how to play because soccer is so prevalent in their countries. And it's something that goes beyond the language barrier."

"Sounds like fun." They pulled into the high school parking lot and Kaitlyn watched as women in burqas walked to the field with their middle school kids. Women clothed in colorful batik and headdresses that accented their mahogany skin.

Luke tossed out a few balls and the kids instantly ran out to kick them around. The field became a melting pot of international faces. Smiling faces. Laughing faces.

Luke blew a whistle, and they all crowded around him. He introduced them to Kaitlyn and explained that she would captain one team and he would captain the other. He had them form two rows, girls and boys together. Then they chose their teams one by one. He tossed red pinnies to Kaitlyn's team and blue to his.

He blew the whistle again, and the play began. Amira tossed the ball in the air. Farid kicked it to Bisimwa, who was intercepted by the red team's Nohbble. She head-butted the ball to Ephraim, who headed down the field to the goal. Kaitlyn let out a yell to keep going.

Babak intercepted Ephraim, whose curly black hair blew in the breeze. Ephraim turned the ball around and headed towards the blue goal. He gained a few yards before the ball went out of bounds. Kaitlyn threw the ball back into play. Bisimwa kicked with the side of his foot. Nohbble head-butted again, and the ball headed towards Ephraim, who volleyed it between his feet to the final kick into the goal.

The blue goalie put his hands on his head and groaned.

Kaitlyn fist pumped and high fived her team, not neglecting to make sure Luke knew what he was up against.

Luke grinned and took on the challenge. Kaitlyn's playful competitiveness was worming its way into his heart. Amira tossed the ball into play. Nohbble got in the first kick and lobbed it to Luke. Luke dribbled it down the field. Kaitlyn edged her way in to block him. She gained the ball and kicked it to Ephraim, who fielded it to Amira.

Farid intercepted and kicked it to Luke, who dribbled it down the field, surrounded by the red team doing their best to stop him. Ephraim dove in front of Luke, causing him to trip and land on his stomach. Kaitlyn laughed. Amira gave the ball a hard kick and landed it in the goal. A cheer rang out. Kaitlyn turned and Luke was still on the ground. She called a time-out and dropped to her knees beside him.

"You okay?"

Luke sat up and winced. The kids crowded around, lines of worry replaced the joy on their faces.

"What hurts?" Kaitlyn asked.

"It's my ankle. I might have sprained it." Kaitlyn leaned down and gently poked. It had begun to swell.

"I don't think it's broken, but you'll need to stay off of it for a while." She turned to the sidelines. "Can someone bring us some ice?"

Amid ran over with a bag of ice and handed it to Kaitlyn. She tied a knot in the top and placed it on his ankle.

"Can you get up?" She held out her hands. Luke grabbed a hold as she helped him up.

Those strong hands. I could get used to those hands. She looked into his brown eyes. He winced.

She placed his arm around her shoulders and limped across the field to the grandstand.

"So, I guess we can concede that the red team won!" Her mouth turned up to a satisfied smile.

"You're going to kick a guy while he's down? Some friend you turned out to be." He shook his head in mock despair. Kaitlyn held up her hands like she was playing a violin.

"Does that feel better?"

"A bit. Are you okay driving a stick shift? Cuz I'm not going to be able to drive with my right foot."

"That I can do. I grew up on a farm. Not only can I drive a

stick shift, but I can also drive a tractor!" She straightened her shoulders in pride.

"You are my kinda woman," he said and winked. The kids looked at each other, covered their mouths, and giggled.

♥ ♥ ♥

Kaitlyn settled herself into the driver's seat of the truck. She had to adjust the seat as her legs weren't as long as Luke's. Kaitlyn breathed in the testosterone smell of the cab. She wasn't sure she liked the smell. But she was sure that she could learn to live with it if it meant having this guy in her life.

"How's this going to work? If I go home first, you can't drive home. If I drive you home, I'm stuck at your house."

"Would that be such a bad thing?" Luke cocked an eyebrow.

"Depends. What did you have planned for dinner?"

"Um."

"Just as I thought. Bachelors. Ugh!" She shook her head and smiled. "Mind if I stop and get some Chinese takeout?"

"I like how you think." He laid his head back on the head-rest and closed his eyes.

"Sore?"

"Yep." He winced.

"I'll check it again when you get home. Might need to wrap it in an ace bandage. Do you have one?" *Now this is why I became a nurse.*

He blinked at her. "I think so."

Luke leaned on her shoulder as she helped him up the front steps to his apartment.

Kaitlyn looked around at the sparse walls. The apartment was surprisingly clean for a bachelor.

The living room held only a couch and lazy-boy, an end table and a lamp. Several books sat piled on the end table, and a colorful hand-woven blanket lay on the couch. She recognized his bike, which rested against the wall. It triggered a memory of him rescuing her when her tire blew. Maybe he had been paying it forward.

She set the Chinese food on the kitchen counter and started rummaging around for plates and utensils. Luke hobbled over and took them from her, brushing her hands as he did. A touch that brought warmth.

"Sit down. I've got this," she said.

"I'm not used to being waited on."

"How did this happen that I'm serving dinner to you two nights in a row? You planned this, didn't you?" Kaitlyn cocked her eyebrow.

"If I were quick enough on the ball, I would have planned this."

"Quick on the ball—get it? You tripped on the ball?"

Kaitlyn opened the boxes and poured the contents onto the plates. Luke held out his upturned hand.

"Pray?" Kaitlyn nodded and gave him her hand. *This has to be from you, Lord.*

He hesitated and grinned. "I was going to sing the silly camp grace, but wasn't sure you'd appreciate it."

"Do it! I want to hear it."

"Okay, here goes. God is great. God is good. And we thank him for our food

We're gonna thank him in the morning, noon and night cuz God, our God is outta site. God our God is dynamite, Amen. Ch ch- ch ch, ch ch ch ch."

Kaitlyn burst out laughing. All of her nervousness burst into joy. And then she started wheenking like a guinea pig. She held her stomach, trying to stop, but then Luke started laughing and she squeaked more. She plonked her head on the table. He put his hand on her back.

"You okay?" He let out another chuckle.

"Yes." She took a deep breath and fanned her face with her hand. Had she just wheenked in front of him? This was sure to make it or break it. She wiped tears from her eyes.

Luke picked up his chopsticks. "Shall we?" She nodded.

"This is fantastic. I should get takeout more often!" Kaitlyn said.

"Tasty, but I still prefer homemade. Say, for example, fried chicken and blueberry pie." Kaitlyn melted in his smile.

"Tell me about Francisco," he said.

She looked up at Luke and froze. "Well," she paused. "We dated for a while."

"What happened between you and him?"

Kaitlyn looked up at the ceiling. "He asked me to marry him." She slid a glance at him. "I thought it was too soon—we'd only been together for a few months. It turned out he just wanted to get a green card and citizenship. Shortly after we broke up, he married one of his professors." She searched his face.

Luke's eyes bore a hole right into her soul.

"He was using you."

"I never saw it coming. I guess I'm just too naïve." She felt the familiar anger and tried to let it go.

"Any other guys in your life? Or are you gun shy now and want to stay as far away for the male species as possible?"

Gun shy. If he even knew. "I tried a dating app. Boy, was that a mistake! Have you ever tried it?"

"Thought about it, but never took the plunge."

"I went on two dates, both duds. One even *forgot* his wallet, and I had to pay for the expensive dinner! How about you?"

"I've had a few girls in my life. None that turned into anything. It seems like they're either all about their looks and clothes, or don't have any ambition in life."

I'd like to be the one to change that!

"Hey, I didn't wrap your foot yet. Show me where you keep the ace bandage."

"In the bathroom. Check the drawer."

Kaitlyn wandered down the hall. The bathroom was so clean. No hair in the sink or scum in the shower. Not exactly the way her brothers had kept theirs growing up.

"Okay, let's see that injury. Put your foot out." She tenderly felt his ankle. He winced.

"It's swollen, but if you take care of it, it should heal in a few days." Her pulsed quickened as she wrapped. "Keep it elevated." She looked into his mocha eyes and held his gaze.

"Thank you. Really. You've saved me today." He held her eyes.

"I really should get home. I'll call an Uber. I've got to get to work tomorrow. You should get hold of some crutches. Don't put any weight on it for a few days until the swelling goes down." She cleared the dishes and washed them. Her phone notified her of her ride.

"I may need a certain nurse to check in on me tomorrow, if that's possible."

"I'll check and see if Tina's free." Luke's eyes widened, and he looked like he'd been sucker punched.

"What? Did you have someone else in mind?" Kaitlyn flipped her head and let her curls fall. She blew him a kiss and closed the door.

Chapter Twenty-Nine

"So, looks like you and Kaitlyn are dating, hm?" Gracie tapped her water bottle on her lips. Luke ventured a smile.

"Maybeeee."

"Eric and I have plans for dinner and a show. You feel up to joining us?"

"That sounds like a real date."

"And that's a problem because...."

Luke held his hands out in a *why not*. Really, what was there to lose? Kaitlyn had made it plain that she had been worried about his sprain. And hadn't she blown him a kiss? If that didn't say she was interested, he didn't know what did. One thing he knew. At the very least, he could become a good friend.

"Okay, I'll pick somewhere fun and romantic," she said with an exaggerated wink.

♥ ♥ ♥

Saturday night rolled around, and Luke tested his foot on the accelerator. Anything he did to exert the muscles in his leg reminded him of his injury. Fortunately, tonight, there was barely any pain.

He caught his eyebrows hitching when Kaitlyn stepped out of her house in a knit teal dress. Her hair was pulled back with a clasp, a few curls cascading over the lacy shawl which covered her creamy bare shoulders. Luke hoped his choice of khaki pants and dress shirt were the right choice. He wished he had his dad's old Ford F150 with the bench seat so that she could sit closer to him.

Gracie and Eric sat at a table for four at the Mongolian Grill, sipping glasses of wine and clearly enjoying each other's company.

Kaitlyn breathed in the tantalizing scent.

"Sorry we're a little late. It was tricky finding a parking place."

"Luke, this is Eric." Eric stood and shook hands.

"And Kaitlyn, Gracie, and Eric," Luke introduced.

"Nice to meet you. Great choice for a restaurant." Kaitlyn waited as Luke pulled out her chair.

He put his hands on her shoulders as she pushed herself in. He held them there a moment longer than necessary. The warmth of her shoulders felt good under his fingers.

She turned her sparkling brown eyes towards him.

They watched as the chef threw bean sprouts, chicken,

pork, and veggies on the grill. The aroma of the sweet Asian sauce was enticing.

"Eric, Kaitlyn was in Honduras at the same time Luke and I were there."

"Really? What were you doing there?"

"I went with a friend whose mom was very ill. I'm a nurse, so he thought maybe I could help her. I'm sure it was the living conditions and the water that was causing the illness. But," Kaitlyn looked at Luke, "It turns out that Healthy Kids has services for elderly. I serendipitously met Maria down there and she was instrumental in getting her help."

"That was really nice of you to go down there with him," Gracie said.

Kaitlyn rolled her eyes. She didn't want to get into the details.

"You're a nurse?"

"Yeah. I work at Mercy Hospital. It's," her eyes went to the ceiling. "Let's just say it has its interesting moments."

"Luke, you should set her up with the Refugee Project!" Gracie said, laying her hand on his shoulder.

"What's that? I mean, I met some of the kids the other day. That was fun."

"Gracie was responsible for setting up a program to help some of the local refugee families. I told you a little about it the other day." Luke twiddled his fork. "You might be interested in helping them with medical appointments."

"Something to think about. I work three twelves, so I have a few days off each week." She glanced at Luke. "And look in on Luke's grandpa. But Tina and a few other friends might be interested as well."

"Eric, tell me about your job." Luke allowed his leg to brush up against Kaitlyn's.

"I'm an engineer with a company that works on products for renewable energy. They also do green building design and construction."

"That sounds interesting. What kind of renewable energy? Turbine windmills? Solar?"

"Yes. But the exciting thing is that we've been working on what we call the "garbage house". They constructed the outside totally from garbage, including 20,000 toothbrushes, thousands of DVD cases, floppy disks and carpet tiles—all recycled. It's really been fun."

"We were just talking about how that might be a way to help marginal countries both rid their garbage and house people at minimal expense. It might be something HK could partner with." Gracie looked adoringly at Eric and took his hand.

Luke snuck a glance at Kaitlyn and put his hand on her leg. She moved her hand on top of his and kept her eyes on Gracie.

"I could definitely see how that could be an advantage in Honduras," Kaitlyn said.

The chef dished up their plates and passed them out. Luke moved his hand to his chopsticks.

"Are you guys married? You're so comfortable together." Kaitlyn stirred her dish with her chopsticks.

"We will be in a few months." Gracie beamed as she held up her left hand to show off her new ring.

"I love that. It's simple, yet elegant. Not too gaudy."

I'll take note of that, just in case we get that far, Luke thought. He was more than enjoying Kaitlyn's company. Every time her gaze met his, his heart turned over in response. It was all he could do to resist running his fingers through her curls.

The full moon cast shadows through the trees as they walked out of the show. Kaitlyn and Luke said their goodbyes to Gracie and Eric and found Luke's truck. Kaitlyn accepted Luke's outstretched hand and sidled up to him.

"Did you enjoy Fiddler on the Roof?"

"I didn't realize it was a musical. I've never been to one before. The dancing was really fun to watch. And Tevia—what a rich voice!"

"Kind of like yours. That show has always been one of my favorites." She started singing, "Matchmaker, matchmaker, make me a match, find me a find, catch me a catch."

She looked up at Luke with a sidelong smile.

"I think we might do just fine without a matchmaker." Luke turned her towards him. Her breath hitched as he stroked her hair. The fragrance heightened his senses. Her eyes sparkled as she turned her face up to him. He dipped his head and let his lips land softly on hers. He longed for more, but pulled back.

"The truck's parked over there." He nodded with his chin. He needed to take things slowly.

She squeezed his hand and smiled. Beautiful girl. Excellent meal. Fun musical. And stars. A recipe for an amazing evening. He couldn't deny his feelings if he wanted to. Which he didn't.

He opened the truck door and helped her in. As he walked to the driver's side, he looked up at the sky, his entire being filled with gratitude.

Lord, I think you've got the matchmaker role covered!

Chapter Thirty

"How's the work going in Honduras?"

Luke took a piece of firewood from Kaitlyn and added it to the growing stack outside Grandpa William's house. Having her come check in on his grandpa once a week was turning out better than he expected. It wasn't hard to find an excuse to be there the nights she showed up.

Luke took another piece from her. "It could be better." He explained about the sex trafficking and Brianna's solution to the pregnancies. Although he and Gracie had talked to Brianna about them, she hadn't told them she had put a stop to the option for abortions. It had been several months since then and he thought she would have taken positive action.

Why couldn't God just step in and fix this? Wasn't that what He was there for? Maybe it was up to Luke. An appalling thought considering what happened when he had tried to fix things in Mexico.

"Woah. Not acceptable." Kaitlyn allowed Luke to brush a strand of hair from her face and smoothed it behind her ear.

"Right? But I'm not sure what to do about it. Brianna thinks the girls have a right to them."

Kaitlyn sat down on a stump. "There has to be a better solution."

"I was trying to figure out the logistics of something like a safe house. The girls need to get away from those men."

"What if you could find a location, maybe somewhere hidden? Do you think Brianna would let you go down there again?" The memory of the Mexican jail made him angry. He rolled up his flannel sleeves, picked up the ax and swung it into a round log. It split in two.

"I had a job in Mexico with another non-profit." He swung the ax into another round, throwing his anger full into it.

"My boss was taking the donor funds and spending them on expensive fishing trips with his buddies and hosting big, fancy parties." He wasn't sure why he was telling her this. He hadn't told anyone in the states about it. She was just so easy to talk to.

"Is that why you quit?" If it had only been that easy.

The crack of the wood splitting sounded and the two pieces thunked to the ground.

"There was a little boy, Zach, about nine years old. Big brown eyes. Black hair wanting to be cut. He needed heart surgery, or he was going to die." Luke's muscles tensed as he wielded the ax again. He swallowed.

"I embezzled money so that he could get the surgery." He met her eyes. Hazel? No, more the color of milk chocolate.

"Did it fix him?" That was all she was going to ask? Not tell him what a jerk he was?

"Uh, yeah. His family was so grateful."

"And did your boss find out?" Luke sat on a large stump,

rested his elbows on his knees, and clutched handfuls of his hair.

"I spent six months in jail." He glanced up at her, expecting to see her scowl. Or back away. Instead, Kaitlyn reached out and touched his shoulder. A whiff of vanilla. Or was it lavender? Whatever it was, it made him forget his pain for a moment.

"That had to have been awful! Six months in a Mexican jail." She shuttered. "And you did it for a good reason. You didn't deserve that." He pulled her down beside him.

"I can say I've had better experiences. Here's the thing. You're the only one I've ever told this to. Not my family, no one at work. So, when you ask if Brianna would let me go down there again..." Kaitlyn twined her fingers through his. "I don't want to make the same mistake— going behind my boss' back." Doing something he would regret. But if he pulled this off, perhaps it would lead to redemption.

"If you decide to go, I could probably get some time off if there's a medical component. That is, if you'd want me to." Want her to? He couldn't imagine anything better.

♥ ♥ ♥

The Honduras sun shone through the banana trees, leaving interesting shadows. A colorful parrot squawked approval of the building project below him.

"Can we get some lunch after we finish? I'm starving!" Kaitlyn lugged another cinder block and hoisted it to the wall, where Luke had just spread mortar to hold it in place. He grinned at her.

"I think I know a great little place in the middle of the village." Only this time, the guy sitting across from Kaitlyn would be him.

It hadn't been hard to convince Brianna to let him return to Honduras. Maybe she wanted someone else to fix the situation. Whatever the reason, he felt anxious to find a solution. And he wanted to do it quick before any more girls were thrown into that horror.

He twisted his shoulders, trying to ease the tension.

Kaitlyn swiped the hair out of her eyes with her forearm.

Luke studied her. "You just added some mortar to your cheeks." Kaitlyn frowned. "It looks cute!"

"Cute, huh? I'll show you cute." She scooped her hand into the bucket and threw a sloppy mess at him. Luke ducked, but not enough to miss his arm. He returned the favor.

"Luke! Why you..." It landed on her chest and oozed its way down the front of her shirt. Kaitlyn's squeal bounced off the cinder block wall. She scooped the ooze off and ran to rub it into Luke's hair. He grabbed her wrist as she jumped to try, exploding into giggles. The tension melted as his laughter joined hers.

Luke let go of her wrist and grabbed the hose, turning the nozzle full force and aimed it at Kaitlyn. Her eyes grew wide as the cold water hit her, washing mortar down her clothes, leaving a muddy mess at her feet. Luke rinsed off his hands and dipped his head as he ran the hose over his hair. He let the hose fall and let his eyes travel from her soggy shoes up to her drenched hair. He locked eyes with her and closed the gap, placing his hands on her shoulders.

"You are adorable." She scrunched her freckled nose at him, and he bent down and brushed his lips to hers.

♥ ♥ ♥

"Let's go look through the market before we head back to the compound. I'd like to see what kind of folk art they have." They had showered and eaten a lunch of rice, beans and carne asada. Luke took Kaitlyn's hand as they wandered through stalls of fresh mangos, pineapple and papayas. They found the artisan market and lingered at cubby holes filled with woven blankets, jewelry, carved masks, and hand embroidered clothing. Several black-haired children played at the feet of their parents manning the booths.

Kaitlyn picked up a blouse and held it next to her, the deep teal accenting her brown curls. As she pulled out a few lempira to pay the vendor, Luke's head jerked, and he ran down the aisle.

"Luke?" She quickly took the bag with her blouse and chased after him. He hid behind a pole, peeking at someone. "Sh." He held his finger to his lips.

"What is it?"

"Remember that little girl I told you about? The one in the video from when I was here last?"

Kaitlyn nodded. "I just saw her. I want to follow her. See if I can talk to her."

"Will it be safe?" He didn't know, but she was the key to finding out about the sex ring.

This girl's black hair was neatly tied into braids, with strands of rose ribbon running through them. She was dressed in a pretty cotton dress, accented with lace and ruffles. A contrast to how she looked in the video. Was this a good thing? Someone was obviously taking care of her. And yet. . .

Luke grabbed Kaitlyn's hand and walked slowly towards her, several rows of vendors between them. They watched her grab a handful of lychee, the soft red tendrils sticking out between her fingers. After a quick glance around, she began to run towards them. As Luke came closer, she startled at someone calling 'Lucinda'. A man with a black mustache and goatee grabbed her arm, his tattooed fingers wrapping tightly around her wrist. She dropped the lychee as he dragged her out of the market.

Chapter Thirty-One

"Hurry!" Kaitlyn followed Luke's lead as they dodged shoppers and nearly stumbled over a stray dog before they lost Lucinda and the man.

Luke ran his hand through his hair, caught his breath, and leaned against a wall. "Probably wasn't such a great idea to follow them."

"That man was awful! He had devil horns tattooed over his eyebrows. Did you see that?"

Kaitlyn shivered and leaned into Luke, where he wrapped his arm around her. "She looked so frightened. We've got to do something, and fast."

• ❦ •

Kaitlyn typed furiously, finishing a medical manual for the staff of Mariposa Proyecto.

She only had another week before she needed to return to

Mercy. It had been a stretch for Delores to grant her a month's leave, and she didn't want to push her luck. Especially since Delores constantly reminded her that she wasn't irreplaceable.

As much as she was driven by the needs of the Butterfly Project, the name they had chosen for the safe house, she was more than enjoying her time and budding relationship with Luke. It had all come about so naturally. She looked out the window at the banana tree—a lizard skittered along the yellow stalk. Maybe the creator of the universe had been fulfilling her desires all along.

"Brought you some coffee." Gabriella set the ceramic mug on Kaitlyn's desk, the steam rising in the early morning sun. "Are you ready for the interviews?"

"Just finishing the training manual. I think I've got everything covered—sections on immunizations, nutrition, exercise. Most importantly, working through trauma and creating joy in their lives."

This was a daunting task. Creating a safe space for trafficked girls while giving them hope and a future. They needed to know they were capable and valued for more than their bodies. Luke had devised a plan to teach them skills to create sustainable incomes. This project energized her. Energized Luke. This. Working together on a common goal.

"We need to choose just the right people that can move forward with the vision. I leave at the end of the week. And Luke can't be here forever." This felt like it fulfilled a greater purpose than working at Mercy, but Kaitlyn wasn't sure she was ready to drop everything and make a change. What about her friends? Her family?

"No worries. You and Luke have done so much to create a solid foundation. Now we'll be able to take it from here."

"I'm only a phone call away." Kaitlyn smiled.

❦ ❦ ❦

Luke unfolded his body as he climbed out of the tuc tuc, lending a hand to Kaitlyn. A motorcycle kicked up dust as it roared by—four people balancing bags and hanging on. Mothers, their babies wrapped in colorful scarves, holding them securely to their backs, picked out vegetables and beans for tonight's supper.

"You haven't told me where we're going?" Kaitlyn looked around for clues.

"It's a surprise. We're almost there." They stepped around a stray dog sleeping on the cracked sidewalk. Music filtered through the open door of a red brick building. Inside was a large dance floor, the polished wood gleaming under the feet of a tango Instructor.

Kaitlyn grinned up at Luke. "We're taking dance lessons?"

He led her to the dance floor, where they mimicked the instructor.

"Watch as I show you how to do the steps." The instructor held his left arm out in front of him. "Forward, forward, forward, sidestep, slide in." Kaitlyn watched as he seemed to glide over the floor, ending with his left foot pointing to the floor.

Luke put his arm on her shoulder and clasped Kaitlyn's right hand with his left, holding it shoulder height. Kaitlyn matched his steps until he sidestepped. She kept going and giggled as she untangled herself from his foot.

"Try it again, please. Like this." The instructor went through the steps again, this time with a partner.

Luke slid his left foot back and toed, then his right foot. When they got to the sidestep, he tilted Kaitlyn back and held her there, just long enough for her to melt into his eyes. He grinned and swung her around, where they continued to the sounds of the accordion and violin.

The sun blinded them as they walked outside into the light. They had only walked a few steps before a girl in pigtails and ribbons ran across the street in front of them.

"Lucinda!" Luke pulled Kaitlyn across the street to follow her. She turned.

"Lucinda!"

"¿Como sabes mi nombre?" She crossed her arms and glanced around. She slid back into the shadow of the building.

"I saw you the other day and heard someone call you. Are you okay? Are you safe? We want to help you." Luke replied, so grateful again he was fluent in Spanish.

Lucinda's eyes darted furtively. "Follow me." She led them down an alley and behind a dumpster. "They stole me." She spoke in a whisper. "Some men stole me. They took me away and make me work for them."

"We can help you." Luke started to reach out to her, but she shrunk back. "We have a place where you can hide and be safe. There's plenty to eat."

Lucinda looked at her feet and scuffed the toe of her shoe on the cobblestone. "I can't. They'll find me and beat me. I have to go."

"I'll look for you again. We can help you." She ran off down the alley and around the corner.

Kaitlyn bit into her knuckle. "How are we going to help her

if she runs off? She must really be afraid." She thought about the man who had grabbed her before. "We have to be careful not to put her in danger." Were they on the right track? She was sure they were, but how to make it happen? That was the question.

Kaitlyn reluctantly packed her bag for her return flight home. There was still so much to do here and, if she were honest with herself, she wasn't ready to leave Luke. Knowing he wasn't here permanently helped. But distance didn't always fuel a relationship. And this was one relationship she didn't want to vanish.

She had been happy with the interviews and felt like Maria and Gabriella had a solid group of women to lead the charge. And what was better, they were confident they could lure Lucinda from the ring and give her a new life.

"Ready to go?" Luke had walked through her door, his lean frame casting a shadow on the floor. Kaitlyn drug her wheeled suitcase behind her. "You're looking pretty glum." She looked up at him.

"I don't want to leave here."

"It's a pretty great project."

"It's a brilliant project. It's you I don't want to leave." Her head tilted forward, and she fell into his arms. Luke kissed the top of her head.

"I'll be home before you know it. You've got work to do. And Grandpa William will be missing you as well."

He hoisted her suitcase into the trunk and looked at the clouds.

"Better get going before the rain comes."

Luke drove to the small departure gate and removed her suitcase. After a tight embrace, he waved goodbye. The vulnerability showing in her deep brown eyes caused him to want to wrap his arms around her and caress that curly brown hair. Thank you Francisco, for freeing her up for me. Or perhaps he should be thanking God.

Kaitlyn reluctantly walked through the revolving doors and looked outside once more. She heard her flight called on the intercom. She ran to the desk, felt her hip pocket for her passport, and quickly checked in.

After passing through security, she rode the escalator to the next floor, where a row of windows overlooked the parking lot. She scanned for Luke as she took her window seat. He was there, waving and blowing her a kiss. As she returned a wave, a shot rang out. She screamed as Luke fell to the ground and the plane backed away.

Chapter Thirty-Two

The eight-hour flight to Portland was excruciating. Tears had stung Kaitlyn's brown eyes as the plane rose to the sky. It was all she could do to not jump out of the plane and run to Luke. Her imagination had run wild—what if he died? What if he were paralyzed? Or permanently injured?

God what is going on here? Like, I don't know if you're trying to show me something, but I got to tell you, I have been waiting a really long time for somebody to show up. You know my track record with guys.

Maybe you are showing me a sign. Is there something you're trying to do here? Because, God, I got to tell you; it doesn't look much like anything good could come from this.

I mean, finally I'm in a relationship with a guy that's really cute. Like really cute. Did you see those dimples? And did you see his scruffy beard? And his curly hair? And his flannel and his little laugh...

She started sobbing again, glad no one was sitting beside her.

♥ ♥ ♥

Tina met her at the arrival gate. Kaitlyn ran to her arms, hiccuping sobs.

"What? What happened?" Kaitlyn pulled away and wiped her eyes.

"Luke. He got shot!"

"No! How?" Tina shook her head. She linked elbows with Kaitlyn as they headed to the baggage claim.

"He was shot as the plane was taking off. I saw him out my window."

Tina dug her phone from her bag. "Do you want to call?"

"Don't you think I tried? No one answered. The phone system is so cranky. It's exasperating." Kaitlyn leaned her head on Tina's shoulder. "I need to know if he's okay!"

Kaitlyn whooshed out a long breath and filled Tina in on the project, Lucinda, and Luke.

"It might have been the gang member that snagged Lucinda. He was awful!" She shuddered. The embodiment of evil.

They grabbed Kaitlyn's bags and headed to the car, dodging passengers and cars.

"I'm really glad you're home. It hasn't been the same without you. Delores has been cranky all week. We're down two nurses and with you gone, it's been a push. There's been a big influx of patients with some kinda virus."

"Glad to know I've been missed. But you don't know how hard it was to come back. I'm so worried about Luke. But also knowing the project was just getting started." Would Luke be able to lure Lucinda to the safe house? He had to be careful. That is if he was still alive.

♥ ♥ ♥

"So, you decided to grace us with your presence?" Was that a sneer on Delores' face? She put her hand on her broad hip. "You know, you could be replaced at any time. There are tons of new grads waiting for jobs."

"Thank you, Delores. I missed you, too. You know you couldn't get by without me. Who would decorate? Who would bring brownies?" She was not going to let that woman get under her skin.

"You think I'm joking?" Delores cocked her eyebrow. Kaitlyn wanted to give her a salute but thought better of it. The fact was, being fired was always on her mind. It would only take one wrong move. Like the one she'd made before.

"Did someone say brownies?" Peter swung his stethoscope around his finger. Kaitlyn shook her head and headed to her first patient.

"Hi there, Manuel. What's going on here? Looks like they sent you up from ICU."

Manuel put his long arms behind his head, making his black hair poof out in all directions.

"Got shot." Not much of a talker.

"Can I take a look?" He moved the sheet to expose a bandage around his thigh, bright red blood oozing through.

Kaitlyn swallowed. This was too close to home. And why couldn't she get through to Luke? Or Maria? Or Gabriella?

"Looks like I better replace that."

She left and returned with bandages and tape. She peeled off the tape where a large, open hole was exposed. *Luke should come home. I could take care of him. I should be taking care of him.*

"So, what's the story here?"

He winced. "Wrong place at the wrong time." Obviously. She wanted to quiz him more, but thought better of it. His story was one she probably didn't want to hear.

Kaitlyn glanced at the TV. The news showed a video of howling wind and rain forcing trees to lean and snap. In Honduras. She gasped.

Chapter Thirty-Three

Luke grabbed his thigh, pain shooting through him, sticky ooze between his fingers. What just happened? A crowd had gathered around him, and a siren wailed. Large raindrops started, and soon drenched the medics placing him on a gurney and into the ambulance.

Had Kaitlyn seen him fall? He hoped not. She would be beside herself. And who had shot him? And why?

A short while later, Maria entered Luke's hospital room with a man in uniform.

"How are you feeling?" Maria pulled up a chair.

"Let's just say the drugs are working."

"Mind if I ask you a few questions? I'm officer Mario." He reached for his hand to shake Luke's.

"Of course." Luke glanced out the window. It had begun to rattle with the wind and rain. What kind of damage might this bring?

"Do you have any clue as to who might have shot you?"

Luke explained about the safe house and Lucinda. And the man who grabbed her.

"My guess is, it was him or one of his gang." Luke remembered Brianna telling him that the police were part of the sex ring. How much should he tell him? Was he a good cop or a bad cop?

"Okay, gracias. I need to get going before I get carried away with the storm."

Maria handed Luke a glass of water. "Have you tried to contact Kaitlyn?" He looked at the clock on the wall.

"She's still on the plane. I tried to leave her a message, but maybe cuz of the storm, it didn't go through." He took a sip, adjusted himself and winced. Her anxiety would put her through the roof wondering if he was okay.

"Okay, I'll try to contact her for you later. We need to talk about our next step. Let's assume it was part of the gang who shot you. They suspect you are trying to *steal* one of their girls. How do we keep Lucinda safe? I'm pretty sure we're not equipped to bring down the mob."

"I don't know. First, we need to find her again. The good thing is, the safe house is nearly finished." And hopefully in one piece after this storm.

"And our staff training is in place—they know how important it is to make the girls feel loved and respected and to create community. I think we're on the right track to train them in skills to earn money, so they don't feel like selling themselves is their only option. Let's face it—they aren't making any money doing tricks and for sure, it's not getting back to their families."

The power blinked on and off. Maria stood and looked out the window. The rain pelted down, and the trees were nearly horizontal in the furious wind. The water was steadily rising in the streets.

"I've gotta go. I'll barely make it home at this rate. Hopefully, you'll be safe here."

"Okay, be careful." The power blinked off. Luke lay back against his pillow and closed his eyes. Getting through to Kaitlyn was looking impossible. He let out a breath.

* * *

Three long days had passed in the hospital. It had seemed safer to remain there than to try and return to the HK compound in the hurricane. Luke, now discharged, stood on the sidewalk resting on his crutches. The rain and wind had ceased, leaving standing water in the streets and trees blown down.

Luke hailed a taxi. He couldn't believe the damage. The small roadside venue he had gotten roast chicken from lay in pieces strewn on the ground. A woman on the sidewalk skirted water sprayed out as the taxi drove past. Evaporated water rose in a mist as the sun shone through the clouds. Luke wiped sweat from his brow.

The taxi driver rounded the corner and stopped suddenly. A palm tree had fallen across the road, sandy loam clinging to its tentacled roots. Luke got out to evaluate his options. The driver said this was the only route to the compound. He'd have to walk. Hobble was more like it, but he would do whatever it took. It couldn't be that much further ahead.

The taxi driver backed up and turned around, leaving him to figure it out. A macaw squawked, scolding him. The palm had knocked down a power line, which lay over the length of it. How was he going to get around? Touching the line wasn't the wisest choice. He crutched his way around the end of the tree and moved brush out of the way with his crutch. He took a step and his crutch sank into the muddy ooze. He took a step back.

Luke's leg was beginning to throb. He reached in his pocket and drew out his bottle of meds. He scarfed one down, wishing he had his water bottle with him.

He looked over the power line again. Part of it was stuck in the branches and left a triangle before touching the log. Could he ease his way under? He had to be successful, or he could be fried with no one to find him or care. He had to find Lucinda and get back to Kaitlyn.

A snake slithered through the grass in front of him and he slapped at mosquitos landing on his arms. *It's now or never.* He slid his crutches under the wire and lay on his back, inching his way, slowly under the wire. Halfway there. He just needed to get his legs through.

He stopped. This was not going to work. He'd land on his head and kick the wire for sure. He slithered his way back out and proceeded on is stomach. *Inch by inch it's a cinch.* Grandpa William's voice in his head. His hands touched the ground where he grabbed a root and pulled himself through. He yelped as he rolled onto his wound.

"You need help, señor?" A man reached out his hand to him, his straw hat shading his dark face. Luke looked to the sky and whispered a thank you Jesus.

"I need to get back to the Healthy Kids compound. It should be ahead a ways." Luke nodded his head to show the direction.

"Sí, is up ahead. I can take you on my donkey. I am Luis."

"And I am grateful!" He helped Luke onto the donkey and grabbed the reigns to lead him.

"My crutches." Luis laughed, gathered them up and handed them to him.

"You want, we can stop at my house. It's on the way. We have mucho mangoes. The storm tossed them down."

His house was small, but the walls were cinderblock and survived the storm. The metal roof was torn off, however, and strewn across the yard. A stray dog rolled in the mud and cocked an eye at a chicken which ran across and squawked.

Luis' wife came out of the house, wiping her hands on her apron.

"Esmeralda, this is my friend Luke. He was stranded on the road. I told him we have mangoes." He gave a big grin.

"Yes, yes, come in."

Luke hobbled in and sat on a crude wooden stool. The house was simple and bright, sun beams shone where the roof had been.

"Why are you here, Luke?" She handed him a plate with sliced mangoes and a cloth napkin.

"I work with Healthy Kids. I was finishing building a safe house for Human Trafficking victims." Luis held Esmeralda's eyes. *Did they know something?*

"Is a big problem here." Luis put his hand on Esmeralda's.

"The storm. It has destroyed many things. Many homes." Esmeralda glanced at a curtained door. Luis gave a slight nod. She got up and slid behind the curtain and returned with her arm around a girl.

Luke's eyes widened. "Lucinda? You're here?" He looked first at Luis and then at Esmeralda.

"We found her crouched in the corner of the alley, hiding behind a rolled over garbage can."

"What happened to your leg, mister?" Lucinda pointed to his crutches.

"I'm afraid someone shot me. But tell me about you. Are you okay? What about that man that grabbed you in the marketplace?"

"A tree fell on our house. I was so scared, but I ran as fast as I could away from there. I think he got killed, but I'm not sure." Luke looked at Luis.

"Lucinda, could you take me there?"

Luke breathed in. "Yes. Yes, señor I could do that.

Chapter Thirty-Four

"Okay everyone, buckle up. The plane will be landing shortly at Portland International. The weather is cloudy with a light mist." Luke straightened up, placed his book in his backpack, and gave the stewardess his empty glass. He checked the screen on his phone. Kaitlyn had commandeered it and placed a photo of her on the desktop. Her contagious grin and brush of freckles. His stomach tightened at the thought of seeing her. Not being able to contact her had been excruciating, but he hoped beyond hope that she had received his itinerary.

He felt the bounce of the wheels and switched his phone off airplane mode.

> Hey babe, we just landed. Meet you at baggage.

His heart thundered in his chest. He was glad his seat had been at the front of the plane.

Kaitlyn met him at security and threw her arms around him.

"I. Am. So. Glad. You're home!" She let out a giggle. Then wiped the moisture from her eye. Luke held her close, breathing in the scent of her hair. His chest filled with emotion. He held on a little longer, giving a moment to hold back his own tears.

"Are you okay walking this far?"

"I still have a limp, but my leg is much better. I'll be fine. And if I'm not, I know where I can find a cute nurse to help me." He winked.

A short while later, they arrived at Healthy Kids.

Luke struggled to get the crutches out. John heaved himself off the curb and lent a hand.

"Sorry about your injury, man. Hope it's okay."

"Thanks, it's healing." *That's the first time John's ever talked to me. Maybe I should have gotten hurt sooner.* Luke fist bumped him. John gave Luke a gap-toothed smile.

Luke struggled to the elevator and pressed the button. After the doors slid open on the tenth floor, he carefully maneuvered his crutches onto the bamboo floor. All eyes from the office focused on him.

"You're back!" Brianna tapped her purple nails on her thigh. *New color, I see.* Crazy as she was, he had missed her. Missed this place. It was good to be home.

"Good thing you have a desk job." Her full lips, sporting red lipstick, today's color, formed a hint of a grin. "And this must be Kaitlyn." She held her hand out to her. "Welcome. We can't wait to hear about your, shall we say, adventure?"

Luke parked himself in a love seat and motioned Kaitlyn to join him. He let out a long sigh. He couldn't believe how much effort it took to get around with crutches. He vowed to be more compassionate the next time he saw someone with a cast.

"Just don't get enough attention, huh?" Gracie adjusted her dangling necklace.

"Yeah, well."

Brianna and the staff seated themselves in the cozy chairs. A gentle rain left rivulets of water streaming down the floor-to-ceiling window.

"Everyone, I'd like you to meet Kaitlyn. We couldn't have made the safe house happen without her." Kaitlyn blushed.

"I didn't do that much."

"Just give us an overview—how you put the project together, what's happening now, what needs to be done." Brianna crossed her legs.

Luke raked a hand through his hair and down the back of his neck. He thought of their mudslinging incident—him squirting water to clean her off. He could feel the heat rising to his cheeks. He couldn't remember ever feeling this way about someone. What was it he was feeling? Hopeful? Like there were possibilities? He took her hand.

Luke cleared his throat. "First off, Maria and Gabriella are great. You can feel confident that they are doing a good job. They, along with Kaitlyn, put together a manual with a code of ethics, policy and procedures for both medical and mental health."

"Get to the good stuff—you know, the stuff movies are made of." Gracie scooted to the edge of her chair. "I want to hear about the girl."

"I saw her again in the market. She was wearing a clean, pretty dress." Kaitlyn continued. "And her hair was in braids with pretty ribbons. Looked like someone was taking care of her." Kaitlyn glanced at everyone. "Luke tried to talk to her—she was pretty scared of getting caught."

"Then a man who was clearly a gang member pulled her away. Anyway, it wasn't until after I got shot and out of the hospital that I ran into a couple who had been keeping her in their care. They had found her after the hurricane. The rest is pretty much history."

"So, she's at the safe house now?" Brianna asked.

"Yes, along with others. Lucinda helped find them. A tree had crashed on their house killing the men in the front house and allowing the girls to escape."

Thank you, Jesus.

Chapter Thirty-Five

"Kaitlyn, what do you want to bring for dad's birthday? Everybody's coming," Maggie said. "Kaitlyn? You there?"

"Yeah. I was just feeling bad because I forgot."

"Okay, and now you remember. You'll be happy to know that Kim is making a salad, so that lets you off the hook." Kaitlyn could picture first Maggie's big-sister comeback, and then her smirk.

"Is mom making a strawberry pie?" Dad would never have a birthday without his mom's recipe of strawberry pie. It wasn't Kaitlyn's personal favorite with the mixture of jello, ice cream and strawberries. She might, however, have been caught dipping her finger in the whipped cream topping and sticking it in her mouth a time or two.

"Of course."

"You're not making this easy, you know. Anyone bringing twice-baked potatoes? I'm pretty good at those."

"Okay, I'll put you down for that."

"And," Kaitlyn paused.

"You don't have to bring anything else. That's good."

"No, I was going to ask if you thought it'd be okay if I brought Luke." She winced, knowing her voice just hitched up a notch.

"Luke, huh. Nice name. I want to hear everything about him, but I've got to go pick up Lizzie from day care. I'll see you soon and we can talk."

Kaitlyn set down her phone. She was really going to do this —share Luke with her family. After the fiasco with Francisco, she wanted as many people as possible to meet him and give their opinion. Wise counsel. That's what she wanted. Before she got herself into another messy relationship.

When she suggested Luke join her for her dad's birthday, it surprised her how willing he was to go.

"You've already met my grandpa." He shrugged.

"And your dad. Yeah, that's a little mild compared to my family. It takes courage to step into our chaotic household."

"Maybe I should reconsider." Luke moved back to avoid Kaitlyn's back slap and laughed.

"Okay, okay! I'm sure I can handle it."

♥ ♥ ♥

Nervous energy had cascaded through Kaitlyn's body, waiting for when she would pick him up. For three days after she had asked him, she had shamelessly counted the hours.

Driving up in her car would prevent the thousands of inevitable questions. If Luke had driven his pickup, a dozen eyes would peer out the kitchen window, wondering who it could be.

She wasn't ready for how handsome he looked—shaved, his chin revealing a slight dimple. And judging by that murmur in her heart, he might possibly be the best thing that had ever happened to her.

"Hey!" Luke slid into the car, adjusting the seat to accommodate his long legs. He drew a soccer ball out a bag. "Do you think the kids would like this? Is there a big yard?"

"Absolutely! They'll go bonkers. My folks live on a farm. There's plenty of room to kick a ball. When we were kids, my folks would take us out in the field for a game of softball." She smiled at the memory. "That is until James ran off screaming because he got hit with the bat. Sam was grounded for a week, the whole while grumbling about how unfair it was." She turned onto the freeway.

"I can't imagine growing up in a large family. There was just me and Ryan."

"You and William are close, though." She glanced at Luke.

"I love my grandpa. I don't know what I'd do if something ever happened to him."

Kaitlyn was getting pretty attached to him as well. She was determined to do what she could to keep his diabetes under control. She put on her blinker and passed a freight truck.

"Should I be worried about what your family will think of me?" Luke shifted towards her, eyebrows raised. She slowed behind a log truck.

Should he? She hoped not. "What's not to like? Just be your alluring, confident self." Luke gave a half smile. "Play with the kids. We can tell them all about Honduras and what a hero you were." She grinned. "They'll want to see your scar. And you can ask my dad about the farm. You know, regular stuff."

Kaitlyn turned off the highway onto a winding road that ran along the slough. A tractor ambled through the field, driving the sweet smell of fresh hay into the air. Scruffy high school boys in their jeans and cut off tee shirts were bucking hay for ten bucks an hour under the counter.

To her right, mallards paddled between black and white male hooded mergansers for an afternoon dip. Something startled them and they skipped across the water and took flight.

"My brothers used to duck hunt. Probably still do. I never was much into it. Tried it once, but you have to get up way early — it's cold and rainy. Not my cup of tea. I'm sure they could take you, Luke, if you thought you'd like it."

"That's not something that's ever occurred to me."

She drove around the curve. "Hey, we're almost there. See those sheep? They're my dad's." She pointed. "This is part of our property. Maggie and I used to take the kayaks out in the slough. And see that tree? That's the one James jumped out of and broke his arm. They tied a tire swing to the branch and would swing out and jump in the water. Until the branch broke."

Someone had placed intermittent signs along the driveway. Happy. Birthday. Old. Geiser.

That looked like something James would do. Strung over the front door was a large Happy Birthday banner. Something Kim and the kids would have done.

Luke gazed at the two-story farmhouse. River rock bordered the foundation, and fir tongue-and-groove siding covered the walls.

"Looks like you added on." He stroked his chin.

"Yeah, my mom said if dad wanted more kids, he was going to have to double the size of the house." Luke carried the large bag of russets and fixings. Kaitlyn carried her dad's present, a new pocketknife. If he didn't need one now, he would before too long. He had a habit of losing them.

"Get ready to be jumped on!" It was only a matter of seconds before all her niblings came running out, hollering about who got to hug Kaitlyn first.

"Easy there, don't knock us down!" she laughed and patted Lizzie on the head.

Luke set everything on the sprawling redwood counter. Her dad's pride and joy. A project that included the cupboards and the kitchen table. Come to think of it, he and William would enjoy talking shop.

"Where is everybody?" Kaitlyn glanced around the kitchen.

"Out on the deck," Sophie said and tugged at Kaitlyn's arm. Liam whispered in James' ear, side eyeing Luke.

"Liam, ready to meet my new friend?"

"Yeah!" Liam jumped up and down.

"Hi! I'm Luke." He knelt to Liam's level and held his hand out for high fives. Liam giggled.

"Looks like you passed the first test!" James announced. Luke's smile crinkled the edges of his eyes.

Luke held his hand out to James. "Glad you could come." James caught Kaitlyn's eye with a quick nod of approval.

After washing and slathering them in butter, they placed the potatoes on a tray and set them in the oven.

Luke stepped into the living room to look over all the family photos. A whole wall of them chronicling each additional kid. Kaitlyn slid her arm in his.

"You're the baby, I see." His right eyebrow rose.

"Yup. And proud of it." Kaitlyn turned as Maggie slid open the glass door.

"She works hard at maintaining her position, too! Come on, everyone's on the deck. I'm Maggie, by the way." She held out her hand and grasped Luke's. She looked an older form of Kaitlyn—dark curly hair, brown eyes, and a killer smile.

Kaitlyn's dad stood up and held out his hand. Why were her hands becoming clammy?

"I'm Dave. Glad you could join us." Kaitlyn looked for any signs in her dad's expression that gave her pause. So far, so good. His hazel eyes twinkled under his now grey hair. She knew he would at least approve of Luke's plaid flannel shirt.

"Luke, glad to be included for your birthday." He watched the kids chasing after each other in the yard. He chuckled, then slid the door open to toss the soccer ball. They squealed and ran in a scramble.

Maggie pulled on Kaitlyn's arm. "Come on, I need help in the kitchen." Kaitlyn looked at Luke and shrugged her shoulders. His solid stance made her confident he could hold his own.

"What do you think?" Kaitlyn said.

"If his personality is as great as his looks? I'd say he's got real possibilities." Maggie stuck a fork in the potatoes, testing their doneness, and set the timer for a few more minutes.

"Okay, Mags. You've been married for five years now. And you're still twitterpated. Tell me what I'm looking for! I need a list. I blew it big time with Francisco and I don't want to make the same mistake."

"Okay, first off, where's his faith?"

"Solid."

"Next, what do you know about his family?"

"I work a few hours a week with his grandpa who has diabetes. I met his dad and his grandpa's the sweetest guy you'd ever meet. Luke adores him." Kaitlyn set out the sour cream and butter.

"Does he like his job? Where does he work?"

"At a non-profit. He loves his job. I went to Honduras with him to help build a safe house for girls who have been sex trafficked. I did the medical training for the staff. It was both fun and scary." Maggie took out the potatoes and gave them to Kaitlyn to scoop and smoosh.

"Sounds interesting. What was the scary part?"

"You probably noticed Luke's slight limp. A gang member shot him. It was terrifying." Kaitlyn filled her in on all the details.

"So, you've spent some time with him. What don't you like about him?"

Kaitlyn's eyes flew to the ceiling. She thought about his deep voice. His singing the camp song grace. His stories of John. The brush of his lips...

"So far, nothing. I like everything about him!"

"Have you had any arguments yet? That's always a true test."

"We've only been together a few months." Kaitlyn glanced out at the deck. Was her dad giving Luke "the talk"? Both faces were pretty serious.

"Let's get this food out. It looks like Luke could use some intervention."

Chapter Thirty-Six

The game of Rummy had continued well into the night, filling the house with the ringing of laughter and teasing. Kaitlyn's mom kept the snacks and drinks coming. Watching her dad strut around the room crowing when he won his hand would be a true test of whether Luke appreciated a sense of humor. And it seemed he did. He appeared to be taking in her parents. Something about the way he looked at her mom. . .

Kaitlyn's mom had suggested they spend the night, Kaitlyn in her old room and Luke on the couch. Kaitlyn was glad they had. Traveling the two hours back to Portland would have put them home at two in the morning.

She couldn't help thinking through the day. Luke had gone down to play soccer with the kids, as much as one could with a bunch of six and unders. Not to mention his limp. When Lizzie had fallen and scraped her knee, Luke grabbed her up, stroked her curly hair and somehow got her to giggling even before he washed and bandaged it. He could probably make it in the nursing world. Or dare she think it, the father world. Be. Still. My. Beating. Heart.

Her mom had sent them off with travel mugs of coffee, cinnamon rolls, and a quick prayer for the day. Kaitlyn had suggested Luke drive. She didn't want to miss any of the gorgeous scenery along Hwy 101.

"Well? You survived." Kaitlyn turned to look at him. She couldn't believe what a great guy he was. And cute. The dimple in his chin. Those eyes. And his passion for his work. Protective of Zach. And Lucinda. Even John.

"That is some busy household!" Luke's lips turned up in a half grin.

"Yeah. I forget how crazy it is until I get back in the midst of it. But I love it when everyone's together."

"It looks like everyone's close. And Sophie and Liam? What a pair. I bet they keep Sam and Kim on the run!" Kaitlyn popped the lid on Luke's travel mug and handed it to him.

And now for the hundred-dollar question. "What were you and Dad talking about?" She slid him a glance.

"I don't have to tell you all my secrets, do I?" He smirked.

"Depends. Do you want to keep our relationship going?" Her expression turned saucy.

"Oh, pulling out the big guns now." Luke guided the car to a viewpoint and turned off the engine. Waves crashed on the rocks below, splashing impressive sprays of water. Seagulls did cartwheels in the air, and they could just see the tips of white pelican heads bobbing up and down in the surf. Their squawks carried through the open windows.

A gust of wind blew her hair, and Kaitlyn pulled her sweater snug around her.

"First of all, your dad is, how should I put it...."

"Unique. Yeah, believe me. I know." Kaitlyn rolled her eyes.

"I took your suggestion, and we spent all kinds of time talking about the farm—the sheep, blueberries and all. You must have had a lot of fun growing up."

"Yeah, there were some good times. Dad can get a little grumpy when working with sheep." Memories of d ad hollering at her and her sibs to keep the sheep from escaping through their human fence or the ram upending them, ran shudders through her body. Granted, sheep had minds of their own and could be exasperating. Let's just say, becoming a shepherd was not in her immediate plans.

Luke adjusted his position to face her. "Your dad asked me if I was the one he and your mom had been praying for throughout your life. And he said if I ever did anything to hurt his little girl, I'd rue the day I ever got involved with you."

"Not quite sure if I should revel in the warmth of my dad's love, or if I should worry that he threatened you." Kaitlyn held out her hand to him and watched his expression—from creases in his forehead to crow's feet at the corners of his eyes. He squeezed her hand.

"Kaitlyn, I want you to know that I would never intentionally hurt you. I suppose sometimes I'm the typical guy that doesn't pick up on cues. But I would never go out of my way to cause you harm." He lifted her hand to his lips. Warmth traveled from her hand through her arm and straight to her heart.

They drove a few miles down the road and pulled off the exit to Cannon Beach, passing the black cannon facing the sea that gave the quaint town its name.

Dozens of people were out and about, meandering through shops, eating ice cream, or flying kites. But, considering the weather was turning warmer, and the sun was out longer, it wasn't surprising.

Luke's phone rang. He looked at it and slid it back in his pocket. Who was that? It appeared he didn't intend to answer it. And he didn't offer an explanation.

Kaitlyn insisted they go to the candy store to watch the taffy machine. Big gobs of soft, gooey taffy rotated between four paddles, stretching it thin. They bought a bag of assorted flavors and wandered down to the beach.

Luke took Kaitlyn's hand as they walked along the water's edge, popping a strawberry taffy in his mouth.

Kaitlyn reached down to pick up a sand dollar, brushed the sand off it and admired the star on its back.

"When Tina and I were teens, her mom got cancer. She was like a second mom to me. We prayed every day that she'd get healed. But apparently that wasn't in His plans. She died a year later."

"That had to be tough. I can't even imagine." Luke picked up a clamshell, smoothed his thumb over it and tossed it aside.

"It was tough. I tried so hard to be strong for her. For them. I'd read Mama Kristina books to take her mind off things. Bought her scarves to cover her bald head. Penciled in eyebrows for her. Tina and I shed a lot of tears. I guess that's why Tina and I are so close."

They sat down on some driftwood and watched the sand-pipers run, creating little pronged footprints in the sand.

"What I'm starting to figure out is that when God says no, something better comes along. Or He has something for you to learn because of it—not always my favorite thing. Or you're prevented from something that could have gone way wrong." She picked up a stick and started doodling in the sand. "I was bummed when it didn't work out with Francisco, but then again, I wouldn't be here with you now, would I?"

"When your dad asked if I was who he had been praying for? I'd like to believe that I am. I'd like to think that God has been molding me into just the right person for you."

A wave came close to their toes, and they bolted back, laughing. Kaitlyn leaned into Luke. Luke turned her to him and guided his lips to hers. Hope warmed through her, touching every awakened nerve within her. He kissed her again. Oh, the softness of his lips... And was she the one his folks had been praying for? She certainly hoped so. Never had things seemed so right.

Chapter Thirty-Seven

Luke drove in comfortable silence as they made their way home. He couldn't believe how much fun Kaitlyn's family was. Adorable little kids and her siblings were great. She seemed to have a great relationship with her mom.

And his mom? She had texted a million times. And left voice messages. Luke worried his bottom lip. He knew he should call her, but at the same time, she had deceived him. That was no small matter. What was he going to say, anyway? Sorry I was such a burden? It's not like he had any choice in the matter either way.

Why did she even have to tell him she was going to abort him? What was the point? Now all he could think about was that maybe he should never have been born. What had his purpose even been? Sure, he had helped Zach, but at what expense? And Lucinda? He was glad she was safe. But couldn't anyone else have made that happen? The world didn't necessarily need him.

Kaitlyn had nodded off. Luke stole a glance at her—brown

curls falling softly over her face, her head tilted, her face smashed against the window. Was that a little drool? He let out a little chuckle.

She startled. "We're almost to your house." Kaitlyn sat up and stretched. Her fingers went to her mouth.

"Did you see me drool?" A look of horror appeared on her face.

"Babe, you look good. A little slobber wouldn't stop me from loving you." Had he just used the L word?

His phone rang. Mom. He hovered his thumb over the answer button.

"Aren't you going to answer it?" Kaitlyn reached over and touched answer on his phone.

"Hello." Luke's voice was stilted. Abrupt even.

"Luke! I've been trying to reach you. Honey, I really want to talk to you. You've been distant since Thanksgiving." Silence.

Luke? Can you just say something?" He pulled up next to Kaitlyn's house.

"Mom, I don't think I'm ready." Luke shut off the engine.

"If it helps, I am really sorry."

"Gotta go." Luke hung up and rested his head on the steering wheel.

"Luke?" Kaitlyn put her hand on his shoulder. "You okay? What's going on?"

He slowly lifted his head and crossed his arms. He turned towards the side window and took a deep breath.

"At Thanksgiving, my brother Ryan told us that his girl-friend was pregnant and wanted an abortion. He was really upset. And then," Luke bit his lip. "Then my mom told me she almost aborted me." He turned towards Kaitlyn. "Can you believe that? How was that supposed to make me feel?"

Kaitlyn slid her hand down his back and started rubbing it.

"That must have been awful. I can't even imagine. Did you grow up feeling like she didn't want you?"

"I always felt like Ryan was the golden child. And now this explains it. She wanted him."

"Babe. Look at me. If she didn't abort you, that meant she wanted you. She probably didn't know how she was going to take care of you. Or maybe she was embarrassed. Do you know who your dad is?"

"It's my same dad. They weren't married at the time."

"You need to talk to her. She obviously loves you. And she wants a relationship with you."

"I don't know."

"Okay. Sleep on it. You can call her tomorrow." Kaitlyn took his hand and kissed his knuckles. "You don't need to come in. Call me tomorrow and let me know how it goes."

♥ ♥ ♥

Luke woke up with the sun shining on his face. He felt surprisingly rested after last evening's angst.

He placed his hands behind his head. Today was going to be another special day with Kaitlyn. Their relationship felt so natural. There wasn't anything they couldn't talk about. Zach. And now his mom.

He even told her about getting expelled in middle school for punching out a kid. He still didn't think he deserved it. After all, he had been defending someone from that bully. At least she seemed convinced of it.

He took a quick shower and threw on his biking clothes. What a glorious day. The sunshine would make the little bits of red in Kaitlyn's hair sparkle. He threw on his shoes and grabbed his helmet.

Hopping on his bike, he headed down the road, welcoming the slight breeze. He checked the time. It would take him a half hour to ride to Coffee Corner and he wanted to be there on time to meet her. He passed the flower stand and thought he should stop and get some for Kaitlyn. He changed his mind when he saw the line. Maybe not, that might take too long.

It was amazing how, when you were in love, everything seemed fresh and exciting. Yes, he was willing to admit that he was being sucked in, consumed, undeniably head over heels in love with this curly-headed girl. He fought the urge to shout to the world that he had found the girl of his dreams. Instead, he maintained a perpetual grin.

Luke's phone rang, pulling him out of his reverie. Kaitlyn? He guided his bike to the shoulder to answer it. Nope. Star Wars ringtone. His dad.

"Hey dad, what's up?"

"Son, I've got some bad news. Your mom has been in a bad car accident and just roused from a coma. We're at the hospital right now. Do you want to come see her?" Luke was stunned. He stared at the screen.

"Luke?" How bad is bad? Was she going to be okay? He should have called her back.

"Sorry, I just wasn't expecting that. I was heading to meet Kaitlyn for a bike ride. I'll be right there. Which hospital?"

"Mercy. We're on the fifth floor."

Luke changed courses and headed north. He'd call Kaitlyn as soon as he arrived.

His mom was in a coma? What did that mean? Was she going to die? She couldn't die. There was a lot more Luke needed to tell her. Please Lord, let her be alright.

A blaring horn startled him, and he swerved out of the way of an oncoming truck. He sped up and hovered in the bike lane. Only two more blocks. His heart accelerated.

Was she alone? How did the accident happen? Was she distracted by her call to him?

Luke parked his bike, adjusted the lock, and flew through the doors. He took the stairs two at a time. At the nurse's station, he asked for his mom's room. A nurse named Daniel pointed him in the right direction.

"Are you her nurse?"

"Yes, actually. Are you family?"

"I'm her son. How is she?"

"She's sleeping soundly. We've given her medication and hope she'll be coming around soon. I'll check in on her in a bit."

Luke couldn't get to room 503 fast enough. He knocked lightly on the partially opened door and went inside. His dad sat watching his mom sleep, oxygen tubes in her nose and an IV attached to her arm. Luke felt the moisture in his eyes and blinked it back.

"Luke." His dad locked eyes. He stood and gave him a hug.

"Is she going to be okay?"

"I don't know. The doctor's been in. They've put her on heavy pain meds. They're not sure yet about the extent of her injuries."

Luke walked over to the bed and took his mom's hand. It felt lifeless. Her face was covered with gashes, her hair sweaty and matted.

"Get well, mom. You have to get well." Could the urgency in his voice hasten the hoped-for results?

The sudden realization struck him—he hadn't contacted Kaitlyn. He jumped up and glanced at his dad. "I have to call Kaitlyn! I was supposed to meet her at Coffee Corner and go on a bike ride. I can't imagine what she thought when I didn't show up."

He stepped into the hall. Punched in her number. It rang for what seemed like forever.

"Pick up!" Luke paced.

It went to her answering machine. "Hey, it's Kaitlyn. Can't wait to get back to you. Beep."

"Kaitlyn, mom was in a bad car accident. We're at Mercy hospital. Call me." Luke walked over to the window and rested his forehead on it. The rhythmic sound of the life support beeped behind him.

"A drunk driver. He got away with barely a scratch. Totally not fair." His dad rested his head in his hands.

"She wanted me to call her." Luke turned. "And I didn't. What if I can't ever talk to her again?" His voice choked up.

"Son, I don't know what's been going through your mind. But you have to know that we both love you more than anything. We always have. We were confused. But God knew that you were supposed to be in this world. And that you were supposed to be in our lives. You've been nothing but a joy to us."

Luke pinched the bridge of his nose. His dad cleared his throat.

"I have to get in touch with Kaitlyn." Luke punched a frantic text to Kaitlyn.

I'm at Mercy with my mom. She was in
a bad accident. Please, please call me!

"Kaitlyn not answering?" his dad said.

"No. And I don't want her to think that I stood her up." Luke said. Lines in his forehead deepened.

"She'll understand when she finds out," his dad said. "Sit down here. I'll go get you some coffee. Are you hungry? I can bring something back for you."

"Coffee would be good. Maybe a sandwich?" Luke said. He checked his phone. Nothing. Would she understand? This was not something he wanted to take a chance on.

He texted again. He couldn't keep his legs from jumping up and down.

Kaitlyn???

"Tell me more about Kaitlyn. Grandpa sure loves her."

"What's not to love? She went to Honduras with me to help with the Butterfly Project—a safe house for trafficked girls. She helped me lay cinderblocks and put together a medical manual."

"Sounds like quite a gal!"

He looked his dad in the eye. "I really like her, Dad. I can't even explain how I feel when I'm around her. I was so anxious the first time I took her out. I was afraid I'd say the wrong thing, or she'd think I was someone I wasn't. Or she'd want someone smarter, or more handsome, or buff." Luke snorted a chuckle.

"That's how it was when I started dating your mom. She was so pretty, and fun, and full of adventure. And boy could she cook!"

"Still can." Luke said. But could she? Would she be okay?

"Hey." His mom's voice was scratchy. The bedcovers moved as she tried to sit up.

"Mom?" Luke hurried to her side.

"Luke. Where am I? What am I doing here?" Her voice raspy.

"You were in an accident." Joe took her hand. "You're in the hospital."

"I am?" She raised her arm and looked at the tube.

"Mom—I was so worried." Luke held her gaze. "I've been a horrible son. I hope you can forgive me."

She held out her hand to him. Luke wiped the tear from her eye.

Chapter Thirty-Eight

Seemed like the entire town had thought to come to Coffee Corner. The sunshine must have brought everyone out. She parked her bike. She couldn't ignore her jostling nerves as she took off her helmet and wandered through the door. A quick glance let her know she had arrived before Luke. Why should she feel so nervous? They had had a more than perfect weekend.

She ordered. White chocolate mint frappe. With whip cream, of course.

Maybe she'd buy a cherry almond scone as well. The clatter of Coffee Corner rose—voices, the rattle of the grinder clinking cups. Conversations.

She carried her order outside and chose a patio table for two. No harm in soaking up the rays. She rummaged around in her little backpack for her phone and checked the time. He was only ten minutes late. Maybe he got caught up in something and couldn't get away. He was probably helping someone that needed it. He was just that kind of guy.

Wispy clouds drifted over the morning sky, lending a brief coolness as it hid the sun.

Kaitlyn scrolled through photos. The Christmas pictures with Francisco. She began deleting them. Why hadn't she done that before? Wait—there was one with Santa. Maybe she should keep that. She cropped Luke and saved it.

She continued to scroll. Playing soccer with Luke and the kids. Her heart swelled—he was so good with them. He'd be a great dad. She could envision him holding their baby or playing soccer. Or a baby in his backpack, on a biking expedition. She smiled and looked around. Still no sign of him. Should she be worried?

Kaitlyn took a sip of her drink and scrolled through Facebook. She checked out Luke's page. A photo of her on the bike trip made her eyes crinkle. Why hadn't they gotten together then? That was before Francisco. She could have avoided that fiasco altogether.

A breeze tinged with chocolate, and almond tugged at strands of her hair.

Did something happen to him? She was legit beginning to worry. He wouldn't be using her like Francisco, would he? She shook her head. There was nothing in their times together that had led her to believe that.

That old familiar zing of anxiety swept through her. Should I text him? No, that would be annoying. But what if something bad happened to him? She checked her phone again. Nothing. No, Kaitlyn, play it cool. You are a strong, independent woman. You don't need a man.

Her eyes traveled to the bike rack—which held only her bike. What if he forgot about me? We didn't confirm this morning. He wouldn't be with someone else? Did I rush things by taking him to the farm to meet my family? Did they scare him away?

It was as if she had the cartoon characters sitting on her shoulders arguing. But Luke said all those nice things to me in the car and at the beach. I was starting to feel like he's the one.

Just stop! You're being paranoid. He's probably just having bike trouble or had to stop to help someone. I'll text him. No, call. She held her finger over the dial pad. I'll give him five more minutes.

She took a bite of her scone. She looked at the park across the street. Kids were jumping and laughing in the fountain.

Luke didn't seem needy. And he had paid for dinner and the show, unlike someone else she had encountered.

Maybe she'd read on her kindle app until he showed up. He was going to show up, right? Why had her favorite coffee become tasteless in her mouth?

She delved into a WWII story about an orphaned girl and her little brother. Her phone popped up a message that her battery was dying. So much for that. She tossed it into her backpack. The reflection of her frown showed in the coffee shop window.

This was a complete waste of sunshine. She had waited over an hour. He could have called. She should just face the fact that she'd been stood up. So much for true love.

And if she had been stood up, where did that leave her with William? Should she quit? She didn't want to take the chance of being over there and having Luke, show up. Nothing says awkward like that. She'd call William when her phone was charged and let him know she wasn't coming back. Make something up, like her hours at work had changed and she couldn't do it anymore.

Kaitlyn strapped on her helmet— her feet leaden as she pedaled home. The brick weight on her stomach made her feel like she wanted to puke. Tears that had been threatening all morning pooled behind her eyelids. The front door opened as she was ready to grab the handle. She bumped into Tina.

"You're home. I was just going to go look for you. Luke called, and he's worried sick. He's been trying to get ahold of you all afternoon."

"He has?" Kaitlyn's voice was just above a whisper.

"His mom was in a car accident. He's a Mercy. Head on over there. I'll let him know you're coming."

Kaitlyn jumped in her car. Why so anxious oh my soul. . .

Chapter Thirty-Nine

"Thanks for doing this. I've never been fishing before." Kaitlyn carried her pole over her shoulder, followed by Grandpa William with his pole and tackle. This would be a good diversion from the anxiety of the past week.

"This will be fun, young lady. Your dad never took you? I thought you grew up on a farm."

"I did. But my dad was too busy with the sheep and u-pick blueberries to take me. I guess I could have gotten one of my brothers to take me, but..."

"They were probably playing sports or riding their four wheelers." His laugh was a low rumble.

She followed him through some alders to a spot where the stream flowed over some rocks. The water was clear, eddying in a deep pool, the sun sparkling like diamonds. A few leaves floated, swirling with the current.

Grandpa William set the tackle box down and gave Kaitlyn a worm to thread onto the hook. Kaitlyn gingerly took the wriggling creature between her thumb and pointer. Considering she was a nurse and saw all sorts of undesirable things, she was surprised at her reaction to impaling the squirming earthworm. She poked it and let out a squeal, nearly dropping it when it squirted something ooey. Grandpa William laughed.

"You are something else. You want me to do that for you?"

"No. I've got this!" She finished, determined to overcome this challenge and threw her line into the water. "I assume you know that Rachel needs a kidney transplant. That accident really did a number on her."

"Yeah, Joe told me. This has been a hard go for her. Hard on Luke, for sure." He cast his line.

"Luke told me that she was going to abort him. That was really hard on him. And yet, the accident seems to have brought them closer together. You know he's going to donate his kidney to her? It turns out it's a perfect match."

"That boy doesn't really understand his value. Maybe at the end of all this, and with you by his side, he'll finally feel whole."

Kaitlyn bit her lip. She hoped she was part of fulfilling His plan.

Kaitlyn's line jerked. "Reel it in. You've got one!" Kaitlyn giggled and wound the reel. She proudly held up her pole, the trout dangling from the line. Definitely Instagram worthy.

* ♥ ♥

A lot had happened the past week. The doctor had scheduled the surgeries and Luke and Rachel seemed to have come out fine. Kaitlyn had been glad to be on duty that week. She couldn't stand the thought of having to get information second hand from Tina or Daniel. And who knew? Rachel could possibly end up being her mother-in-law. She needed to see that her coworkers were taking good care of her. And Luke. Kaitlyn felt her cheeks grow hot at the thought.

She arrived early for her shift and checked in with Daniel.

"How are Luke and Rachel doing?"

"Not bad for just being out of surgery for two days. They seem to be sleeping okay. Then again, the meds have kicked in."

Kaitlyn carried in some balloons and set them in the corner. She stood over Rachel's bed. Her hair had been washed and the cuts on her face were beginning to scab over. She was a little pale. When was the last time her vitals had been taken? Her chart said she wasn't keeping food down. That was a concern.

Rachel roused and smiled weakly at Kaitlyn.

"Hey Rachel. How are you feeling?"

Rachel gave a slight nod, as if every movement took a special effort. Kaitlyn squeezed her hand.

She moved to Luke's side of the room. He had some serious bed head going on. It brought a smile to her lips. His sheet was pushed down to his waist, revealing his muscled arms and chiseled chest. It was all she could do to resist running her hands along his arms. Apparently, hospital gowns were not his thing.

"Hey." Her voice was soft. Luke opened his eyes. "How are you feeling?"

"Like crap." He ran his hand through his hair and rubbed his hands over his stubbly face

"Well, friend, I have to say you look like crap." Kaitlyn grinned. "On a scale of one to ten, how does this compare to a gunshot wound?" Kaitlyn cocked an eyebrow.

"This is way worse." Kaitlyn gave him a light kiss on his forehead.

"But it was worth it, right?"

Luke started to tear up. He looked out the window. "I think I found my real purpose. I was supposed to be here to save my mom." Kaitlyn reached for his hand and brought it to her lips.

"Can I bring you some breakfast? Coffee?"

"That would be good."

"Let Daniel get your vitals first." Daniel placed the blood pressure cuff on his arm and wrote down the reading. Looked good. His 02 stats were on target.

"When can I get out of here? Do you realize how much I've been in a stupid hospital the last couple of months?" That was a quick turn from tender to ornery.

"Yeah, I know. It's not fun. Probably a couple more days. I'm sure you're anxious to get back to work."

"I'm not really a big fan of hospitals." Wow! Mister cranky pants! Must be hangry.

"Sometimes I'm not either. I'll go get you some breakfast." *And give you a break.*

Kaitlyn stopped at the nurse's station.

"Good morning Delores." May as well start the day on a good foot. "It looks like Rachel isn't holding down food. Is she doing alright otherwise?"

"She's going to need a feeding tube. Get your other patients checked and then I want you to do that."

The color drained from Kaitlyn's face. *A Dobhoff? No. I can't do that.* Her hands began to shake as she walked to the cafeteria. Especially on Rachel. Not only would she lose her job, but she'd lose a friend. Surely someone else could do it.

Kaitlyn looks over the breakfast options and chose an omelet and hash browns. The coffee wasn't the best here, but hopefully Luke would be out of here soon and they could return to Coffee Corner.

She returned to the room. Grandpa William and Ryan had showed up.

"So, Luke was filling me in on your weekend." Joe looked at Kaitlyn. His sly grin made the heat rise to her cheeks. She stole a glance at Luke. Had he told them everything? Like, everything?

"You've got quite the family. And to be raised on a farm? That had to be a great experience."

"Yeah, mostly. I can drive a mean tractor!" She put on a Rosy Riveter stance.

"It would be a great place for grandkids to visit," Rachel shot Luke a look. It was Luke's turn for pink cheeks.

"Did Luke tell you about when he was... how old were you, Luke? When you won your first soccer game?" Joe took a bite of donut, then handed it to Rachel.

"Six. He was in first grade. He kicked in the winning goal. He's always been good at sports," Rachel's lips turned into a proud smile. She took a bite.

"Or what about the bike races he organized in middle school? You couldn't get him off a bike." Ryan smiled.

William laughed. "He cleared out a whole section in the field behind my house for a dirt trail complete with jumps. Surprisingly, he seldom ended up with scrapes. I would have thought sure he'd end up with a broken arm or something."

Luke looked down and palmed his forehead.

"Sounds like you had a fun childhood, Luke. Nice your family feels like I need to know that side of you." Kaitlyn grinned.

Rachel started to retch. Kaitlyn jumped up and brought a container to her just as Delores walked in with the Dobhoff.

"See, I told you this is what we needed to do. All you guys clear outta here. We need to take care of this little gal." Delores waved her hand to shoo them away. Luke yanked on a t-shirt and slowly made his way out, giving Kaitlyn a worried look as he passed.

"Okay Rachel. You're not keeping food down. We're going to place this tube through your nose and down to your stomach." Rachel's eyes widened. "You shouldn't feel any pain."

Delores opened the package and handed it to Kaitlyn. *Please God, you've gotta help me here.* She took a deep breath, administered some numbing medication, and slowly inserted the tube. Her heart was beating wildly. When the tube reached the right length, Kaitlyn leaned over, her hands on her knees, and let out a whoosh.

"You're good. Let's roll her to x-ray to make sure it's placed properly." Delores moved aside as transport entered.

"Can I go with her? I just want to make sure it's right."

"I don't know what's got your panties in a bunch. No, you've got other patients to care for. You'll know soon enough."

She doesn't know. How the last time I inserted the Dobhoff, Janey died. How my preceptor told me I would never be a good nurse. Kaitlyn passed Tina in the hall.

"You're white! You okay?"

"Just had to place a Dobhoff in Rachel!"

"Oh!" Tina took Kaitlyn by the shoulders and held her gaze. "It's going to be okay. This isn't like the last time." Kaitlyn nodded as a tear trickled down her cheek. Tina wiped the moisture away with her thumb.

Kaitlyn's shift was nearly over when she heard the bed alarm. Rachel? What might be going wrong? It had seemed the feeding tube was working okay. She hurried into Rachel's room and saw Luke's mom, arms spread, face slack and unresponsive. Kaitlyn willed herself to keep calm. She gently shook her and stepped back as Rachel began coughing up blood, gasping for air. Kaitlyn reached for her vocera and called for Daniel. He quickly checked her oxygen saturation—02 and 70%. Daniel locked eyes with Kaitlyn and said,"

"Call a Rapid Response and page the doctor!"

Luke stormed out of bed and marched over to Kaitlyn. He grabbed her arm. "What is going on? What did you do to her? After all we've been through, I'm not about to let her die because you messed up a stupid procedure. I thought you knew what you were doing!"

Kaitlyn's whole body shook. She fastened her eyes on Luke's. What she needed right now was a warm, comforting hug—not his anger. It wasn't enough that all the memories of Janey had flooded in. And now Luke was beside himself, thinking she had ruined everything for his mom. And what if she really had? No. Rachel dying was not an option.

Chapter Forty

Kaitlyn awoke on the couch, disoriented by the darkness. She shivered and wrapped her arms around her nauseous stomach. Why was she on the couch, wrapped like a hotdog in her quilt? Where was Tina? She threw off the blanket and sat up. She raked her fingers through her disheveled hair. And why did her face feel wet? Had she been crying?

Rachel! A crippling agony squeezed at her heart. It was not something she wanted to feel again. Ever. First, watching Luke get shot. Now watching his mom go downhill. She wrapped the quilt tighter around her, hoping to ward off the chill traveling down her spine.

Kaitlyn switched on the light and drug herself over to the fridge for something to eat. She pulled out some leftover pizza and slid it into the microwave, noticing the clock. Two a.m.

How could things have been going so well and now, suddenly, she's been thrown over a cliff? Things had been good with Luke, hadn't they? And now, just when he was mending things with his mom, everything tanks. She leaned against the counter and crossed her arms, a vee forming on her forehead.

How could you do this to me, God? It's like you dangled a carrot in front of my nose and let me start falling in love with a guy that was going to let me down. And on top of that, I'm forced to do that stupid Dobhoff thing. Again! What the heck? This is so not okay. Sometimes you make me so mad! She made a fist and swung her arm at her vision of Jesus.

A pang of guilt washed through her as she pulled out her pizza. She shouldn't be getting mad at God, right? If Tina weren't sleeping, she would remind her He had her best interest in mind. But did this fall into that category? If so, she definitely wasn't feeling it.

She sat vacantly staring at her plate, bit into her pizza, and shoved it aside. She laid her head on her arms.

She obviously wasn't supposed to be in a successful relationship. This was it. No relationships again. Ever.

***

Kaitlyn awoke to Tina stroking her hair. She sat up and rubbed her eyes.

"You've got wrinkle marks on your cheeks." Tina smiled. "You okay?"

"How am I supposed to be okay when the world is falling apart around me?"

"Well, there is some good news." Kaitlyn sat up straighter. "Rachel is out of ICU and is stable. And it wasn't the feeding tube that caused the problems. You did everything right."

"Really?" Kaitlyn frowned and bolted up.

"Delores told us. She wanted me to make sure you knew that."

"Delores did?" Kaitlyn shook her head. Unbelievable.

Bentley jumped out of his bed and ran to the door, barking. "Who's that? You expecting someone?" Tina shook her head and answered it.

Luke stood there with a sheepish smile and two cups of coffee, the caramel flavoring wafting through the hole in the lid.

"Luke?" Tina stepped aside and let him in.

Kaitlyn shrunk back. She didn't know what she was expecting, but it certainly wasn't Luke. Coffee? Was he offering a peace treaty?

"Hey." Kaitlyn ran her fingers through her messy hair.

"Hey back. Can I come in?" Kaitlyn gave a slight nod to the table. Luke offered a coffee to her and one to Tina. He set a white pastry bag on the table and leaned against the counter. Tina pulled out a chocolate filled croissant and a cinnamon roll. If this was a peace offering, he certainly had learned her sweet spot.

"Daniel released you from the hospital?" Luke nodded.

"I think he was tired of hearing me whine." He gave a sheepish grin.

"And your mom?" Kaitlyn glanced away, afraid to ask. Even though Tina had assured her she was fine, she had to hear it from Luke.

"I think she'll be in for a few more days, but Daniel said her vital signs were good, and she's been able to eat. Even said her poop looks good." Kaitlyn snorted a giggle.

Tina put her hand on Kaitlyn's. "Does he know about Janey?" Kaitlyn shook her head.

"This was more than just about your mom, Luke. When we were doing our practicums, Kaitlyn had to administer a feeding tube to a patient named Janey . Normally, when the Dobhoff is inserted, the patient gets an x-ray to make sure that it went into the stomach and not the lungs." Tina paused and looked at Kaitlyn. Tears were welling in her eyes.

"Kaitlyn's preceptor told her it wasn't necessary, even though Kaitlyn knew it should be done. Her patient ended up dying."

Luke stood, closed his eyes, and let out a breath. "So, that had to take all the bravery you could muster to administer that to my mom. And it didn't help that I was a jerk to you—it panicked me." He shook his head.

"I am so sorry, Kaitlyn."

She stood and walked into his open arms. Luke put a hand to her cheek and wiped a tear with his thumb.

Kaitlyn fell into his chest. Luke wrapped his arm around her waist and ran his hand slowly through her hair.

Broken. This is what it was like to be held by strong arms when you were broken.

"Luke, I'm so sorry..."

"Hush now, it's okay. There's nothing to be sorry for. I'm the one who should be apologizing. I had no right to treat you that way." He wiped another escaped tear. She reached her hands around his neck, stood on her tiptoes, and pressed her lips into his. He returned the favor. Warmth spread from her heart down to her bellybutton. He placed small kisses on her forehead, each cheek, nose, and back to her lips. No way was she ever going to let this guy get away.

"Okay, enough of that. Your coffee is getting cold!" Tina shook her head, hiding her grin behind her roll.

Chapter Forty-One

L uke rested his elbow on the open window as he drove to Grandpa William's, glad for the longer days of spring. He was grateful for the warming weather, opening more opportunities for long bike rides where he could smell the freshly mowed fields and soak in the rays. He was sure he could talk Kaitlyn into helping him plan another Bike Meet-Up. Maybe this one could be with the refugees.

A gentle breeze danced through the fresh growth on the peach trees, causing blossoms to swirl like snow showers The first buds of peaches gave hope of filling canning jars and eating rich desserts.

"Do you think you could make as good a peach pie as you did blueberry?" The memory of the night she brought dinner to Grandpa's. The night he realized the possibilities before him. That was what, only three months ago? It didn't seem possible.

Blessed. That's what he was.

"I might be persuaded to do that." She gave him a saucy grin.

Luke stood a minute and examined the outside of the

house. He and his dad had done an acceptable job of painting. It sure looked better than before. They stepped onto the porch. Looks like the next job would be to strengthen the porch rail. He'd talk to his dad about that. Pretty sure Kaitlyn would be willing to help.

Kaitlyn had gone through the fridge and cupboards with Rachel and Joe and guided them in replacing food with diabetic friendly options. She'd made a chart of what he should include in each meal and when he should take his insulin. That way, when she wasn't there with him, they would know what to do.

"Keep up the excellent work, and you'll be here till you're a hundred," she said and winked.

"Grandpa, would you mind if I started Kaitlyn in a little project in your workshop?"

"Why, yes, go ahead. What do you two want to make?"

"I thought, if it was okay with you, that we could use some of those cedar boards and I'd help her make her hope chest."

"A hope chest? Now you're talkin'. Your Grandma Alice would be so happy if she could see you two right now. In fact, I bet I have one of her handwoven throws you could put in it."

Luke glanced at the throw on the couch. Having one of those to snuggle up with on the couch with Kaitlyn and binge watch Bones. Yeah. He'd be okay with that. Add a little popcorn. Glass of cider.

"I wish I could have known her. She sounds amazing," Kaitlyn said.

Luke wished she could have too. But then again, at that point in time, God hadn't brought him to the place where he was ready for the right relationship. And quite possibly, God hadn't had Kaitlyn in the right place for him, either.

Kaitlyn's hand felt warm in his as they walked to the shop.

They simultaneously breathed in the cedar's smell when they entered. Luke looked at Kaitlyn and chuckled.

"I love that smell. Something about it," she said. "My mom has a cedar chest. Sam and I used to crawl inside on top of the blankets when we were little. We must have liked the smell."

"It's fresh," Luke said.

They picked out boards and laid out the plan on the work-table. Kaitlyn placed the protective goggles over her eyes that Luke held out to her.

He stood behind her, his heart speeding up as he guided her hands on the chop saw.

She turned to look at him for approval. Approval for a job well done? Of course. But what welled within him was approval for this girl who had won his heart. This girl who was fun, full of integrity, and let's just be honest, absolutely adorable.

He turned her towards him and brushed sawdust out of her hair.

"Looks like you were made to be a carpenter," he said. "Wood you like to build a future with me?"

Her smile turned into a giggle. "I wood if..." If? What did he need to do to make her say yes? He'd do anything.

"If?"

"I just want us to spend more time together. Not rush into anything. I mean, if we have any plans to, you know, the M word? I would hope we would be together for the rest of our lives and another six months, or a year, will only make us sure it's the right decision."

He melted at how the corners of her eyes crinkled. And that lopsided smile. He could live with that for the rest of his life. She was a thousand kinds of perfect.

"You just take all the time you want. It gives me more time to prove how much I love you." He kissed her and marveled at the pure rightness of it all.

Chapter Forty-Two

K aitlyn held Luke's hand as they walked through the gates of the Oregon Zoo. A peacock, his stunning tail fanned out, strutted proudly before them. Kaitlyn giggled. "Just like a guy—struttin' his stuff!"

"Hey now. If a guy's got it, he needs to flaunt it."

A young boy was tugging on his mom's hand. "Come ooonnnn, mom. I want to see the lions." She quickened her pace.

"Let's go see the birds of prey show. I think it's by the elephants." Kaitlyn made her way over the well-known sidewalks. She had grown up going to this zoo and had always been one of her favorite things to do. It was so relaxing.

They watched the elephants, the mom scooping dirt and hay and tossing it over her baby. She could never figure out why that was a thing.

"Let's grab a snow cone. It's getting warm out here." Kaitlyn let the flavored ice melt in her mouth as they sat on the grass.

"Ladies and gentlemen, boys and girls. I know you've been

waiting to see the show, so get comfortable." A teen girl walked out wearing a thick leather glove upon which sat a falcon.

"How many of you think falcons only live in the wild?." A show of hands rose.

"Well, actually, many live in large cities. In the wild, they make their nests on cliffs. Skyscrapers are like cliffs to them and so build their nests there."

The girl walked in front of them, slowing so they could see the beautiful black and white breast feathers and yellow beak. "Another reason they like cities is because some of their favorite foods are pigeons and doves."

"Okay everybody. Watch. Mary is going to release the falcon, where it will fly over your heads to land on Heather's wrist behind you. Ready?"

Oohs and awws were heard as it flapped its wings, flying just a foot above them. Kaitlyn let out a giggle and leaned into Luke. After a loud applause, he held his hands out to her to help her up.

Two women approached them.

"Do you know them?" Luke asked.

"I don't recognize them."

"Kaitlyn. Is that you?" Kaitlyn shrugged her shoulders.

"I'm Jesse and this is my sister Julia."

"I'm sorry. I don't remember you," Kaitlyn said.

"We know you from St Mary Hospital, where our sister was a patient," Julia said. "It's okay. We didn't expect you to remember us."

"But we definitely remember you," Jesse said. Kaitlyn searched her mind, reaching back to when she was a preceptee. Nothing rang a bell.

"We were just talking about our sister when she was in the

hospital. You were such a wonderful, kind nurse. She really appreciated your thoughtful care," Julia said. She brushed her strawberry hair out of her eyes as a gentle breeze blew.

"What was your sister's name? Maybe I'll remember her," Kaitlyn said.

"Janey." Kaitlyn jerked as if she'd been sucker punched. She placed her hand on her open mouth.

"She died. And it was my fault." Kaitlyn's voice was barely above a whisper.

Jesse and Julia exchanged glances and frowned. "You thought it was your fault?"

"Yes. I placed the feeding tube into her lungs."

"No, no, no, no, no. She didn't die because of you. Don't you remember all the tubes in all her orifices? My poor sister had a lot going on. And the feeding tube you placed had been applied correctly."

Kaitlyn fell to her knees and covered her face with her hands. A sobbing breath escaped her.

Julia squatted down. "Kaitlyn. Look at me." She lifted Kaitlyn's chin. "You were not at fault. We were actually relieved when she died. She was finally free of years of pain."

Jesse said, "We have always hoped we could find you and thank you for the wonderful, compassionate care you gave her."

"And now, serendipitously, we have." Julia looked at Jesse and smiled.

Luke helped Kaitlyn to her feet and wrapped his arm around her waist.

"I can't tell you how grateful I am that you've told me this. Thank you. This might be one of the best moments in my life." A moment of redemption.

Chapter Forty-Three

Time passed quickly when you were having fun. It had been a year since Kaitlyn and Luke had built the Hope Chest. She had filled it with all types of household goodies, along with a king-size quilt her mom had made and dishes from Rachel.

Even though Luke had not proposed, she felt solid enough in their relationship that she knew the hopes wrapped up in her hope chest would not be let down.

She thought about all that had transpired in the last couple of years. The near miss at the altar with Robbie. And then Francisco and what she had now understood a healthy relationship looked like. That had been a near miss. And Tina. She couldn't think of anyone who could fit the role of a bestie like her. Peter and Daniel had really made working at Mercy so much more enjoyable. Their friendship had grown and made them into truly invincible human beings. Just a year ago, they had been excited about passing their NCLEX and looking for the perfect job. It hadn't turned out to be perfect in every way, but there was no substitute for working with the people you loved.

And what about William? Wasn't he a peach? She marveled at how God had led her to him, not only to fill a void, but to have another mentor in her life. That was back when she had told God she just wanted a companion. And look how great that turned out.

And then there was Luke.

She still felt tingly every time he held her hand. Or rubbed her tired shoulders.

Every time he kissed her.

He was such a solid guy. Full of integrity. Fun. Adventuresome. That was totally a legit word, right?

Bentley started barking and wagging his tail as he heard Luke's truck pull into the driveway.

"You like him as much as I do, don't you?" She opened the door and held her finger up, letting Luke know she'd be a minute. "Come back into the house." Bentley dutifully followed her in and ran to the window to watch.

She grabbed a sweatshirt and her phone. It might be warm now, but it could get coolish at the top of Mt. Hood.

"Hey!" Luke bent down and kissed her. "Ready to go?" He'd shaved. That was unusual. And that scent of musk. All that for a hike? Whatever he was thinking, she was just fine with it.

"Yeah. You picked a gorgeous day!" Wispy clouds drifted over the early morning sky, allowing golden sunlight to shine through in golden streaks.

"I had dinner with my folks last night."

"Yeah? Did they ask about me?"

"Of course. They were so grateful that you had been my mom's nurse. And also that you accepted the job with grandpa. They were sure that he was as healthy as he was because of you."

"Aw. That was sweet. I love that old guy. You're lucky to have him close by. I hardly ever see my grandparents."

"Who knew if we'd have ever run into each other again if you hadn't been taking care of him?"

"We did have a few times we'd met before. I just wish we'd connected way back then instead of me hanging out with Francisco. At least I figured out what I didn't want in a guy." She laughed.

He freed one hand from the wheel and reached over to grasp hers.

A comfortable silence accompanied them as they drove to the trail.

She jumped out of the truck. "Ahh, now this is enough to make a girl want to twirl." She side-eyed Luke. He smiled and shook his head.

"Don't you just love the fresh smells of damp moss and sorrel?" She bent and picked what looked like a large three-leaf clover and bit into it. She handed one to Luke.

"Taste it. It's good in salads."

"Did you just say that? I thought you didn't eat salad."

"Okay, well, I don't, really. Tina thinks it's good in salads."

"Phew. For a minute there, I thought you were turning into someone I didn't know."

They followed the trail to the stream where they rested on a boulder. Luke sat with his legs dangling down the curve of the rock. Kaitlyn sat between his legs and rested her back against him. An eagle swooped down and snagged a fish, then flapped its massive wings as it flew off. The wonder and goodness of God, seen in nature. Seen in answered prayers.

"Come on, we want to reach to the top by noon, so it's still daylight when we come down." Luke scooted himself up and reached his hands down to pull Kaitlyn to a stand. He brought her close and planted a kiss on her lips.

"That's just a little something to keep you motivated to keep hiking." He grinned.

"Just a little farther and we'll be at the peak," Luke said. "Mind if I speed on ahead? I can't wait to see the view."

"Of course. I'm fine." And she was. Kaitlyn took her time, relishing every step. Being in the woods renewed her soul. She realized she hadn't thought once about work.

Kaitlyn caught up with Luke. "It's so beautiful up here. I can't believe I haven't been hiking more."

"We can change that." His smile held a twinkle.

The view from the top was breathtaking. Kaitlyn could see for miles. Slivers of sunshine shone through the puffy white clouds, illuminating the ragged rocks, and causing sparkles to ripple through the lake.

Luke slid his arm around her waist, and she rested her head on his shoulder.

"I love you, Luke McCarthy."

He beamed. "Funny you should say that. I was thinking the same thing."

"You love you?" she said, her eyebrow raised a notch. The sparkle in his ever-shifting, teasing eyes pulled her to him.

"Well, yeah, that, but no. You are the best thing that ever happened to me, Kaitlyn Monroe." He kissed her. Looked into her eyes and ran his hand through her hair. Kissed her again, more deeply, causing ripples of longing to course through her.

He led her to sit on a granite rock. They watched a blue jay land, pecking the ground for something to eat. It hopped onto the branch of the pine.

"Is that something shining? Look, over there, where the

blue jay is." He pointed. "I wonder what it is."

Kaitlyn walked over to where he pointed. Something was indeed shining. It looked like it was stuck in a pinecone. She lifted the pinecone, sitting loosely on a branch. Luke followed her.

She put her fingers to her parted lips and held it up to him. He looked like the cat that ate the canary.

"Is this what I think it is?"

Luke broke out in an enormous grin as he took it from her. He knelt at Kaitlyn's feet and took her hands.

"I would be honored if you would consent to become Mrs. Luke McCarthy and be my companion for life."

Kaitlyn's eyes grew misty. She wiped under her eyes with the back of her fingers.

"I thought you would never ask!" A small hiccup escaped.

Luke took her left hand and placed the simple platinum engagement ring on her finger.

"It's beautiful!" She held his eyes, lost in the windows of his soul. She was breathtakingly sure this was the moment she'd been waiting for all her life. This. Yes, this was the guy she had saved her heart for. "How did you know what I would like?"

"I've spent a year holding onto everything you say, Kaitlyn. That was just one of those things."

Kaitlyn stopped, trying to hold in her elation. It danced in her eyes and her face glowed.

She placed her hands around his neck and kissed his forehead. She moved her hands to rake through his curly dark hair. He stood and wrapped her in a satisfied embrace.

How had she doubted that the Creator of the universe would know what was perfect for her? The desires of her heart had been met, and she felt nothing but gratitude.

I hope you enjoyed Book 1 of the Mercy Series.

Reviews are gold for authors— would you mind writing one for me on Amazon or Goodreads?

When Dorothy attends a reunion she encounters an old flame and reveals a long kept secret.

Sign up for my email list and this story will be on its way.
jan-johnson.com

You will also have access to my podcast, Women of the Northwest, where I interview ordinary women living extraordinary lives.

About the Author

Photo by
Jody Rae Photography
jodyrae.com

@jodyraephotography

Jan Johnson has been writing since fourth grade when her dad published her first book, *The Little Red Man*, a space story. That was back in the day when we were all sure aliens lived on Mars.

Jan lives on a sheep farm in Brownsmead, Oregon a mile from the Columbia River with her husband Ed. Don't mistake living on a farm as meaning she likes animals. Well, she actually does— from a distance.

She's passionate about building relationships, meeting new people and hearing their stories. You know what they say—Love God, Love People.

When she isn't writing, starting something new, or podcasting, she catches up with her ten children who are scattered hither and yon.

Connect with Jan
jan-johnson.com
Women of the Northwest podcast
Feel free to text and say hi: 503-791-0850